LOSING NEVERLAND

EVELYN MONTGOMERY

For the girl who never wants to grow up & still leaves their window open at night.

For the girl who still believes in thinking happy thoughts, even if sometimes, it takes just a little bit of pixie dust.

For the girl who dreams of flying amongst the stars to a world filled with make-believe with a boy they can't help but love.

A boy who has magic in his eyes, and danger in his soul.

This one's for you.

INTRODUCTION

This book is a retelling of the story Peter & Wendy by J.M. Barrie.

Triggers contain underage sex, graphic violence, strong language, explicit sexual scenes, kidnapping, noncon, dubcon, and child endangerment concerning drug abuse.

Reader discretion is advised.

"TWO IS THE BEGINNING OF THE END."

PETER & WENDY BY J. M. BARRIE

CHAPTER 1
WENDY

"There was never a simpler, happier family,
until the coming of Peter Pan."
Peter & Wendy
- J. M. Barrie

I jump as thunder crashes outside the large Victorian window across the room. Rain pelts angrily against the glass. A bright flash of lightning illuminates the space, the accompanying thunder rumbles through the night filling the air with its raging growl. My body shivers. A tingling feeling starts at the base of my spine and immediately travels north, spreading across my skin in an all-knowing way I haven't felt in years.

Someone's here.

Another flash, another crash of thunder and I spin around quickly as a dark figure scurries across a different window on the left side of the room. My hand trembles as I grab the knob to the drawer of desk behind me. The one that keeps my letter opener, my only defense against the unknown tonight.

But is it really unknown when this foreign feeling is something I've wished for, dreamed of, obsessed about for years since the last time I felt it.

Since the last time I felt him.

I push the yearning, the wanting, the desire aside, replacing it with the rage that's built since he's been gone.

He'd never return. Never come back. It's just my imagination.

Isn't it?

Sweat breaks out across my skin as I worry my bottom lip between my teeth. Slowly, I pull the drawer behind me open as another flash of lightning illuminates the room. A crash of thunder sends me bouncing slightly to my right, shaking, trembling, before I can grasp the object I'm searching for. For a split second I make out the figure of a man standing in the dark corner across the room.

I stop what I'm doing. Time stands still.

It wasn't just my imagination, someone *is* here.

And It's not just someone, not just anyone.

Turning around quickly, I frantically search the drawer as I hear the spark of a match. My heart rate spikes. My breathing becomes rapid, shaky. My palms sweat as I toss aside paper, letters, scraps of notes I haven't bothered to look at in years. The smell of tobacco is strong as boot steps echo through the room behind me. The sound is oddly disturbingly louder than the storm raging outside as it pounds in my ears. My hands search faster. Left to right, front to back, all around the inside of the drawer, but it's no use.

It was never any use fighting the inevitable.

Fighting him.

Finally, my fingers brush across cold metal. I tighten my grip on the make-shift weapon just as an arm snakes around my waist, a hand reaches up tightening against my throat, and the letter opener slips through my fingertips.

He pulls me back tight against his chest as I hear my only defense clatter to the floor. I gasp for air, but it doesn't come fast enough. He tightens his palm letting me know who is in control — *who was always in control* - before loosening his grip ever so slightly and pulling me closer against his firm frame.

He steps back swiftly, making my feet stumble as I try to match his large strides. Just as I start to tumble, just as I swear I am about to fall, his strong grip around my waist keeps me upright, keeps me grounded, anchored to a fate I hate to admit I always dreamed I'd one day meet.

I try my best to fight the war of conflicting emotions inside me. The heartache, happiness, despair. I claw at his hands desperately, attempting to break free and then feel his light chuckle feather across my neck.

"Darling," he breathes into my ear, my skin instantly tingles from the sound of his voice after so many years. "You always were a hard one to fucking tame."

The sound of his voice paralyzes me.

I stop fighting.

He loosens the grip on my waist. Bringing his smoke up to his mouth, he takes a long drag.

I don't move. Don't speak. I couldn't even if I tried.

With ease, he hooks me to him. The hold he has around my neck is strong, crippling, as he takes another inhale of his smoke. I wait in sweet agony, desperate to hear his voice say my name one more time.

Please. That's all I want after all the years. After all the time he's forced us to be apart. Just to hear my name one more time fall from his sinful lips.

I feel the fast rhythm of his heart against my back as it beats furiously in pace with mine. My body trembles. I swear I feel his strong grip slightly shake. My eyes widen as he anchors me to him, until there is no way we could get any closer, except one. His arousal is evident as he presses it against my ass. A low groan escapes his lips.

That sound. The knowledge of what I do to him shakes me when it shouldn't, makes me weak in the knees. I try to force all thoughts of desire aside, but it's almost impossible after how long I've yearned to be right back here again. In his arms. Surrounded by his smell. Engulfed in his touch. I'm melting into him more and more by the second, unable to hold onto any logic that could stop me from falling for him again after all he put me through.

After a moment, he slowly exhales a cloud of smoke, then tosses the butt of his cigarette to the floor. Spinning me around in his arms, my eyes meet his for the first time in decades and my breath catches in my throat.

"It's been a long time, Darling," he seethes.

His eyes search mine, a darkness I don't remember clouds them. My heart speeds up in fear. My mouth feels dry. I know my voice will be weak if I try to speak, so I wait. I wet my lips, trying to remain calm. The second I do, his eyes flash to my mouth. When he looks back up, the darkness in his gaze turns completely black. His eyes widen, his nostrils flare, and he harshly backs me up against the dresser.

Instinct kicks in, I push back, fight him when I know there is no use. His low laugh spurs me on as I shove against him harder. Stronger than ever before. After a minute of attempting to wrestle out of his hold, both his hands wrap around my neck, and he yanks me into the air. Anticipating, I jump and wrap my legs around his waist, and my palm smacks quickly across his strong jaw. Before I have time to register what I've just done, his grip around my throat tightens and he slams my body back into the furniture behind me.

I don't back down. Staring back into his evil glare, I somehow, finally manage to conjure up all the hatred inside and claw at his face. His eyes flare, but the darkness in them clears for just a moment, before his grip on my neck tightens further.

"I came for what you stole, Wendy," his voice feathers against my lips as he loosens his grip ever so slightly on my throat. "I've been waiting a long time, and I'm not a patient man. Give it back, and maybe, I won't take what you hold most dear."

His eyes flash to the picture frame behind me on the dresser. It's the one of my daughters. My twins. Jane and Margaret. The last one I took before they went off to college a week ago. Graduating early, they shocked everyone when they were accepted into an ivy league college at seventeen.

Seventeen.

The same age Peter and I were the first time he came to steal me away to Neverland.

"It would be a shame," he taunts when I still don't find the words to speak. With eyes still fixated on the frame, he releases a heavy sigh. "Such pretty little things. They look just like their mother used to at their age."

At that, I fight back harder than before. My hands come up and dig into his throat as I force his head back as far as I can. He releases his grip on me and pries my hands off him, forcing them behind my back and keeping them there in his strong grip.

He presses into me, the bulge in his slacks straining, harder and thicker than before, as he forces it harshly up my slit against my clit. I swallow hard, attempting to deny the sensation that instantly brings me such pleasure, and he grins. His eyes dance with a menacing mischief as he leans back slowly, then deliberately forces his length up my center again.

On instinct my eyes close and I desperately try to stifle a moan. His low laugh rings through the room a second later, making my eyes flash open to meet his in anger.

"Never had someone fuck you like I can, isn't that right Darling?"

"Fuck you, Peter," my unsteady voice rasps out.

His left hand reaches up, tightening around my throat again. Warning me. Testing me. But he doesn't cut off my air supply, just stares me fiercely in the eyes, controlling my next words. My next breath. I force my hips forward, attempting to put some space between us, but all that does is force his cock where it doesn't belong. Where I won't ever let him put it again. I bite down on my bottom lip and he leans in smiling, testing me, taunting me to say *that* name again.

I was the only one who ever got away with calling him Peter. By the look in his eyes, I'd say that freedom is no longer mine. The years we've been separated have been unkind to him. Slowly, I back as far away as possible while he proceeds to cage me in, crushing me between him and the dresser.

I can see he's fallen, given into his darkness, more than he ever has before.

He's flung himself into the black cloud that always haunted him in the past. Hooked, I can see he's addicted to the darkness that now consumes him. He's stayed there, in his nightmares, the same way I've been living mine.

Jas Hook has a death grip on the only man I've ever loved, just like I always feared.

I know, because I'm the only person alive that knows the secret most don't.

Peter & Hook?

They're the same man.

Except, I see only one staring back at me now. The one that I always feared would win if the Peter I once knew allowed him in.

"Years," I choke out when he doesn't respond. "Years you could've come back to me. Years we... Years that are lost."

His eyes hold mine. Cold. Detached. His palm shakes on my neck, giving me a break into the devil lurking inside him. He's affected. He tries to hide it, but I swear I can see a little bit of the Peter I once knew hiding in the shadows of his eyes.

"Why now?" I demand. He searches my face, just as I

search his. Time stretches in a torturous way while I wait for a response.

After a moment, he whispers with a wicked smile. "I grew up lost, Darling. I wasn't going to come for you before it was time." He gestures over my shoulder at the picture frame. "One lost soul doesn't justify making another."

My daughters. He stayed away because of them. I shiver as his grip on my neck loosens. His left hand falls to my hip just as his right raises between us, brushing lightly across my lips, almost tenderly. Somewhere deep inside, despite my better judgment, I feel my heart begin to ache.

We stand in silence a moment, the air thick between us while I attempt to study him more closely in the moonlight. He's a boy who is so much more a man than any I have known since he's been gone. He's still the same yet somehow changed. His body is broader, built on muscle and strength. His jaw is stronger than I remember. His dark hair is longer, falling into his eyes, yet short on the sides. He's forever *seventeen*. Forever ingrained in my heart, in my mind, the way he was when I first saw him. Still, something's different. I can't quite put my finger on it, but in a way, he's changed.

It's more than just the hook Jas has in him now. An alter ego he once liked to play around with when it suited him with the lost boys. He seems older. Hardened. Aged in a way simply growing up could never have changed anyone.

It's something I fear has altered the boy I once knew in a way I will never understand. Never grasp. In a way that threatens both my future and what we once had.

As pathetic as it is, I've been holding onto hope all these

years praying he'd one day come back for me. Staring into his eyes now, I fear I will never get the boy I once knew back.

The boy I once loved.

All of his light. His darkness. His good and his bad.

He had been forever seventeen long before I ever was. Long before he stole me away to Neverland when I was the same age as him. Long before I lost myself in him, fell in love with the myth before being discarded as if I meant nothing when a choice I *had* to make called me home.

Yes, I left, but he could've come with me. We could have still been happy.

When we both haven't spoken for far too long, I inhale hope and release all fear as my gaze falls to his lips.

"You've changed," I whisper, and another wicked smile tugs at his mouth. "You're not..."

"Listen to me, Darling. Listen close," he murmurs, his thumb caressing softly across my bottom lip.

With his eyes trained on my mouth, our chests rise and fall quickly. Our breathing syncs. The temptation between us shows to be just as strong as it's always been, even after all these years.

"When you left, everything changed," he whispers.

His gaze rises and the look he gives me steals my breath away. The darkness has cleared, the light blue eyes I fell in love with almost two decades ago stare back at me.

"Darkness is all I know now," his voice shakes. "A darkness you made. One you created."

I try to argue but he stops me by placing a finger against my lips.

"I can't find it," he confesses, his voice trembling as

demons surface in his eyes. It's another slight break into the new man that's holding me in his arms. A man that is still so much and yet so little the boy I fell in love with. "I need you to help me find it."

Find what?

"Do I have a choice?" I blurt out.

Anger brews under my skin for all the years that have passed since I last saw him. As much as it hurts me to see him suffer, in his absence, I've suffered, too. Still, despite that, I want to help him, but I don't have any clue what I'm getting myself into, especially since I have no idea what he lost.

What's more, my world's a mess since he's been gone. Always has been, in fact. My memories of him, as well as the ones I've made with my daughters, are the only things that have gotten me through the past seventeen years. I forced myself to grow up without him, become a woman, no longer the little girl he once knew.

I can see he's hurting, but I've been hurting, too.

As far as aging goes, I look much older than him now that I'm in my mid thirties. But in years, Peter was always much older than I was, even if he's spent his whole life trying to deny it.

The longer I don't submit to his demands, his eyes begin to cloud. A black, hollow gaze stares back at me and I know I've said something wrong.

"You always had a choice, Darling," his voice rasps angrily. "This time, let's hope you make the right one."

He backs away so quickly I fall to my knees at his feet. He laughs, and I curse under my breath, embarrassed and hurt because the Peter I knew would never have let me fall like that. He also wouldn't have stood by and watched as I lay broken, a shell of what I once was at anyone's feet, especially his.

When I don't rise right away, he takes a fist full of my hair and slowly pulls me to my feet.

"I... I don't know what you're looking for," I stammer as I find my footing and square my shoulders, attempting to seem stronger than I feel before I dare to look him in the eye.

"Yes, you do," he taunts, taking a step closer. He releases my hair and grabs my chin harshly in his palm. "It started with you, and it will end with you. One way or another. Fight it, and it will only make it harder for both of us."

He grabs my arm and pulls me harshly to the window. There is no time to think. No time to decide. Before I can catch my next breath, he's stepping up onto the bench seat. I watch wide eyed as he kicks at the glass. It shatters instantly into a million pieces around our feet.

"Second star to the right, remember?" He gestures out into the night, dropping my hand and staring deep into the eye of the storm.

The thunder crashes as rain blows through the shattered glass. I'm drenched instantly. Crossing my arms over my chest, I attempt modesty as my baby blue nightgown clings to me like a second skin, the fabric leaving nothing to the imagination.

"Say 'goodbye' to what you made of your life here while you pushed what we had away. It'll all be a dream come morning."

When he finally turns to look my way, I don't miss the

way his eyes flash with heat as they roam around the curves of my body. I'm filled out in ways I never was when I was seventeen. He notices instantly, and the look he gives me when his heated gaze finally lifts to meet mine makes my knees go weak.

My heart constricts as I stand before him torn. I can't leave, abandon my life here. I can't abandon my daughters.

I take a step back, which earns me a dark scowl. He reaches out and pulls me quickly to stand opposite him on the bench seat as the lightning flashes illuminating every curve of his haunted face. I see hurt, pain, a lost look he's drowning in filling his eyes.

"I thought you said I had a choice," my shaky voice pleads.

His hand snakes around the back of my neck as he pulls me into his chest. Glancing down at my lips, he smiles, "And did you decide?"

I take a look out at the storm. I glance quickly back inside my room. They're both the same. One, the darkness I've been living in. The other, a daunting threat of what's always been inevitable.

Deep down inside, I guess I always knew one day he'd come back for me. One day, we'd be forced to finish what we started. My journey with him led me home once before. Maybe it will again. Maybe, this time, I won't be forced to come back alone.

I glance up at him through the rain pelting against the side of my face. My lashes flutter as a gust of wind picks up, and thunder crashes angrily in the distance.

I don't know what he's looking for. What's more, I'm not

sure I can help him find what he's lost. But I do know I've felt more alive in the last five minutes than in the past two decades we've spent apart.

I swallow over a lump in my throat. My right hand shakes as I wrap it around his waist. A grin pulls at his lips as I reach up with my other hand and do the same, locking my fingers behind his back like I did all those years ago.

His gaze roams the curve of my face before landing once again on my lips. A lightness sparkles in his eyes a moment later when they lift, once again, to find mine. The darkness is gone. Maybe I can help him find whatever it is he lost.

Before I have time to dwell on the idea too much longer, he holds his lips against mine, and whispers, "Good girl."

Jolting us forward into the black of night, my body feels weightless as it slices through the air. Everything rushes me at once. The pain. The longing. The heartache. What we lost. Memories crash against me like the wind whipping dangerously against my body. Before I can tell Peter I changed my mind, before I can scream for Hook to take me back, suddenly everything fades to black.

CHAPTER 2
HOOK

"I'll teach you how to jump on the wind's back, and then away
we'll go."
Peter & Wendy
- J.M. Barrie

My teeth grind together as my head lightly sways side to side with the tide. I watch her frame wrestle in her sleep. In her darkness.

Our darkness.

The dream she's having is relentless on letting her go.

Raising my glass to my lips, I let the rum burn as it slowly slips down the back of my throat while I continue watching. Waiting. Mesmerized and fucking terrorized knowing she's once again by my side.

Wendy Darling, what the fuck am I going to do with you now?

"You can stare at her all you like, never helped you before, it sure as shit isn't going to help you now," John,

Wendy's younger brother, says from the shadows in the doorway.

I look up as he enters with a tray, regarding his sister with no more than an irritated shake of his head. He sets her meal down on the table beside the bed, pulls a pack of cigs from his pocket and lights up a smoke.

"Now, *Smee*, is that any way to welcome a guest back to the Jolly Roger?" My disturbed voice shocks me slightly when it grits out through clenched teeth as my eyes raise and catch his. He regards me with concern, to which I want to tell him he can fucking keep his pity. I will not be controlled by Wendy. Not a second time.

I set my glass down on my desk just as the boat rocks harshly against another wake. The wind and storm outside beat angrily against the glass window behind my head. Just like it did when I arrived in London and brought her back with me. It's almost as if the whole of Neverland is revolting against having Wendy back on the island.

I look to the floor, wrestling with the reality myself. I'm still not sure it was the right choice to make to bring her back here after Tink told me Wendy now lived alone. Her daughters had moved across the country. Her husband...

My heart stings at the thought of the man that, for almost two decades, had what I wanted most. The man that took what was always supposed to be mine. I shake my head, unable to force my thoughts any further, to the thought of them sharing a bed. To his hands on places I'd just as soon gut him for if I ever learned he touched. I lean back in my seat, listening to the girl I would once give up anything for cry softly in her sleep across the room.

Once loved. Once cherished. That is, before she left me *cursed* in her absence. Haunted by her fucking memories.

I still love her. I know I do. And it's that one fact that has spurred the darkness inside me into a savage, raging storm. Unhinged. Uncontrolled. Just like the one howling outside in Cannibal Cove.

I study her, laying in my bed after all this time, and my hands begin to shake.

Drowning quietly in my thoughts, my eyes lift and find John's. He hasn't looked away. He's been observing, watching, studying me the whole time I've been consumed, once again, with thoughts of his older sister, Wendy. He studies me with an inquisitive glare, making me almost grow nervous, when I'm never fucking nervous. It's almost as if he can read my thoughts.

"Keep staring at me like that, Smee, and I'll take away your whore privileges for a fucking week."

That gets him, and he looks away quickly. John likes to loose himself in a sweet, wet cunt, just as much as the rest of us. As for myself, the harlots on the island have never come close to filling the void since Wendy's been gone.

When she deserted us years ago, John stayed behind in Neverland. Loyal to a fault, it seemed only fitting I make him my first mate after everything that happened. Everything which was inevitably stolen in a blink of an eye and ruined, tainted forever.

"Traitor," John exhales slowly a moment later, looking down at his sister spread out on my sheets. The smoke from his cig circles above Wendy's restless body as she continues to writhe in sweat on my bed. "Not a guest. Traitor, Captain," he clarifies. The sting of his words pierce my black heart, reminding me of why I took so long to go back for her. "Of all of us, *you* know that best," he adds.

Fuck yes, a traitor. A hypocrite. Someone who betrayed me worse than I thought anyone ever could. Deceived me even worse than Tink did all those years ago.

As the words take hold, memories resurface, and my breath becomes shallow. Having her here, so close after all this time, my last nerve threatens to break. My hands shake as I reach out and grab ahold of the rum, quickly bringing my glass back to my lips.

When Wendy left, the darkness took hold and quickly consumed what was left of our world on the island. I thought nothing could make me feel worse, more dead inside, as the light everyone loves Neverland for was destroyed. Watching Wendy breathing across the room, lying in a bed we once shared, I know now I was so fucking wrong.

"What do you plan to do with her," John sighs, gesturing towards his sister.

She lets out a soft, sad whimper as the pixie dust wears off and she's thrust back into a world I know she never thought she'd visit again.

My blood boils bitterly as it rushes through my veins. Thoughts of Wendy and I the first time we were together in Neverland have haunted me since the second she turned her back on us all those years ago.

A curse fell on my life when she walked away, and I've never been the same since.

"What I *always* planned to do with her," I seethe. "Use

her. Break her. Take what I want from her. The only way I know how."

"She never liked your dark side, Captain," John says, as he turns and makes his way back towards the exit. "Always frightened her. She took better to Peter."

That fucking name.

With a heated glare, I look up and catch John's eyes as he stands in the doorframe. No one has said that name since the day she walked away. Now, since hearing it fall from her lips earlier tonight, I've had to endure the piercing way it stabs me in the heart twice.

"Sorry," he says, holding up his hands in surrender. "Won't slip again."

"Make fucking sure of it."

He glides his hands in his pockets with unease, his eyes downcast to the floor at his feet as I turn my attention back to Wendy. She looks to finally be at peace. Her breaths come out more easily. Her chest rises and falls with grace. Her demons are quiet. But they won't be for long.

"Time is not on our side this time, Hook," John whispers after a moment, and my breathing quickens. "The clock is..."

"Ticking!" I boom.

Rising from my seat, I throw my glass at the wall and overturn my desk in one quick thrust. It cracks as it makes impact with the wooden planks below my feet, but it doesn't break. Not like my heart does knowing the woman I swore to never allow into my life ever again has now managed to upturn my whole world in a matter of mere seconds when I was told she was living alone after all the years we've been forced to spend apart.

"I know, Smee," my nostrils flare as I force myself to calm down. Fists clenched at my side, my hands shake as I suck in a breath that won't come fast enough. "Now, show yourself out before I put a bullet through your fucking head. You are, after all, a Darling. Regardless of where you stand. Traitor runs through your veins, John. No matter how loyal you've been these past seventeen years, I won't forget that."

He shows no emotion, only glances back at the bed across the room. A wicked smile lights up his face a second later, causing me to glance up quickly and catch the wide startled eyes of Wendy. She's propped up in the middle of the black sheets, tears staining her pale face. The bed linens are pulled up to her chin as she takes in her surroundings and starts to shake.

"Told you," John grins as he turns and takes his exit. "After all these years, darkness is *not* on our side, Hook."

This time, he's smart enough not to mention the name that's been banned since Wendy flew out of my life seventeen years ago.

The door slams. When he's gone the room immediately fills with a sharp, desperate tension. A strong, electric energy wrestles between Wendy and I, stealing all reason from my brain. I stare into Wendy's eyes, confusion etches itself across her beautiful face before she sucks in a breath and her bottom lip begins to tremble. Clutching the sheet to her chest, as if it's her only armor, only defense against what she fears most, me, she waits for me to speak.

But I can't.

In this moment, words won't fucking do.

I want to make her see, make her feel. All the pain. The

misery I've felt these past seventeen years since she's been gone.

I want to force her, break her, destroy her, fuck her senseless until all that's left is the truth.

I want to watch as she's crushed underneath me, under the lies, the darkness that she created.

I want to memorize the hurt in her eyes as she's forever marked by my nightmare, filled with my cock, and cursed just the same by the black heart that now beats in my fucking chest.

A heart that will never again show her love, only pain, for the hell she has inflicted.

Her chin raises in defiance when I still haven't spoken a word. I smile knowing I'll find so much pleasure in breaking the little strength she believes she has left. She stares into my eyes with so much courage, I can tell she actually believes she has a chance. A chance at winning. A chance at making me fall to her feet like I did all those years ago. When I was her pathetic Peter. A boy who believed the lie that she could be the only women he'd ever want.

She's wrong. She's seen a bit of my darkness once before, but that was back then. When she knew me as a boy.

She's never known me as a man.

Never as Hook. A captain. A king.

The person she fell in love with once was a fucking child.

Peter *fucking* Pan.

The boy she knew is dead.

She'll learn. Oh, how she'll learn. Starting right fucking now.

I take slow, calculated steps towards the bed, intensely

watching her gaze the entire time. It isn't until I reach the frame that I see her flinch slightly back into the shadows in fear. The boat sways, and the room grows darker. Her decision to join me back in Neverland lays heavy between us right now. Her indecision over her choice is evident. Much like the shadows growing as the time nears midnight.

"Regretting your choices?" I taunt, pulling a pack of cigarettes from my pocket and casually lighting the end of one. The smoke trickles from my lips as I watch tears drip down her cheeks. Watching her break should phase me, but it doesn't. All it does is fuel the need for destruction. The need to inflict pain for the suffering I've endured in our time apart. "I must admit, with the rumors I've heard over the years, they sure are a disappointment in my eyes, Darling."

Her gaze locks bitterly on mine. Her eyes flare with a sort of violence I've never seen in her before. She straightens her spine and wipes the wetness from her face.

"I regret nothing," she whispers causing the heart in my chest to beat savagely against my rib cage for the first time in nearly two damn decades.

I've been dead so long, how can one fucking sentence make me feel like I'm burning alive?

"Hm," my lips murmur as my heart continues to hammer out of control. I attempt to buy time, studying her silently for the truth I know is hidden deep inside. Gesturing towards her with my smoke, I whisper, "You sure about that?"

"I did what I had to do."

I place my cig between my teeth and make my way towards the bar. With my back to her, I take one final long drag and set my smoke down in the ashtray before pouring myself another two fingers of rum. I shoot it back quickly, refilling the glass and cracking my neck from side to side as I watch the amber liquid quickly fill to the brim.

What she *had* to do cost us both everything.

How can she sit there and say she *doesn't* regret that?

Unless she's bluffing. Wanting me to break, become the boy she once held so fucking dear. But it would take more magic than is in all of Neverland to bring *him* back to life.

I think twice before pouring her a drink, but eventually concede against what I know is my better judgment, then turn to make my way back toward her.

When I do, she looks to her right and brushes a few strands of her auburn hair behind her ear. The ring on her left finger catches my eye, and just like the magic I swore didn't exist anymore, I feel my heart start to beat again. This time, it hammers against my chest harder than fucking before. The ring reflects in the low light of the sconces on the nearby wall, stunning me, stopping me from moving forward. It steals the breath from my lungs.

My heart, though finally beating again, feels pierced, hooked, bleeding out as a coldness rushes through my veins and my jaw clenches in rage.

I thought it was lost.

"Did you love him?" I blurt out before I can help myself.

My thoughts immediately go to the man who took her from me. The man I selfishly hunted down, intent on tearing apart, limb by limb, before stealing her away to finish what we started.

To my horror, her disgrace, I never found him.

She startles, then looks at me with big beautiful blue eyes and considers the question for way too long.

"Did you?" I demand.

Her chest begins to rise and fall quickly as we stare off against each other. Her bottom lip trembles and I feel my hand start to shake.

"Answer me," I yell. "Did. You. Love. Him. Darling?"

She jolts at the authority in my tone, but still doesn't say a word. I throw her drink to the side and the glass instantly shatters as it hits the wooden floor. Shooting mine back quickly, I throw it just the same and take two large strides to the side of the bed. I cage her in, one hand on each side of her sinful frame. She tries to back away from me as best she can, but there's nowhere for her to move. The devil in me *delights* at the fear that's shining bright in her eyes and I grin.

"Where is Peter?" she whispers finally, her eyes searching mine as her breath feathers against my lips.

Her smell consumes me. Coconut. Vanilla. Mixed with the rum on my breath it's fucking intoxicating.

Maybe I will fuck her. Make her see. Make her feel. All the Pain. The Misery. The brutal blow of rejection that I felt when she left me, married him, grew up and had her twins.

It could be fun, making her embrace the regret she swears she never felt. Maybe I will use her the only way I've grown to know how to use any woman since she's been gone. Only problem is, I could never deny her. Not *my* Wendy. A fact I'm beginning to realize never changed as my resolve crumbles and the urge to hold her tight roars to life while I continue to look into her scared eyes.

She pleads with me, begs me to show her the boy she once knew. But it's no use.

"Please," she whimpers again. "Where's Peter?"

"Dead," I growl, then smile as a shiver courses through her trembling body.

"I don't believe you," she cries, sitting up straighter, she blinks away tears, attempting to seem stronger than she really is.

I cock my head to the side and study her. In one tiny heartbeat I could take her, any fucking way I like, and there is no way she could stop me. She used to like that, I remember. Even as her *precious* Peter, she always preferred the way the darkness I kept buried inside fucked her. But what she remembers, the tiny glimpse of the man I was one day destined to become, is nothing compared to the way I'd take her now. The way I'd make her see all the ways she's been so damn wrong about everything.

"You sure about that?" I hiss as I reluctantly back away. "Well, you should know, Darling. After all, you're the one who fucking killed him."

Turning, I cross the room and quickly make for the door before I can decide to do otherwise. Before I make a foolish mistake and take what I want. What I can't and won't let myself have.

"Remember, you agreed to help me find what I'm looking for," I toss angrily over my shoulder. "For your precious daughters' sake, it's best we get on with it. Be ready at dawn."

I slam the door behind me, and the second my feet cross the threshold, I turn and lock it quickly. Stashing the key in my pocket, I close my eyes, rest my head back against the door, and flinch when I hear her crying just on the other side. Releasing a heavy sigh, it's hard to admit but having her here, I feel more cursed than I ever have since she's been gone.

I try to breathe deep but I feel the air catching in my chest.

That ring.

My heart, my head, they're a fucked-up mess from the sight of it on her finger after all this time.

Bringing her here might very well be a mistake. She's too close. Too real. Too tempting.

Seeing her on the Jolly Roger after almost two decades is making me feel. Making me believe. Making me want more when I haven't wanted anything since she walked away. Since she abandoned *us.* Since she gave *us* up.

I won't go back on my reasons for bringing her here. Not now. I won't let her change me. I need to stick to the plan to find what I've lost. And yet, I can't stop my head from wondering or going where I don't want it to.

My hands grip my hair with bent up rage as my back slides down the door and I quickly slump to the floor. Digging my fingers in deeper, I self-inflict a torturous pain as a deathly reminder to stick to the fucking plan.

Only problem is, Wendy was always the plan.

My favorite thought. My biggest victory. The only thing in life I ever yearned for more than anything else. More than Neverland.

CHAPTER 3
WENDY

"When you are sleeping in your silly bed you might be flying about with me saying funny things to the stars."
Peter & Wendy
- J.M. Barrie

TWENTY-TWO YEARS AGO

A soothing, rhythmic, humming noise nudges me from my dreams. I smile knowingly, feeling, and understanding, the shift in the room before I even open my eyes. The music is gentle, low enough for only me to hear and not wake anyone else in the house. I sit for a moment, a blush creeps across my cheeks. My body awakens in a different kind of way than it ever has before for the boy who I sense is sitting on the edge of my bed.

When I still don't move, his foot gently rubs against mine and my smile begins to grow. The bed shifts with his weight as he sits down on the comforter, and I smile. My head lulls from side to side with the rhythm of the music he plays, but it only lasts a few more moments before he stops suddenly.

"Keep playing, Peter," I whisper. "I haven't heard enough. You're almost at my favorite part."

"What part is that, Wendy?"

His body shifts again. I suddenly feel his fingertips against my inner thigh. My breath catches. Feelings, emotions I am not sure how to put into words, simmer in my lower belly. I don't move away as his palm gently caresses where his fingers just touched. My eyes flash open as he scoots closer on the bed.

Swallowing over a lump in my throat, I search his gaze and wonder if he understands the way he's making me feel. Something I don't even fully understand yet myself. After all, Peter is only a boy. A boy that ran away from home when he was born. Or so he tells me. These feelings, they're all new to me, new to him, I think. And I can tell by the look in his eyes that whatever I am feeling, he's feeling, too.

If it was really true that Peter ran away from home the day he was born, the boy sitting in front of me, the one who looks to be the same seventeen years I am, would instead resemble a child. Not the boy, almost man, sitting across from me now. A boy on a dangerous cusp of exploration, playing recklessly too close to the unknown. A boy currently staring back at me with so much heat in his gaze, I feel slightly embarrassed for the both of us.

This is new.

This isn't the way our meetings normally go.

For as long as he's been coming to sit with me, what must be several years now and playing his pipes at the foot of my bed, I never once thought he'd be staring back at me the way he is now.

Recently, I had wished for it. Dreamed about it, even.

However, *every dream I've ever had pales in comparison to the look he's giving me now.*

"You've changed..." Peter says as he leans in closer, setting his pipes aside and bracing his hands on either side of my body. He brushes a strand of hair out of my eyes, and I tremble. With a smile, he steals my next breath when he whispers, "Want to know my favorite part, Wendy Moira Angela Darling?"

Nervously, I stare at his mouth and whisper, "Part of what, Peter?"

He grins, making my thighs clench together on an instinct I have never known before. Glancing up, his eyes roam across my face, down my neck, to my breasts that have gotten larger since the last time he was here a few months back. Heat settles between my legs, and I bite my bottom lip as his gaze finally finds mine.

"Of you, Wendy."

My laugh comes out shaky as I glance away, but he cups my chin gently in his palm and slowly forces my stare back his way.

"Everything."

He brushes his thumb across my lips, and I swear *I might die from the way my body starts to tremble. My heart beats out of control.*

I try to talk myself down to reality, to ease the tension building between us. Peter always says whatever comes into his head, so how can I know what he's saying true?

"Everything about you is my favorite part," he whispers, as his thumb caresses the right side of my cheek.

"Part of what?" I whisper back, before silently kicking myself for being such an idiot. He already answered that. Anxiously, I start to stir in the bed, excitedly anticipating what he'll say next.

28

"Part of living for," he says without pause. "Breathing for. Dying for."

I have to tell myself to breathe as he backs away, acting like what he just said didn't change the course of my entire life. He picks up his pipe, ignoring how much what he just said changed me forever, and brings it back to his mouth. He shrugs. And as if it should be as evident to me as it is to him, he says, "Favorite part of living, Wendy."

He looks at me over his instrument and starts to play again. My heart soars, my body feels numb. His words just took me to heaven and back and he doesn't even know it. When he gets to my favorite part of the song, he gives me a wink that almost makes me do something crazy. Almost makes me shoot out of bed, grab the pipe from his hands, and cover his lips with my own like I've wanted to for months now. I suck in a shaky breath, my mind playing back his words as he continues to play his music before he slowly rises from the bed.

He walks over to the window, and I watch him for a moment, mesmerized by the difference of what's happening between us since the last time he was here. He's always been older than me all the years he's stayed by my side. He's always seemed out of reach. A part of a different world. That is, I guess, until tonight. Something has changed. As he looks back my way through the shadows of night, I sit up in bed and don't miss the way his eyes fall and take me in again.

I've matured since the last time he was here. Blossomed a little, almost overnight. I didn't resemble a little girl last time he was here, but I was far from a woman, too. Now, my face is slimmer, my breasts larger, my hips wider, and my heart is beating faster than it ever has before any of the nights when

29

Peter has come to my room. Thoughts I swear I shouldn't be thinking keep creeping to the forefront of my mind. An impulse I know one day will get the better of me no matter how hard I try and fight it.

As his song finishes, I rise from the bed and Peter takes a bow. A giggle escapes my lips as he stands to his full height and starts to come closer.

"What about me, Wendy?" He smirks. "Have I changed?"

I want to tell him, yes! He has!

The look in his eyes. The feeling I get when he comes closer. The possession I feel as he reaches out now and takes my hand pulling me toward his chest.

It's all new.

Flustered, I look to the floor and say, "No, Peter." But the new emotions coursing through my veins gets the better of me, and I end with a whisper, "You're just as perfect as always."

"That's right," he boasts. "Flawless, Wendy."

Looking up, I raise my brow in challenge at him. He's always been conceited. But that's also one of his most fascinating qualities. A look of amusement spreads across his face as he pulls me in a small step closer towards his chest.

"Everyone has flaws, Peter."

"Not you, Wendy," he smiles, so sure of himself, and then adds, "And not I."

"How can you be so sure?" I tease.

"I just know," he winks, his hand guiding me to spin as he slowly twirls me around in the middle of my room.

"Do you?" I tease. "I bet you know everything." I laugh as his eyes catch mine when I turn past him. On the next turn, I notice his gaze traveling down my body. Desperate. Unabashed. My

hand in his begins to shake, my voice trembles as I force myself to ask, "Am I right, Peter?"

He just smiles, his eyes never finding mine again as they continue their appraisal, then he backs away quickly, dropping my hand and making me fall back on my feet with a slight stumble. I try to shake the way he's making me feel, like I matter one second and don't the next. He brings his pipes back to his lips and plays a short tune, acting as if everything that was just consuming us was merely a dream, not reality. Shaking my head, I force my thoughts away from mature things and focus on the way things have always been.

It's just Peter Pan. The boy that's been coming to my bedroom randomly for about three to four years now. The boy that says whatever comes to his mind and is so conceited, there is no way he could think of anyone before himself. All he's saying is just typical Peter babble.

Then why is it affecting me differently than it ever has before?

"I have something for you," he says randomly as he stops playing and abruptly drops to one knee.

My eyes grow wide. He's played around like this before. After all, everything is a game with Peter. What's more, he believes all games are real. But the sight of him on one knee does something to me that it shouldn't. That it hasn't any time we've played around like this before.

Holding out his hand, his fist clenched tight, he smiles. "Guess what it is."

My mouth is too dry to speak, so I just shake my head no.

"Come on, Wendy," he rolls his eyes impatiently. "Guess."

"I'm not good at guessing."

"Just try, please, for me."

31

He gives me a sexy smirk that almost makes me drop to my knees, so I concede.

"A thimble?" I ask, but he just laughs, so I try again. "Pixie dust."

He glances over his shoulder for Tinker Bell, almost as if he's nervous. When he looks back my way he shakes his head no, scrunching up his nose and closing his eyes in disgust. When they open again, they're even more impatient than before.

"Um," I stammer. "'I told you I wasn't good at this, let me see. A... a mermaid."

"Wendy," Peter laughs. "A mermaid wouldn't fit in my hand."

Delighted with his joke, he stands and takes a playful step towards me. Reaching out, he takes my hand in his and opens his palm. In the dark, I try to focus on what he's trying to give me, but I can't tell exactly what it is until he slips it into my hand and pulls me a step forward into the moonlight cascading through my bedroom window.

An acorn button. My heart skips a beat. Our first kiss. A playful one when I was just a kid. I look back up at him quickly, but his eyes are still trained on my palm as he gently rolls the button around, and amusement still dances in his eyes.

"What... why?" I begin to ask.

"So you never forget me, Wendy. So you know, I'll always come back for you."

He walks away and a piece of my heart forever goes with him. Just like that, I know no matter what happens between us, I will always wait for him. Regardless of if he tells me to or not. If we were ever forced to part, I could never stop wishing, hoping, one day he might fly back through my window.

Picking up his pipes, he walks away towards the boy's room while I study my hand more closely.

What does this all mean?

"Don't lose it, though," he warns and I look up startled. "If you do, I might one day forget my way back to you."

"But Peter..."

He stops and studies me intensely.

"Always wait for me, Wendy. If you do, one night, you'll eventually hear me crowing."

He gives me a wink over his shoulder just as he disappears into the jack and jill bathroom separating my room from my brother's. I scurry after him, bumping into my dresser as I go, and tripping over a bathroom mat. The sound of his pipes grows louder as I enter my brother's room and see him stop at John's bed.

Every night he's come, he's never ventured into their room. Why now?

Suddenly, Peter flies up onto John's bunk and kicks him to the floor. My hands cover my mouth in shock, as I desperately try to keep the scream inside that wants to break free. I don't want to wake my mother or worse, my father. But what Peter just did was so wrong and...

"I say!" my brother, John, startles awake a moment later as he rubs sleep from his eyes and looks up at Peter. "Wendy, is that really him?"

I look between the two, John not much younger than Peter or myself. I lower my hands and I'm about to answer when...

"Michael!" John shouts. "Michael, he's here!"

Michael bolts out of the bottom bunk and my brothers wrestle each other out of the way, trying to get closer to Peter, the boy they've heard so much about with the stories I've told them the last couple years. Through their questions and their bouncing around, Peter's eyes hold mine. Suddenly cocooned in a separate world, just the two of us, an anchor in the middle of all the madness, he gives me a playful wink before he jumps off the bed and takes a couple steps towards me.

"You ready, Wendy?"

"For... what, Peter?"

"The best part," he smirks. Leaning in further, I stop breathing as he whispers, "My favorite part."

It's only Peter and I as I stare into his eyes and on a breathless reply, whisper back, "I've been waiting my whole life."

My words hold more weight than he knows. The way his eyes grow wide in understanding makes my heart swell. It makes me wish Peter and I were somewhere else. Someone else. Some other boy and girl who stood a chance at growing up together, falling in love, growing old with one another and never letting go. Just two old souls who never have to worry about waiting, and never have to think that one of us is moving on, without the other.

As long as I stay here, I will always be growing up. I will always be moving on, even when I don't want to. In a few years, I'll grow older waiting for him to come back to me, all while Peter forever stays the same.

"I lied," Peter says, breaking me from my thoughts. My brow furrows as he takes a step forward and takes my hand, the one with his acorn button in it, and wraps it in both of his. "About my favorite part," he whispers.

"You did?" I ask, slightly alarmed. He nods his head yes and my throat closes up, but I manage to get out one question. "Why?"

"Because, my favorite part hasn't happened yet."

He pulls me back towards my room and my brothers follow.

They're quiet now, wondering what's happening, eager to hear everything that's being said. The window to my room is open and I study it wondering how, until I hear the faint jingle of bells overhead and look up. A twinkling light dances above our heads and I smile in awe.

It tickles as the fairy flies and the dust dances down across our skin. My brothers giggle as they follow Tinker bell towards the open window, then quickly up and out, into the night. I go to yell, to protest, to stop them from possibly getting hurt, but Peter pulls me close up onto my window seat, wraps his arms around my waist and all thoughts cease to exist, except one.

I'm tired of waiting.

My nipples rub against his strong chest as he pulls me flush against him. A foreign feeling flutters at the base of my spine, igniting in my core the second I look into his eyes. It travels to my lower belly and causes me to bite my lip anxiously with desire.

"I want to show you my world, Wendy."

I know the words aren't meant to sound so seductive, but they do. I watch his tongue wet his lips as his grip around my waist tightens.

"I want to show you..." my breathing quickens as I stare in his eyes, waiting for him to continue, "how complete it feels with you finally in it."

"Peter," I breathe, but he leans in, his lips suspended over mine and I suck in a sharp breath.

"That's my favorite part, Wendy. You. Me. Neverland."

I blink a few times, trying to clear my head. "How do you know you'll still feel the same when you finally have me there?"

"I don't have to see you to feel you," his breath feathers against my lips and that foreign feeling I've been experiencing

35

since he flew through my window tonight ignites into so much more. A yearning. A burning. An ache that will only be cured if I go with him.

"I feel you with me every day. Every adventure I take. You're always with me."

I curl my other arm instinctively around his waist. "Really?"

He smiles mischievously.

"I want to feel you in ways I've never felt before," his eyes lower and graze across every inch of my skin.

Hot. Heavy. Exposing me in a way I've never known before. Felt before. They're doing just as he says. Touching me, teasing me, leaving their mark, changing me, keeping me from ever being able to forget the way I feel when he's admiring me like he is now.

He hesitates for a moment. His eyes lift to meet mine. His chest rises and falls quickly.

Is he nervous?

"Do you want that, too?" he asks. "For me to feel you, know you, all of you, Wendy?"

I can't speak. I can't breathe. So, I give him a nod. Just one simple tilt of my head.

Yes.

"That's my good girl," he smirks, as he pulls me quickly to the window and jolts us forward, out into the night.

To the second star to the right.

CHAPTER 4
HOOK

"'Wendy,' he continued in a voice that no woman has ever been able to resist, 'Wendy, one girl is more use than twenty boys.'"
Peter & Wendy
- J.M. Barrie

PRESENT DAY

I force the hook deeper into one of my mate's right side, twisting and smiling when I see the light fade from his eyes. His death grip on my arm loosens as his inevitable end takes over. Blood spills out from his wound, leaving a fucking mess, drenching the floor at my feet, but I don't stop. I twist the hook under his rib in a full circle, my jaw clenched tight, his life deliciously slipping through my fingers as my eyes grow wide, his fade closed, and I watch him take his last damned breath.

With no regard for how precious life is at all, I toss his cold body to the floor and turn towards my men. Hatred brews under my skin. A hostile need to take one of their lives next increases with every breath I take. I stare them down and wait for one of them to speak. Yet, none of them seem to have the fucking courage.

"We could have handled it," John eventually starts. Yes, they could have. But not in the way the fucker deserved. Then, my first mate makes a mistake and says, "Though, getting your hands dirty always did help you de-stress, Hook."

"Who says I'm fucking stressed?" I hiss as I wipe the bastard's blood off my favorite weapon on John's tunic and then stash it back on my belt. The hook's weight sits heavy on my side, just like the thought of Wendy laying in my bed after all this time sits heavy in my gut.

Or is that my heart?

Shaking my head, I glance up and wait for John to answer. The stand-off between me and my first mate intensifies the longer he takes to answer my fucking question. The other crew members in the room sense it and back into the shadows. Hell, she may be his sister, but I'll be damned if he tells me what's what. Especially when he has no fucking clue what really went down between us all those years ago.

"You just gutted one of your own men for no reason..."

"There was a damn good reason."

"Telling Tink that Wendy is back on the Jolly Roger is no reason to..."

"Keep running your fucking mouth, Smee, and you'll be next."

His jaw ticks as a few of my men quickly clear out of the room. They're obviously worried I'll start a killing spree that they won't have the chance to escape once I get started. Wouldn't be the first time. And shit, it damn sure won't be the last if John keeps pushing his luck.

"Tink forgot about Wendy long ago, Hook," he grits out as he takes a step towards me. But that's not true. John doesn't know all he thinks he does, seeing as Tink was the one who tipped me off to her living alone. "Honestly, I think she's more pissed at who has been warming your bed since Wendy than a ghost from your past."

"Tink warms it often enough herself, when she's in the right mood to share."

"But not as often as Tiger Lily."

"Speaking of which," I hiss out, annoyed with the conversation. I glance out the window and see the sun setting, "It's about her time too, and fuck if I don't still need another damn release."

I shoulder past John and continue out into the corridor, hoping to put this conversation behind me. Although, I'm not that lucky as I hear John quicken his pace the second I enter the hallway. My men scatter, startled, panicked, fearful as they duck into various rooms. I stalk angrily towards the stairwell leading up to the first deck. The boat sways as I hear their whispers, their uncontrolled chatter about what's got me so fucking fired up, but I let it slide against my better judgment. My mind is too full of puzzles I've never been able to piece together. Starting with Wendy.

If my intuition on the sunset is right, Tiger Lily should be bare naked, tits down, ass up, spread across my bed in the guest quarters. I've kept her waiting long enough. My dick hardens at the thought, and I pick up the pace, climbing the stairs two at a time when John finally speaks again.

"You can't outrun it this time, you know."

My feet hit the deck just as a gust of wind picks up. I have to duck in order to not be tossed overboard by one of my ship's sails. Rolling my eyes, I let another one of his insubordinate outbursts go when I really shouldn't, and don't give him the satisfaction of a response. I look down at my blood-stained clothes as I make my way across deck and start to unbutton my shirt, pulling it from my slacks in the process.

Tiger Lily's never minded me fucking her dirty before. But something about sinking into her wet cunt covered in the aftermath of what Wendy does to me feels wrong.

"You brought her back here for a reason, Hook. Burying yourself in the same damn pussy you've been fucking for the past seventeen years isn't going to fix whatever the hell you fucked up."

In less than a second, I turn and have my hand wrapped tightly around John's throat. With one flick of my wrist, I could break his bloody neck. With his body pushed up against the nearest wall, I'd debate doing just that if it wasn't for Wendy. I tighten my grip into a painful vice, glaring fiercely into his eyes. The darkness that grows within me is intent on making sure he's just taken his last breath for continuing to run his fucking mouth. I've already told him to stop once, already given him more than enough chances over the years to shut the fuck up about shit he has no damned clue about, but still he keeps on talking.

"Who says *I* fucked it up?" My wild eyes bore into his.

Jaw clenched tight in rage, my grip tightens, continuing to cut off his air supply.

Fuck it. Maybe I am on a rampage. Maybe I will end my first mate after all and unleash hell on my men. All for a past I can't change and a future I'm screwing up more and more with each second that passes. Just the thought of Wendy makes me fucking destructive. Deranged with the knowledge that she's here, just a few steps away, and I still don't know what to do about it. I still don't know how to get back what I lost.

What we lost.

It's killing me after all this time to have her so close and yet so far away.

Subconsciously, my eyes lift to the top deck, catching a light on in my master's quarters. I'm instantly drawn to her, like I've always been. Without realizing, my grip on John's throat starts to loosen. He starts to suck in a sharp breath. Startled, I release my grip. Taking a step back, I hear him cough, suck in air, desperate to reclaim his life that was seconds ago slipping through my fingers.

I, however, only have eyes for her as I watch shadows begin to move in my upstairs quarters.

Shoving him out of my grip, I turn to leave, hell-bent on putting both Wendy and her brother behind me. But when he sucks in a deep breath, regains the strength to work his damn tongue, his words pierce through any solace I was going to find by letting myself go balls deep in Tiger Lily's pussy tonight.

"I do," he finally grits out. "I say *you* fucked it up."

Turning back around slowly, I watch him push off the

wall. After a tense moment, he stalks past me, rubbing his neck, still trying to regain his breath. The look in his eyes as he passes makes me stand down. It's the look of death. Death for any man that crosses him right now. I know because the darkness that breeds that kinda of destruction, that need for vengeance no matter the cost, lives in me, too. Although I know I can take John in any fight, I let him pass, respecting Wendy and what we had too much to bring him any more harm.

If that's not enough. His words paralyze me because they're true. He turns back to look at me just as my eyes lift once again and catch Wendy's shadow in the window overhead.

"She may be a traitor, but she's my sister first," he hisses. "You've had seventeen years to fix this, Hook. I stood by your side because I couldn't bear the thought of going home. As long as I was here, she might come back, and you might finally fix a chance you screwed up with a girl you sure as shit never deserved."

He takes his exit, the door across the way slamming shut just as Wendy pulls back the curtain to my quarters. She stares off into the quickly fading sun and my heart constricts, strangling me as I'm forced to watch her from a distance. For the life of me I can't take my eyes off her. Hell, I never could.

"Hook," Tiger Lily's voice calls to me from beyond the door at my side. But all it does is make my dick shrivel as I watch Wendy's eyes travel slowly down to meet mine.

I expect them to be filled with hatred. I expect her to walk away, to back down like she always did. Always has. What I don't expect is for them to be filled with sadness. To be filled with tears. She bites her bottom lip, a lonely tear drop slips from her beautiful eyes and falls slowly down her left cheek.

I expect her to look away.

A piece of me, though, is not surprised when she doesn't.

Tiger Lily's voice calls to me again and a sickness builds in the pit of my stomach. Never dropping my gaze from Wendy's, I stalk across the deck, away from Tiger Lily and my past, and quickly take leave of the ship. Pulling a cigarette free from my pack of smokes, my eyes fall to my hands and I stop dead in my tracks once my feet hit land. Lighting up, I study them with a cold heart. They're stained with the vengeance I just took out on an innocent man. What's even worse, I'm stunned when I see them start to shake.

They don't shake because of the blood. They shake because Wendy being back here in Neverland does something to me it shouldn't. Makes me fucking care when I haven't cared about anything but fueling the pure rage and vengeance that's been building in my soul the past seventeen years. It's true he was a man that didn't deserve to die. But since I took over the Jolly Roger, I've never cared who was on the other side of my hook, and I damn sure won't start caring now.

I glance back up and see Wendy's stare hasn't faltered. She gazes back at me from across the ship with the same sadness, the same regret that filled her eyes seventeen years ago when she told me she had to leave Neverland. When she pushed me away. When I desperately wanted to stand by her side. The only slight difference is, this time, there's something else in her stare that pulls me in and makes me nervous. It's something I can't quite put my finger on as her spine stiffens and she stands up a little taller, intent on not turning away first.

Fuck this, I won't start caring now. Especially not about a man that may or may not have deserved to die.

We all die.

But not all of us really live.

Not when your reason for breathing refuses to give you the things you can't survive without.

Her heart. Her soul. Her future. No matter the cost.

Exhaling a cloud of smoke, I give in and concede, bowing, I glare up at her and offer her the satisfaction of winning this round. Turning, I feel Wendy's eyes on my back until I am completely out of sight.

With all the bullshit intent on tearing apart my soul these last twenty-four hours, there is only one place I feel like being right now.

I wish I could save myself the walk and fly, but I haven't been able to soar above land and into the clouds without the help of pixie dust since a few weeks after Wendy left. In fact, I had to sneak some from Tinker Bell and the other fae to even get back to her so I could bring her here last night. Plus, that would let her see where I am going. Where I have gone every damn day since she's been gone.

A place even my darkness isn't an escape from.

One where I first felt the magic start to leave me.

One that forever changed both of us, and ruined me from *ever* being able to move on without her again.

CHAPTER 5

PETER

"'See,' he said, 'it is the kiss I gave her. It has saved her life.'"
Peter & Wendy
- J.M. Barrie

SEVENTEEN YEARS AGO

"Be careful, Wendy. I won't be able to live with myself if you get hurt."

Reaching out to her quickly, I wrap my arm around her waist and hoist her up against my body into the air, barely saving her in time to keep her from tumbling off the rocks and into the crashing waves.

"Oh, my, Peter, thank you," her breath is warm against my lips as her eyes lift to meet mine.

Her grip on my biceps tightens. Something stirs in my lower stomach as our bodies heat to an unbearable high while I stare down into her eyes and hover with her in my arms above the rocks.

"You know, the lost boys say you always wait until the last minute to save someone."

Her eyes twinkle in the moonlight. I can't help the grin that spreads across my face because I'm absolutely in love with the look that's staring back at me. Flushed cheeks. Startled eyes. It's thrilling. Breathtaking. That's what she is. Nothing has ever been able to take my breath away before. Until Wendy.

"They say you like the rush of the risk, the cleverness in the catch, more than the life you're saving," she continues, her mouth hanging open as her eyes travel to my lips and she wets hers with anticipation.

Leaning in, my dick stirs as she waits with bated breath for me to respond. I've grown to like her best there, desperate, waiting for me to give her what she needs. "You're the only life worth saving, Wendy."

Her body trembles in my arms, and I tighten my grip around her, pulling her closer, not able to get her close enough.

"More than your own, Peter?" she whispers.

"Without question. I'll always put your life before mine."

With a wink, I take flight. I can't tell if her breath is rushed from my words, or the swiftness with which I flew her up in the air. But as I start to descend through the mist, her arms tighten around my neck, and I feel her same rushed breath feather against my skin as she holds on tight and closes her eyes.

"One day, Wendy, you won't be so scared when I steal you away and out into the stars."

"One day, Peter, I'll be able to breathe again when I'm around you, and not feel like I'm about to faint."

Ducking quickly into the eyes of Skull Rock, I set her down softly on her feet and force her to look me in the eyes as we stand on a rock ledge.

"You feel faint? Why didn't you tell me you couldn't breathe, Wendy? If I knew..."

"Oh, Peter," she laughs, swatting me away playfully, then turning and taking a step out of my reach. "Not everything someone says should be taken so literally."

"Why not?"

My back stiffens, my stance hardens, because I would never tell her anything that was untrue.

She spins on her heels, her eyes lock on mine for only a second before anxiously darting around the dark rock cave we're hidden away from the rest of the world in. She looks... nervous? Hesitant? Did I say something wrong?

"Oh no, not like that. It's just that..." her voice trails off as I stare at her with hooded, questioning eyes, and take a step in her direction. She instantly takes one back. So, I take another one forward. Again, she backs away.

Normally, I love games, but not right now. Not when I feel like Wendy could ever be untrue to me.

Her back hits the stone wall behind her and she looks away startled. "What is this place," she asks as her eyes scan the dark tomb.

"Skull Rock," I whisper, taking a stray strand of her corn silk hair and brushing it behind her ear. Her body trembles, and it does something to me. Something I can't put into words yet. So, I continue, "It's where we take the ones we kidnap when we're playing pirates. When the boys know me as Jas Hook."

"Do you kidnap a lot of people, Peter?" Her eyes finally find mine in the shadows and it's my turn to feel faint. Stepping into

her, I suck in a shaky breath and go to speak, but she continues. "Before you kidnapped me, that is?"

"You came willingly, Wendy," I correct her with a smile. Brushing her cheek, my thumb touches her lips as I say, "Something tells me, you'll always come willingly, Wendy."

Resting my palm against the stone at the side of her cheek, I lean in and wait for her to answer me, but she won't even look me in the eye as she places both her palms against my chest and attempts to hold me at a distance.

"Please," she begs, and something deep inside, something that feels dark when I've only ever felt light, begins to stir.

I like the sound of her begging. A lot, I decide, as I cock my head to the side and study her. Her breath comes more rushed than before. Her chest rises and falls quickly as I slowly tip her chin up, forcing her to look me in the eye.

"Do you feel faint now, Wendy?"

My thumb brushes against her bottom lip. A foreign feeling builds, pumping through my veins as my cock lengthens between us. I've felt it harden for her before, but not like it's doing now when she's pressed tightly up against me, her breasts, nipples, brushing lightly against my chest, and her thighs noticeably shaking.

My Wendy.

My beautiful breathtaking Darling.

A carnal need rushes through my body as my right-hand snakes behind her neck and pulls her from the wall, crushing her frame securely against mine. She gasps out when she feels, finally understands, she does something to me, too. I haven't been able to think straight since the night I flew back and noticed how much she'd changed. Blossomed. Developed into something so mouth-

watering, so tempting, so fucking addictive I know I won't be right again until I have her.

Her eyes plead with mine, craving something we know we're on the cusp of discovering, but don't know how to grasp it just yet.

Maybe that's part of the magic.

Maybe something so strong, so perfect, can't be contained.

My thumb brushes across her bottom lip and a whimper escapes her, echoing through Skull Rock, floating through the air between us on a tempting breeze. Maybe the only way to believe in the magic is to let it consume you, control you, dominate you, like my Wendy has somehow managed to find a way to rule over me.

"Are you nervous?" I whisper.

"Should I be?" she asks cautiously.

Her body shakes. She tries to hide it. Tries to stare into my eyes confidently, but I notice her shyness. I feel her insecurity. I understand her need for modesty without her even having to say a word.

Though, I don't think I can honor it tonight.

"I told you I wanted to feel you, know you, all of you, Wendy."

"Peter, I've never..."

"Never what?"

She sucks in a breath. Her eyes drop hesitantly between us. She tries to back away, but I don't let her go. Tightening my grip around her waist, a carnal need I've never embraced before beckons to let it be unleashed. If that wasn't enough, something about the way she denies what she wants makes something inside of me snap.

"Feel that?" I growl as I push her back up against the wall and force my thick length up her inner thigh.

She closes her eyes, bites her bottom lip, stifles a moan, and nods her head.

"I've never either, Wendy. Felt this. Wanted this." She stops breathing. "I don't know what I'm supposed to do, either." My head drops to her neck, her skin breaks out in goosebumps as I gently place a kiss to her trembling skin. "What I'm not supposed to do?"

I stare at her neck, my breaths come out in rushed, heated waves against her skin. Goosebumps break out across her collarbone, and my eyes travel lower. They graze hungrily down to her full breasts and instinctively I press my body harder against hers. She lets out another whimper. One filled with pain, with pleasure. My eyes flash back to hers, and I notice they're still closed.

What's more, she still hasn't taken a breath.

"Wendy," I whisper, leaning my face down, drawn to her more than ever before. I lick my lips, my gaze studying her mouth. "If you need air, Darling, all you have to do is ask."

She gasps, sucking in a breath just as I fist her hair in my hand, her fingers desperately grip my scalp, and our mouths crash against one another for the first time.

Her right leg wraps around my waist and I push her back up against the wall, instinctively bringing my hand up under her other thigh and lifting her into the air. She wraps both legs around my middle as my hands rise up her curves, settling against both sides of her face.

Should I take this slow?

Fast?

She fists my shirt harshly and pulls me closer, answering my need with a greedy moan of pleasure.

More.

We both need more.

In sync, our mouth's part, deepening the kiss and I brush my *tongue against hers. She stills. My eyes open and catch her startled stare. She doesn't pull away. With my mouth held against her lips, I repeat the motion, then ask, "Is this, ok?"*

She doesn't respond, only leans in and slowly kisses me back. Her tongue strokes mine seductively, making a sound escape my lips I've never heard.

I've never craved something before like I crave Wendy.

A frenzied need suddenly mixes with a demanding urge to take, and our bodies grind against each other surprisingly knowing how to respond.

I hold her for minutes I wish were hours as we explore each other in a way we've never thought of before. Her lips on mine feels mind blowing. Earth shattering. I'm obsessed. Hooked for life, instinctively knowing I will never get enough. Could never get enough.

She's the only girl for me.

From my first memory, it has always only ever been my Wendy.

Taking a step like this feels so right, inevitable. We can't deny each other any longer.

"Peter," she whispers, as my mouth falls back to her neck. I kiss, taste, suck a trail to her collarbone, across her clavicle, down her chest, to her breasts that I haven't been able to stop thinking about. Not since the night I flew back through her window, noticed them large, round, mature, and carried her back with me to Neverland.

Setting her down on her feet and taking a step back, I ask, "Can I touch you here, Wendy?"

I run my fingertip along the lace at the top of her light blue nightgown. She shivers. For the life of me, I can't tear my eyes away from her breasts or the nipples I see piercing through the thin fabric. Finally, my gaze lifts long enough to see her nod her head with approval. I hold my breath as I step back into her and slowly start to unbutton her shirt.

"Have you ever had someone touch you here?"

My fingers get to the last button, and I wait, realizing how much I need her to say no. How much I need to be the only one that has ever touched her like this. Ever will touch her like this.

My hands raise gently to her shoulders, but I don't look away from the fabric still covering her chest.

"No," she finally whispers.

A smile spreads across my face as I push the top of her nightgown off her arms, exposing her to me for the first time. I run my fingertips down, across her curves, holding her breasts in my hands and groaning at the weight of them in my shaking palms.

"Have you ever had anyone taste you here, Wendy?"

She sucks in a breath. I take her nipples in between my thumb and finger and gently roll them, my dick hardens, strains, as her head falls back and a moan escapes her lips.

"No," she whispers again. Before I can respond, she begs, "Please, Peter..."

My head lowers to her breasts, but just before I suck her nipple into my mouth, I dip my hand to her center and rub between her thighs. She gasps out loud as I fill my mouth with her smooth pale skin and run my fingers back and forth across her most delicate spot.

"And here?" I groan, pride filling my chest when a wetness begins to coat my fingers. "What if I taste you here, Wendy?"

"I," she pants, "I don't... I don't know."

I pull my fingers up to the top of her center, to a sensitive nub, and notice she bucks her hips off the wall wanting more. Smiling, I take her other breast in my mouth and suck down harder. My fingers rub circles as I commit to memory the spot she likes me to touch most.

"I've never..."

I cut her off, dropping to my knees and pulling up her blue nightgown. "Remember, Wendy, neither have I. But I want this." I suck in a breath. She smells sweet. So delicately delicious I can't wait to get my mouth on her. "I need this."

My vision blurs. My mouth waters. My dick throbs as I take in her wet velvet skin through her white panties. Looking up, she blushes as her chest rises and falls quicker than before.

I slowly pull the white lace down to her knees, shaking, trembling with the need to move faster. But I want to take time with Wendy. I want to remember every second of feeling her, tasting her, for the very first time. I blow against her center, loving the way her fingers dip into my hair and she pulls me closer.

"Do you feel faint now?"

"No, Peter," she whispers.

I run my fingers through her wetness. Licking my lips as they're coated instantly with her arousal.

"I want to make you feel faint, Wendy," I confess in a whisper.

Her thighs shake again as I continue to run my finger through her center, stopping at her opening to press up inside her as my eyes lift and catch hers. Her mouth falls open, her eyes widen, and I groan as I force my finger further into her warm center.

"I want to make your world go black and be the only one that breathes you back to life. Gives you air, Darling."

"Oh, God," she pulls my head closer.

"Will you let me?" I whisper, watching as my fingers pull in and out of her heat.

The wetness coats them thickly. Without thinking, I press another finger inside her determined to make the wetness grow.

"Please," she whispers as my face comes closer to her center. "Please, Peter. Please try."

"Oh Darling," I groan, closing the space between her throbbing center and my lips, "Remember, all you have to do is ask."

Covering my mouth over her velvet skin, I groan. She cries out as my tongue parts her center and I force my fingers quickly inside her. Even though I've never done anything like this before, instinct takes over and I grab one of her thighs and throw it over my shoulder.

Licking up to her sweet spot, I suck down hard, like I did on her plump nipples and hear her scream. She loves it, I can tell, just as much as I love doing this to her, so I repeat what I did again. This time, she purrs my name. I groan as I pull my fingers in and out of her quicker, faster still, not able to take it slow like I first wanted. I'm too turned on by how wet I can make her pussy as she begins to drip down the back of my hand.

"Oh God, Peter, I think I am going to faint..."

Something inside me snaps as I finger her harsher, demanding more from her. My lips suck harder on her nub before I release her favorite spot and lick up her center quickly.

"Do you like it when I lick you?" I ask. She only whimpers. "Or suck you, Wendy?"

"Suck," she pants. "Suck me harder. Peter, Please."

I do as she says, hooking my fingers inside and running them in and out quickly. She explodes into screams a moment later. Her thighs start shaking, her center pulses, her wetness covers my *hand, dripping down my wrist. Slowly I feel her world fade to black then finally, I hear her suck in a sharp breath of air, frantically coming back to life.*

When she's breathing steadier, I place a kiss against her favorite spot, now my favorite spot, and rise to meet her stare. A beautiful, sexy haze clouds her eyes and I groan loving the look of satisfaction I put on her face. My cock throbs between us, needing to feel a release like she just did. Taking my hand covered in her wetness, I trail it across her lips. Her eyes widen as she realizes what I've just done.

"Taste it," I demand. She does as I say and something about the way she complies makes my dick twitch. "God, that's beautiful," I hiss as I watch her lips suck my fingers into her mouth, cleaning her taste off my hand with frenzied greed. Before I can stop myself, I confess, "I need you to suck me, Wendy."

She instantly stops breathing. Leaning in, I lick her wetness off her lips, successfully breathing her back to life when she finally sucks in another breath. This time sharper than before.

"Good girl," I whisper. "Just like that."

Pushing her to her knees, she complies to my wishes, and I eagerly unzip my pants and pull my dick free. This is all new to me. I'm not sure if we are doing this right, but something in her eyes tells me she wants it just as much as I do.

But just to make sure...

"Do you want to, Wendy?" I groan as I fist my thick length in my hand and stroke it, rotating my hand around my throbbing crown. Fuck, it feels so good, so I pump my dick faster while staring into her lust filled eyes and almost explode across her tits.

She nods her head. Her eyes flare as she looks at my straining length and wets her lips.

"Stick out your tongue."

She does so quickly, and I waste no time slapping the head of my cock against her warm, wet, willing tongue.

"Wendy," I hiss out, overtaken by the sight of her on her knees doing what I needed her to. My heart pounds knowing she's about to suck me off. She looks up at me with startled eyes. "Do you want me to tell you what I want?"

She nods.

Eagerly, I coach her on what my body tells me it needs. What it's never needed before, only whenever I thought of her.

"Close your mouth around the tip," I growl.

She does and my head falls back as my world fades a little to black. Addictive. That's what this feeling is. The quick fade to darkness before the rush back to light.

Opening my eyes and looking back down, I brush her hair out of her eyes and smile.

"Wrap your hand around it," she does, and I suck in air through clenched teeth. "Stroke it, good girl, just like that."

I feel a tiny bit of my wetness leak out into her mouth and know the second she tastes it too because the vixen begins to purr.

"Do you like that, Wendy? The taste of me."

She nods her head just as my hand comes up around the back of her neck and I pull her forward, and my dick fills her mouth completely. Both of us hiss out simultaneously from the perfect feeling of my length hitting the back of her throat. My body screams for me to fuck her mouth hard, but I hold back.

Once again, tell myself to take my time.

"Again," I demand, and she complies.

Bobbing her head up and down. Taking me all the way down

the back of her throat and holding me there. Tears prick her eyes as I throb, letting go a little more in her mouth.

"You like that?" I hiss, pushing her head down further until I hear her gag. She nods and my head falls back with a groan. "Keep going, Wendy." I growl as I look back down into her tear-filled eyes, "Suck me like I sucked you."

She does. She sucks me until I explode down the back of her throat. The sound of myself thundering, crowing, screaming her name bounces off the stone walls.

My world goes black for the first time, and I lose myself to Wendy. To the darkness.

When I do, something inside me changes. Something inside me snaps. I feel a part of me grow up as I look down and watch her wipe her lips, the taste of my cum still lingering on her tongue.

It scares the shit out of me, growing up, so I lose myself to the darkness a little more and promise myself it will never fucking happen again.

CHAPTER 6
TINKER BELL

"Then they had to tell Peter of Tink's crime, and never had they seen him look so stern.
'Listen, Tinker Bell,' he cried, 'I am your friend no more. Begone from me forever.'"
- Peter & Wendy
J. M. Barrie

PRESENT DAY

"You came to us with a problem. We gave you a solution."

Rolling my eyes, I take a moment and breathe deep before focusing back on the mortal in front of me.

"You understood your obligation when you accepted our gift," I hiss. "It pains me to have to remind you, yet again, of our arrangement."

"You thought, as well as I, that the spell would work," he

hisses back. "But it didn't. That's not my problem. I shouldn't still be under any obligation."

"The time to make that decision is not after the fact," I snap. "The spell worked. For a season." What he wasn't told won't hurt him. "Now that Wendy is back in Neverland, you are required more than ever to make good on what you promised in exchange for what you want most."

"I won't lead her to the faerie ring..."

"Perhaps we'll put you there ourselves then. Starve you out until you've gone crazy and are forced to give us more information."

Silence stretches between us. My ultimatum hangs thick, hopefully forcing an understanding because I'm tired of the good guy act. This mortal sold his soul to the devil, and I'll be *damned* if he doesn't give me what I need, even if I do plan on killing him in the end anyway.

"Let's not forget, we've already renegotiated once," I seethe. "You originally promised us Margaret and Jane. However, we never were successful at stealing them away. Maybe if we had been, none of this would be an issue now. Wendy would have gone crazy. Peter would have long forgotten about her after witnessing her inevitable downfall. That would have given him the extra push he needs to be the Hook Neverland deserves. To fully succumb completely to his darkness. Instead, inside him, there always lingers a small amount of light. A small piece of hope. A reason to remember their past when we've worked so hard trying to get him to forget it."

I take a step forward and the coward before me steps back in fear. Eyes widened, fists clenched, I watch with delight at the torment I see staring back at me. The pain. The suffering. The power only I can inflict.

Neverland was a prize Peter didn't deserve to inherit. A gift Hook will never be man enough to reign over. I see that now and it only fuels my rage. My need for retribution.

"The spell worked perfectly, just like we wanted," I confess, and his eyes widen. "Not telling you the end game, is not my problem."

"Wendy?" he anxiously questions. "If I had known…"

"Must I remind you why you came to us in the first place?"

"No matter what I wanted, Tinker Bell, your plan was always to let Peter win in the end. You'd drink poison for him. You're so obsessed, you can't see straight. Even when he constantly pushes you away. Even after he banned you for interfering. For stealing his magic and…"

"I took what I needed to in order to save Neverland."

"Neverland doesn't need Peter Pan," he shouts. "And it sure as hell never needed Hook."

His words pierce with a brutal force as I square off against him. Quickly, I take a few steps forward, intent on doing him harm, and only stop when I hear my name called out behind me.

"Tink," Tiger Lily shouts. "We still need him to live if we have any chance of the plan working."

I cock my head to the side and let what she's just said roll around my mind. Studying the person in front of me, I contemplate all the ways I would find joy in ending him right now, and how that might affect our progress after all this time. In the end, I decide the princess is right and take a step back.

"You give us what we want," my teeth clench in anger as I stare deep into his eyes, searching his soul, "and I'll give you the opportunity to prove you're more worthy of ruling Neverland."

His eyes light up. It's an offer I know he can't refuse. One that's undoubtedly a lie. There is no way I would let this mortal rule a world like Neverland. But, in the end, I know he'd never deny the chance to try. Ultimately, I know he wouldn't be ruling so much as pretending to rule like they all pretend when they cross over to our side. Mortals. They're all puppets, doing as I tell them to, because their lives would be empty without the magic only I can provide.

"How do I know you're not lying?" he questions quietly.

With a shrug, I turn and make my way across the room. "You don't," smiling, I add, "But come, let's seal it with a drink."

"I know better than to take food or drink from you, Tink."

A sinister smile spreads across my face as I turn back his way. He's already bound to us. Mind, body, and soul. A piece of meat, a slice of bread, or a sip of wine won't change that.

"Well then, let's cut the bullshit. Do we have a deal?"

Stepping forward, his eyes hold mine sternly as he says, "You give me the chance to prove to you that I am better than him, and I'll fucking prove it. Every damn time. All I've ever wanted was that chance, Tinker Bell," I hear Tiger Lily shift restlessly behind me on her feet. I let the poor bastard in front of me go on, hoping it fuels her vengeance as much as mine. "You give me a chance to rule at your side, and I'll help you take down Hook. Do what you must, but don't harm Wendy."

Again, what the fool doesn't know…

"Then it's a deal," I smile.

He gives me a curt nod and my need to finish what we once started grows.

"Good," I exclaim, turning Tiger Lily's way and giving her a sympathetic smile, reassuring her with my gaze that the end game is still the same.

The poor fool in front of us is just a steppingstone to get there. With a heavy sigh, I start for the door with vigor in my step and a grin.

"I do love playing tricks, and Wendy was always my favorite form of entertainment."

CHAPTER 7
HOOK

"Would you send me to school, and then to office, soon I should be
a man?" Peter inquired craftily.
"Very soon."
"I don't want to go to school and learn solemn things," he told her
passionately. "I don't want to be a man. O Wendy's mother, if I
was to wake up and feel a beard!"
Peter & Wendy
- J. M. Barrie

I n the early morning hours, after my inflicted self-
torture down memory lane, I lazily scrape a razor
across my face and watch my eyes darken in the
mirror. Memories, horrors, nightmares I'll never escape rush
through my mind as I stare back at my reflection. The blade
presses harshly into my skin, drawing a slow trickle of blood
from underneath the flesh. I smile as it slides down my cheek
and drops into the basin of the sink. It turns the water

crimson as I shake off the shaving cream and rinse the blade. My mind grows numb for only a second as I rid myself of any evidence that I too, eventually grew older than I ever thought I would.

No one knows. No one has seen this part of me since I came back to Neverland. And that is exactly the way I'm going to keep it. My secret. One I will undoubtedly take to the grave.

My jaw clenches as I watch the water turn a darker shade of burgundy the more my blood pools, mixing with it slowly. My vision blurs. The terror from my past rapidly pulls me under. Grabbing hold of the porcelain, the blade slips from my fingers and falls to the floor. I lean against the sink, begging the nightmare to please, leave me be, as panic rises under my skin spreading quickly across my flesh like a plague.

But it wasn't a bad dream. It was real. And just like always, after all the years we've spent apart, her voice comes back to haunt me.

"I'll be waiting, Peter. Forever."

"Forever might not be long enough, Wendy."

"Then I will wait for you in this life and in the next. I promise. I'll never stop waiting, Peter. I'll never stop believing you'll come back for me."

The thing is, I did come back for her. I waited. Watching. Observing. From Kingston Gardens across the street from her house. Days turned into months. Months turned into years. Until one day, I couldn't watch anymore. Not after what I witnessed. One day, I couldn't stand the way I had willingly changed for her, a destiny she'd be overjoyed to learn that I embraced, if only she hadn't turned her back on me first. A fate I can never show her after what happened. Because one day, I had to force myself to turn away and return to Neverland, without her.

"Aren't they the most beautiful babies you've ever seen?" her mother exclaimed that day as I watched Wendy finally emerge from the house.

"Perfect in every way," he had said at Wendy's side.

My Wendy.

I couldn't understand why they were talking like that with *my* Wendy.

I watched from afar as her eyes cast to the ground and sadness reached from her heart to mine. I felt the cold hands of death in that moment as it grabbed ahold of my soul so tightly, I willingly gave myself over to it, wanting the darkness to swallow me whole if it meant it would stop the pain. But it didn't, not yet anyway, and so I grasped onto the last piece of life I had left inside my soul as I emerged from the gardens, desperate for her to look up and see me after all the time I hid there waiting for her.

Although, even if she had, she wouldn't have recognized me. A boy who started the transition to becoming a man. The beard I once feared was now thick and long on my face. I don't know how long I had sat there, waiting for her, just like I had asked her to wait for me, but she didn't. The irony still takes my breath away to this day.

"You'll feel better once you've had some fresh air," her mother consoled Wendy again, patting her arm and leading

her away from where I stood, before guiding her further down the street with *him*.

"Trust me, darling. Mother knows best. You know I always know what's right for you, just like I'll always know what's best for your daughters."

Daughters!

"Absolutely right," *he* agreed, following quickly behind them and putting his hands on *my* Wendy once he reached her side.

I can still feel the jealous rage that boiled inside that day, rushing madly through my veins as I watched them turn the corner and usher Wendy out of my life.

Coming back to the present, I focus on my hands, and watch as my knuckles turn white from gripping the sink. Harsher. Tighter. In anger for not being man enough to go after her.

Man enough.

A bitter laugh fills the room as I think about the fact that that day, I had become a man.

Sitting, waiting for her, I had grown up without her knowing. I had become old enough to be considered an adult, yet young enough to still pass for youthful. My body broader, my face more defined, yet I still looked close enough to the way I had when I first left Neverland to be with her. To stay with her. I was unwilling to leave until one day, when they emerged from that house pushing two infants in a stroller, I knew I couldn't convince her to return with me.

Looking up, I force myself to take a breath as my eyes meet the dark soul staring back at them now in the mirror. The evil that consumed me when I gave myself over to the inevitable that day glares back. The day I turned away bitterly from what we had and returned to Neverland with the little bit of pixie dust I had left. I've never been the same after that day. Never forgotten. And I promised myself right then and there that when I came back to Neverland, I'd never forgive anyone, including myself, for what we lost.

Mother knows best, the thought rings to the forefront of my mind and grabs me back into the past.

This coming from the mother who pushed Wendy and I apart. The one who kept her from me. Night after night when I would go to her window, she'd push me away, tell me Wendy didn't want to see me. She kept her hidden in that house until that day she emerged a mother.

A wife!

"Listen to your husband, Wendy," I had heard the witch say as they walked out of sight, *"And everything will finally be right."*

With a force unknown to man, I yank the sink from the wall, and it crashes to the floor with a fatal blow. It shatters at my feet as water immediately begins to pool around my ankles, and rises quickly in the small space I've imprisoned myself in.

Hidden away from my crew so they won't see the truth.

I slam open the door and stalk across the hall. John suddenly appears in the corridor and hurries to see what happened, he calls for a few of my crew to hustle and help piece back together what I broke.

But nothing can fix the damned.

Nothing can mend the condemned.

I learned over the years that Wendy's calling on my soul

was nothing but a doomed fate. A careless enchantment that I couldn't help but follow to my inescapable downfall.

With one swift kick, the door to my main quarters flies open. I don't need to search for her. Like a looming punishment, I already feel where she is as my eyes dart to the left and I watch, scanning her partly naked frame as she tries to cover up. She attempts modesty as my intrusion interrupts her getting dressed.

Modesty.

A smile pulls at my lips just as more memories surface and a defiance flares in her eyes. I take three large strides across the room, pulling her tight against my frame and feel nothing but sheer delight when she doesn't put up a struggle.

"A new day calls, Darling," I seethe, gesturing to the window and the sun that's slowly started rising. "Time has never been on our side, so let's agree not to waste it, shall we?"

She studies me for a moment, annoyance growing, bitterness brewing just under her stormy eyes before she begins to wrestle, trying to break free with all her might. The blouse she was holding in her hands falls to the floor in the process. I can't help but look down at her tits as they bounce back and forth, causing my mouth to water and instinct to take over. I push her up against the nearest wall. Her palms press harshly into my chest as she tries to force me away. The laugh that breaks free from my lungs a moment later only spurs her on as she starts to kick, grunting with all her strength to escape my hold. The inevitable.

Because that's what we've always been.

Inevitable.

"Who gave you these clothes," I hiss as I pull away slightly and yank her skirt quickly down to her knees.

She tries to escape my hold, digging her fingers into my hair and forcing me aside. I manage to hold out and take each blow, each scratch from her nails as they dig into my skin, adding pain to punishment. I take her defiance with honor, with pride, for being able to draw the animal out in her so easily. Rising fast, I spin her around to face the wall. Looking down, her bare ass makes my mouth water as I quickly take her wrists in my hands and force them above her head, slamming them and her naked body back against the cold wall.

"I prefer you in your blue nightgown," I growl. "Not some hand-me-down rags any whore could wear."

"They came from John," she hisses.

Who's the traitor now, Smee?

But my thoughts are cut off as she presses her ass back against my groin in a means for escape. Although, all it does is make me want to take her, rough and hard against her will. It's a thought that has my dick painfully hardening because I never did get the release I craved last night. And no one in my life has ever been able to give me a release like Wendy.

"Besides, why do you care what I wear?" She looks over her shoulder and gives me a heated stare. "As you said, time is ticking. Tick. Tock. Tick. Tock."

My body crashes against hers so hard I worry for a split second I may have hurt her. When she doesn't give me reason to believe she's injured, I wrap her hair in my fist and pull her backwards across the room. She kicks at me. Grabs out to maim me, but being just out of reach, I watch the show like the fucked-up monster I am inside, entirely too delighted with the scene. My cock grows harder noticing all the ways she's filled out. All the curves she didn't have as a young woman.

"Let. Me. Go!" Wendy screams just as I reluctantly release her, and she bounces back against my bed.

Out of breath, naked, legs parted, hands braced at her sides gripping the sheets, I swear I have never seen anything more tempting in my life. Pussy bare. Nipples hardened. I tell myself to look away before I fuck her senseless like I've been craving to for seventeen years.

"The blue nightgown," I insist. "Nothing else."

"Why?" she shouts, standing and taking a step towards me.

My eyes graze down her frame before raising and meeting her stare. She notices and smiles, and fuck if it doesn't do something to me. Her confidence is enticing. Her maturity, fucking breathtaking, as she places her hands on her hips in challenge. She tempts me. And fuck if it doesn't almost push me over the edge.

"Because. I. Fucking. Said. So," I fume.

I can't tell her the truth.

Because it was the last thing I saw her in before she was hidden from me. Because it was the last thing I held her in the last night we spent together. Because it's the image of her I held onto all these years, wishing, hoping, secretly praying, one day we'd finish what we started.

"Is that how this is going to be?" she taunts, rendering

me speechless for reasons I can't yet understand. "Your crew may take orders from you, Pan, but I. Never. Will."

With an authoritative glare, I step into her and wait until I have her complete attention before lowering my voice. "I have ways of making you comply. I won't stop at getting what I want."

"I don't believe you," she counters quickly. "You told me that once before, and then you broke your word."

"I think you'll realize through your time back in Neverland, it was you who broke your word, not I."

"Bullshit."

My eyes widen. I've never heard Wendy swear before and I begin to realize the sweet innocence I fell for seventeen years ago might just have been replaced with a damaged soul that matches my own.

"I call fucking bullshit."

"Ugly words for such a beautiful mouth." I lick my lips as I take another step closer, until I can feel the heat of her body on my skin. "Don't tempt me, because you'll quickly find, I play dirtier games than you were used to."

"Try me."

A mischievous smile spreads across my face as I lean closer, my lips resting above hers, my grin grows. "Gladly."

Pushing her back against the bed, I grab her nightgown, previously discarded and tossed across the mattress, and slip it over her head. I'm surprised when she doesn't fight back, and even more stunned when she lets me continue to dress her. My eyes catch hers in a tender way that starts to shake the chains I've locked around my black heart. The intimacy of the moment tempts it back to life as I slowly lower the garment down her bare chest, across her slender stomach, and mouthwatering full hips. Pulling the gown down her thighs, I grasp the rope at my waist and start to wrap it around her wrists tightly.

Strangely, she still doesn't fight, just stares up at me with a kind of revulsion, and it does something to my soul. Fascinates it. Intrigues it. Lures it back to life.

"Maybe you like it dirty," I antagonize, needing to know what she's thinking. "Filthy, perhaps? Is that right, Darling?"

She doesn't say a word as I drop to the floor and tie her ankles next. Hastily, I finish tightening the rope, giving it one last tight tug for good measure when her voice pulls my attention back up to her bewitching gaze.

"In the end, all I ever got from you was rotten love anyway." My eyes widen with rage, warning her to take it back, but she goes on. Leaning forward, her breath feathers across my lips in challenge as she whispers, "Do your worst, Peter. I died the moment you walked away and never came back. Maybe saying goodbye to you a second time will finally bring me back to life."

Before I can respond, her eyes suddenly start to fade. Her lashes flutter as they softly close and she falls back against the sheets. I barely have time to catch her as she starts to slip off the edge of the bed. The dead weight of her body forces us both to the floor. Glancing up quickly, I watch as a twinkling of lights flutters out of the room and then curse the fae who put a spell on her under my breath.

It'll be hard to keep them from Wendy until I get what I want from her. But not impossible.

Lifting her in my arms, I lay my ear against her mouth

and wait to hear her breathing. When I finally feel the warmness of life against my skin, I walk her gently across the room, my heart and mind now tearing each other apart from the words that just fell from her lips.

My worst?

Oh Wendy Darling, you don't have any fucking idea.

CHAPTER 8
WENDY

"It is humiliating to confess that the conceit of Peter was one of his most fascinating qualities. To put it with brutal frankness, there never was a more cockier boy."

Peter & Wendy

- J.M. Barrie

I could hear them, but I couldn't see them.

"She's coming around now."

"Did you tie those fucking ropes tight?"

"Any tighter, and she wouldn't be able to breathe, Hook."

"Good. Maybe this time she'll remember who, and who *only*, has the right to breathe her back to fucking life."

My hands struggle against my restraints. The tie around my eyes tugs my hair sharply when I attempt to look in the direction of their voices. The gag in my mouth stops me from being able to swallow properly and I choke on my own spit as my hands wrestle to loosen the rope tied around them. But it's no use. The rope is secured multiple times around my wrists, then tied around my middle just as many ensuring I have no chance to escape.

"Fuck, that'll make you hard, right Captain? The sight of a woman choking on her knees."

"Shut your fucking mouth Rufio."

The voices are quiet for a moment. Fear rises in my chest and spreads like wildfire across my skin as I wait for them to speak again. As I wait for a sound, any sound, to clue me into where they are, or what they might want with me. Rufio's last comment has my mind racing with thoughts and memories I never want to relive.

"Shit," I hear Rufio laugh. "When Tink told us you said to meet you here," my body goes rigid with the mention of her name and I stop breathing, suddenly alert and awaiting the worst, "she made it sound like you were willing to share. Like you do from time to time with Tiger Lily."

"Fucking Tink," I hear *him* rasp out again.

Him. He's just him now. No Peter. No Hook. Just a cruel mixture of something so familiar yet so far out of reach I fear I will never be able to understand *him* ever again.

"And maybe," I hear him continue. "Maybe that is not a bad idea after all. Get her on her fucking feet."

I try to suck in a breath around the gag but it's no use. Before I can finish my useless attempt, I'm grabbed by each of my arms and hoisted up onto shaky legs in loose gravel. I push outward as best I can at each of my sides, but my pathetic attempt at escape, at fighting them off is only met with roaring laughter.

"Untie her eyes," I hear him say, and then notice, he didn't laugh with the lost boys just now.

No, I didn't hear the sound of his voice mocking me. All I heard in his authoritative tone is the utmost displeasure.

For what? Bringing me here? Restraining me? Sharing me? Oh God, please don't let it be that. He wouldn't, not after the past. Not after he knows the nightmare I've lived through before at the hand's of his mates.

Or would he?

I'm realizing since being back in Neverland, I don't know the man who kidnapped me. I'm starting think, I never really knew the lost boy he once was, as well.

One of the crew harshly grabs at the tie around my head and start to unlace the fabric. Every thought, every feeling inside me screams that I'm not ready for this. That I was not ready to return.

I thought I could do this, but I was so wrong. There are so many memories here. So many things I have been attempting to suppress. To hide. My whole life since *he* left me and never returned, I've been fighting off the memory of this nightmare.

What they once tried to do to me.

Shaking with fear, I know now I am not ready to confront it. Not like I thought I was.

"Fuck, she's prettier than she used to be, am I right Captain?"

"One more fucking word, Rufio, and I'll gut you with my hook."

"Yes, Captain."

As the fabric falls from my face, and my eyes attempt to adjust to the darkness,I blink quickly, worried that if I don't get my bearings fast, I'll meet a fate I barely escaped the first time.

My mind is still trying to make sense of everything, my eyes still adjusting to the low light, when I see a figure step forward. I push everything else aside and focus there.

My shoulders stiffen as my eyes finally fully adjust and I take in the deep scowl on his face. He lifts a cigarette to his lips and takes a long drag as his eyes roam lethally across my body. Up. Down. Stopping on my most intimate parts. Shuffling my weight on my feet, I glance behind him and see the grown men of his crew, who were once lost boys, staring, ogling, undressing me with their hungry eyes.

My vision adjusts finally to the lonely light coming from the lantern Rufio carries, my head swivels and takes in where we are.

Skull Rock.

"It's where we take the ones we kidnap."

"Do you kidnap a lot of people, Peter? Before you kidnapped me, that is?"

"You came willingly, Wendy. Something tells me, you'll always come willingly."

My body begins to tremble as the memories come flooding back. He was right. I did. And once again, I was a fool and fell for his magic. His charm. Just like all those years ago.

Only this time, I've found myself bound and gagged in Skull Rock as horny crew members of the Jolly Roger look at me like a feast they're about to devour. Something completely opposite from the first time I found myself here alone with Peter.

The memory shakes me. Forcing my eyes back to meet his as a cloud of smoke slowly leaves his lips, I try to hide a shiver that rushes up my spine when he says, "Seems fitting that we start at the beginning, don't you agree?"

My eyes widen. I struggle with my restraints and take a step back. He takes two steps forward. Grabbing my throat, he pulls me towards him with one strong yank.

"This is the first place I felt it leave me. The first place I felt you steal it from me, Darling." He cocks his head to the side and studies me. "The first place I felt your submission."

I hear a murmur amongst the crew behind him and my heart speeds up with fear.

"Don't tell me, Wendy, that you don't remember?"

I shake my head no, not wanting to remember any more than I have to as every word, every damn memory he brings to the surface threatens to pull me into a slow hell I'll never recover from.

I barely survived the first time; I won't stand a chance the second.

Throwing his smoke to the ground, he spins me so quickly, my back now flush against his front, that I close my eyes and stumble slightly trying to catch my feet. He wastes no time in pulling me back tighter against his frame. When he does, I hear a slight moan escape his lips as my ass hits his hardening length. My eyes flash open. How can he be aroused? Fearfully, I look down at the lust filled eyes of the lost boys in front of me, and start to pray for help.

"Fuck, I liked giving it to you, Darling," his low raspy

voice flutters against my ear. "Taking it. Feeling you. Tasting you. For the first time."

His hands roam up my inner thigh. I push back against his stomach, struggling to break free as my gaze flicks from one lost boy to another in horror. They take a step forward, eagerly wanting to share the goods he's intent on sampling, and I tense in his arms.

"Maybe if I see the way they finally give it to you," he grits out. His hand hovers above my center, making my heart race in panic before he slowly lifts it further up my lower stomach, "take it from you, feel and taste what was the beginning of my end." His harsh words get louder as his large palms stop at my breasts, he molds them in his hands briefly, before he raises them to my neck, tightening his grip, "Maybe then, I'll finally see, finally understand, finally get back what you fucking stole from me."

He spins me around quickly.

"After all, it's not like you kept your promise." My heart stops as he steps closer, so close his nose brushes against the tip of mine. "You let another man touch you." I tell myself to breathe, but it's no use. When I try to look away, his eyes darken. He harshly cups my chin, and forces me to face him. "You let another man taste you." I try to close my eyes, to deny everything he's saying, but he jerks my chin angrily in his hand. His low angry voice feathers across my skin a moment later as he whispers, "You let another man's cock inside your wet willing cunt, Darling. How do you think that made me feel?"

A tear escapes my eyes before I can stop it.

"Maybe I should go back on my promise too."

I violently shake my head no, which only earns me an evil smile as my heart breaks into a million pieces.

"So, you do remember?"

My eyes plead with his as he studies me in the dim light. I can't take much more. The anxiety. The memories. It's all too much.

I try to take a step back but stop when I hear footsteps behind me. The crew is coming closer.

A bitter anger rises in my soul.

I didn't stay away all these years living in fear to have everything end like this.

To get to the end of whatever this is between us, to find whatever he's searching for, to finally make him understand he turned his back on me too, I can't live in fear any longer.

"You have no clue what that does to a man," he growls. "Losing you. All those years. Knowing. Watching."

Watching?

"Understanding that what I once believed, what I once," he pauses and my heart stops, "loved," it comes out barely as a whisper, his face full of pain as it leaves his lips, "was only a joke. Make-believe. Fucking pretend."

He pulls on the ropes around my middle, tugging me towards him. I feel the cold prick of metal against my neck a moment later and suck in a sharp breath.

His hook.

"I wasn't fucking pretending, Wendy," he whispers softly.

I shake my head, blinking quickly, struggling to understand what I'm hearing.

It's a confession meant only for the two of us.

Raising his hook, he slides it between the gag around my mouth and my damp skin. I feel it pierce my cheek and flinch from the sting of it gently scratching through my flesh as he lowers the constraint finally from my lips. His eyes trace the fabric as it falls. An eerie silence builds between us as he licks his lips.

Before he can say anything else, I gather as much strength as I can to face my fear head-on, take a deep breath and blurt out, "I was never pretending, either, *Pan*."

Hushed murmurs sound behind me as his eyes flash up to meet mine. I didn't call him Peter, and I refuse to call him Hook. For once, he's going to listen to me. Even if it costs me what I've always feared most. Even if I eventually have to tell him the truth I know he's not ready to hear.

One he may never be ready to hear.

His nostrils flare, but the darkness in those once beautiful eyes lifts momentarily, giving me a gateway to his soul, and so I go on.

"The difference between us, *Pan*, is you believe everything and blame everyone else but yourself."

His hand on the rope shakes slightly. Is that anger, or fear in his eyes? Before I can decide, I say, "Me? I believed in the wrong boy at the wrong time."

Hurt flashes through his bitter gaze before his eyes begin to darken a moment later, washing away all feeling, any clue that his heart is actually beating.

"It cost me more than he will ever know because," I take a deep breath, take a small step closer, and whisper just between the two of us, "he'll never be man enough to understand what he once lost."

His scowl deepens as he looks to the floor for a moment. The crew once again attempt to come closer, but he holds his hand up stopping them for the time being. When his gaze lifts and finds mine, a sadness fills his expression. It strangles my heart, tempts it to break for him. But I hold strong. Hold onto the past. All the hurt and pain that losing him inflicted on me all those years ago.

"Believing in everything means not living in denial, Darling," he softly whispers back. "As for blame, my intentions with you were always honorable. Your refusal to accept the past, to be honest with yourself, will always bring you more shame than any pain, any suffering, I could ever inflict."

He looks beyond my shoulder, a menacing grin stretching across his face as he studies his crew just a few steps away.

"The boy I knew would never disgrace me for his own victory."

His gaze locks bitterly on mine. Resentment hangs in them as his jaw ticks with bent up rage.

"The boy you knew lost everything. His fall from grace was your doing." He leans in close. His breath falls across my lips in a heated, passionate, anger that has my head spinning. "You humiliate me with your lies, Wendy. The lies you tell yourself. The way you tarnish our past. In your own mind, own selfish ways, you'll always win. Just know, fools surround themselves with lies so they don't have to look at the truth." My hand shakes slightly, my knees grow weak as the past comes crashing back to the present. He cocks his head to the side and smiles. "It hurts, doesn't it?"

I exhale a shaky breath. "What?"

"Realizing your own world is full of make-believe, pretend." His grin deepens, his eyes lower, study me, roam over every inch, every curve of my face. "I'm not the only one who has been living a lie, Wendy. I'm not the one who's always been wrong. It's time you fucking accept that."

CHAPTER 9
WENDY

"...Peter's peculiarities, which was that, in the middle of a fight,
Peter would suddenly change sides."
Peter & Wendy
- J.M. Barrie

SEVENTEEN YEARS AGO

"And then what did he say?" One of the lost boys, Slightly, whispers.

My eyes beg me to open them, but sleep attempts one more time to pull me under.

"I heard him say she tastes like sweet pineapple bursting on his tongue."

"I wonder what she feels like," Cubby whispers in response to Slightly.

"Did he say anything about that?" The twins ask in unison.

"Shh," Slightly tries to hush the group as I'm pulled from a *perfect dream into what I'm worried might be one of my darkest nightmares. "Don't wake her."*

Peter took John and Michael out to fight the Indians early this morning, and by the way the lost boys are talking, it's safe to assume he hasn't returned home yet to Hangman's Tree.

"When did he tell you this?" Nibs whispers back irritated.

I burro into my bed and pretend not to hear them across the room.

Maybe they're not talking about me. Maybe they're not talking about Peter. But some all-knowing feeling that I refuse to accept tries to tell me otherwise.

"He didn't," Slightly confesses. "I heard him down by Crocodile Creek when he thought he was alone. Talking to himself. Doing things to himself in the dark that I couldn't quite make out, that I've never seen before."

"Like what?" the twins ask together again in unison.

My breath catches as I wait for Slightly to go on. My mouth waters. What... what was Peter doing? My thighs clench together in anticipation. My center dampens. I'm sure I know what.

It's the same thing I've been doing since that night at Skull Rock after everyone goes to sleep. When Hangman's Tree is quiet and all I'm left with are the agonizing thoughts of Peter and me. I touch myself, thinking of him. Wanting him. Needing him to fill an ache I can't myself.

"Like I said, I couldn't completely make it out, only, I've never seen or heard anything like it before. He kept going on and on about Wendy."

I hear the boys shift in their seats, no doubt looking in my direction. I keep my eyes closed and my body curled up into a ball in the center of my bed. My heart soars knowing Peter's thinking of me and doing things I'd rather be doing to him instead. But the thought of the lost boys behind me brings me nothing but dread.

"It sounded like he was in pain. But... The best kind of pain. The kind of pain that..."

Slightly trails off and I bite the inside of my lip, trying to make the anxiety I feel in my gut go away. It's been two weeks since the incident at Skull Rock. Peter hasn't touched me and he has barely looked at me since. He leaves me alone every chance he gets. He always seems like he is on the run from something.

From me.

We've barely been in the same room together, let alone spoken more than a few words to each other since.

"Whatever it was, it made me want it, too," Slightly finally continues.

"Maybe we should see for ourselves," Cubby questions and my heart races with fear.

"Yeah," Slightly agrees. "Maybe we should."

I hear a chair scrape across the floor, followed by four more. My hands shake as I clutch my blanket tighter around me, as if it'd be any protection against them all.

"I don't know."

"Yeah, I don't know," one twin echoes after the other. "What if Peter finds out and gets mad at us?"

Still, I hear their footsteps inch closer and my breathing stops.

"He's never not shared with us before," Slightly encourages the group.

"Yeah, but didn't you say this was different?" Tootles butts in. "We don't know what he was doing, so how are we supposed to know how to make him share?"

Tootles. I haven't heard his voice until now, and I hang on to it like it's a lifeline. He's suddenly the voice of reason when he's normally anything but. I just hope the others listen to him, but as they continue to inch closer my heart speeds up because I know they won't. They never do.

"There is only one way to find out," Cubby rasps out.

His voice is so close it sends chills down my spine.

"Should we try it? Take her when she's sleeping? Maybe she won't wake up."

As if doused by cold water, I turn over, opening my eyes quickly. All five lost boys stand at the edge of my bed peering down at me eagerly. It's almost as if they believe I will manifest into something for them all to divide amongst themselves. When that doesn't happen, their eager faces turn to frowns.

"What is it?" I ask, trying to sound startled but my voice comes out shaky and filled with fear. "Do you need something? Where is Peter?"

"Out," Slightly grins.

"Yeah, out," the twins agree.

My eyes dart between Slightly and the other two boys at his right, before my hands instinctively grab the blanket at my waist and pull it up higher as a shield.

"We should go look for him," I blurt out, attempting to rise from my bed but I stop when Nibs takes a step forward and pushes me back against it.

"What do you want?" I shout out.

"Whatever it is you gave Peter," Tootles grins on my left.

My gaze snaps to his and widens.

"I didn't, we didn't..."

"What else did he say?" Cubby demands from Slightly.

"Wet, he said she was so wet. He wanted to make her wetter."

"Doesn't look wet to me," Cubby frowns, studying me as his eyes gaze up and down my body. Instinctively, I close my thighs. It's a terrible mistake, because out of the corner of my eye, I see Slightly's stare flash to my center. A wicked smile tugs across his face.

"There," he points. "That is where Peter was touching himself."

His eyes lift to mine and what he sees flash through them gives him whatever answer he needs, and assures him he's right. I go to bolt off the bed and hear him shout, "Grab her boys!"

I'm harshly pinned down by the twins as Slightly and Cubby lift my nightgown. I kick at them, making contact with Cubby's stomach, but Slightly grabs one ankle, and when Cubby recovers, he grabs the other.

"Peter!" I yell. "Peter help!"

"Tootles," Slightly demands, and my eyes flash to him before falling on Tootles in the corner. Nibs stands a little further back in the darkness. His face looks angry for whatever his friends are intent on doing, but he doesn't stop them. "Raise her night dress. See if she's wet. If she is, taste her and tell us if she tastes like pineapple."

My heart races. My breathing matches it. I suck in another breath and scream as Tootles comes closer. "Peter!"

"Hurry," Slightly yells. "She's hard to hold."

I thrash against the lost boys harder than before, but their grip only tightens into a vice I can't escape.

"Is it bad that I like the way she's fighting us?" one of the twins asks.

"Me too," the other says, "makes me feel... different."

I anxiously glance to my right just in time to see him greedily palm the center of his pants. The bulge there grows larger.

"Me too," the others say in unison.

Oh my God!

"Peter!" I yell again. "Peter! Help!"

"Hurry up, because I want a turn," Slightly urges Tootles on. "I want to ... to do other things to her, too."

"Me too," the boys' voices darken as they tighten their grip and Tootles closes in on me. He proceeds to lift the hem of my nightgown. I try to push him away, but all I end up doing is bucking my hips off the bed. The lost boys let out a hungry groan at the same time, obviously loving the sight.

"I don't see anything wet," Tootles says.

"Maybe you can make her wet," Cubby decides, and I cry out for Peter louder than before.

"How?"

"Touch her," Slightly whispers. "See if anything changes."

Tootles' eyes meet mine as his hand raises. I scream for him to stop. I yell for him not to come any closer. I try my best to kick, scream, break free, but a second later I feel his hand brush against the inside of my thigh. I flinch as his fingertips trail up to my heat. I close my eyes as they reach the outline of my panties, and then...

"Make one more move and I'll slit your fucking throat, Tootles."

Peter!

Releasing a shaky breath, I open my eyes. The lost boys still have me held down against the bed, but Peter is standing behind Tootles, a hook raised at his throat, and for the first time since we met, the look in his eyes terrorizes me. He hasn't glanced my way yet, but I see the evil lurking in his features, brimming at his surface.

When he finally looks my way, his gaze glides up and down my frame slowly taking in what they've done. The devil flashes through his blue irises turning them completely black. He pulls the hook harshly across Tootles throat and my entire body freezes. Blood spurts out, splashing drops across my nightgown, splattering onto Cubby and Slightly who still hold my ankles.

They jump back immediately. My body trembles, convulses, I can't believe my eyes. I can't believe what Peter's just done. The twins jolt back too as Tootles falls to the floor, and his eyes slowly fade as death consumes him.

I try to catch my breath. I try to steady my racing heart. I try to remember Peter as I have always known him. Sweet, kinda, caring. Not the villain standing before me now. Peter takes one step forward as the others desperately take a step back. He slowly pulls my nightgown down, his hands gently push my legs back together, and he pulls me from my bed and tucks me into his side.

Still not sure how to process what just happened, I slowly look up to meet Peter's stare as Tootles' blood pools around our feet. Biting my lip, I try to forget what I just saw. Try to think happy thoughts. Try to tell myself that wasn't Peter that just ruthlessly sliced through one of his best friend's throats with no regard for his life or the friendship they shared together, regardless of what he was doing to me.

Peter cups my chin gently in his hand and sternly looks deep into my eyes. "Are you ok?"

I nod yes, afraid to tell him otherwise, as tears prick the back of my eyes.

"No," he rasps out in anger. "No, you are not ok. Who started it?" he demands.

I know I shouldn't care about giving the ringleader away. I know I shouldn't want to protect the boys who just did this to me. But for some reason a sense of mothering them, protecting them, stops me. They didn't know what they were doing. But it doesn't make it right. It doesn't make vengeance right, either.

Or does it?

"Who?" Peter demands again, this time louder than before.

I shake in his embrace, my mind still petrified, panicked, from the change in him that I just witnessed. My eyes drift to the floor, and when I still won't look up, he tries again more tenderly.

"Please Wendy," he whispers, "Tell me, who did this to you?"

My heart beats faster from this side of him. The tenderness. The need to protect. Before I can stop myself, I look up at Slightly who immediately takes a step back in fear. Peter tenses as he takes in where my eyes fell.

He leans into me, places a kiss on my cheek, then whispers, "Good girl."

Gently releasing me, he spins quickly, pulling a sword from his waist and slices off Slightly's raised hand as he begs Peter to stop. A gasp falls from my lips as I jump back in panic. My mind screams at me to run but my feet are glued to the floor as I watch this new side of Peter unleash hell once again on the lost boys. He runs his sword through Slightly's heart a second later and he quickly falls to the floor. My hands raise to my mouth, and I muffle a scream before Peter turns on Cubby.

"Him too?" he addresses me, never taking his eyes off the boy who was once his friend.

Cubby's eyes plead with me to lie for him as they anxiously

find mine over Peter's shoulder. They beg me to save his life. I feel sick, my mind clouds, I think twice before Peter looks over his shoulder and eyes me sternly.

"Answer me," he demands in a way that has me complying instantly.

Taking a deep breath, I bow my head, unable to look up at the fate that Cubby is about to meet, and whisper, "Yes."

A second later, I flinch as I hear Cubby take his last breath when Peter's sword pierces him right through the chest. Peter turns toward me, and I feel the twins tense at my back. He takes a few steps forward, passing me with a stern look, and then wipes his blade on each one of the twins' chests.

"Touch her again," he hisses. "And I'll fucking kill you."

Peter stashes his sword at his side, then grabs my hand. Pulling me gently into his embrace, the twins release a shaky breath behind me as my eyes lift and catch Michael, John and Nibs. A lost boy who thankfully wanted no part in his friend's games tonight.

"Thank you," the boys behind me cry in unison.

"You were spared as witnesses," Peter says angrily. "To tell others what happens when they touch what's mine."

I look up into his eyes, and the darkness I saw there a few moments ago begins to clear. The Peter I remember, the one I've always known, starts to resurface.

Peter begins to lead me away. Out of the corner of my eye, I see Nibs, John and Michael scurry towards the twins. Their hushed murmurs of what to do with the bodies is hard to hear over the pounding of my heart, the warning in my brain, as Peter leads me further through the house and into his bedroom.

"You'll sleep here," he demands, closing the door behind us and stalking across the room.

"But," I whisper, still fearful from what I just witnessed. His body stiffens when he comes to a stop in the center of the space. "Where will you sleep?"

His gaze drifts to the large master bed in the center of the room, just as mine does, too.

"There," he says matter-of-factly, "with you."

"But," I stammer, still trying to forget what I just saw. Who Peter just became. "Peter, I..."

He turns and takes two large strides towards me. Anger fills his eyes. Resistance builds between us. I can't just give him what he wants. Not after what I just witnessed. But my body has other thoughts, and submission simmers in my lower stomach from the danger lurking in his gaze. A give-and-take sort of magic swirls around us, making me feel dizzy. I stumble backward like an idiot. He steadies me, and his eyes soften slightly.

"Turn around," he whispers.

The heat in his gaze makes me weak in the knees. The tenderness with which he reaches out and guides my shoulders, urging me to do as he says, makes me comply. His fingers shake at the nape of my neck a moment later before he starts to unbutton my nightgown. This time, my knees really do give out, right before his strong arms wraps around my waist and anchor me to him keeping me upright.

"Let me take care of you," he says gently into the crook of my neck as his fingers continue to unbutton my night dress.

He pulls it from my shoulders, and it quickly pools around my feet. I look down, notice the bloodstains on the dirty fabric and suck in a shaky breath. His fingertips are on my panties a moment later. Slowly, tenderly, he pulls them down my thighs and instructs me to step out. My center dampens as I do as he says. His shaky breath on the backs of my thighs sends chills up my spine. He stands to his full height, and my mind races, wondering how I could feel this way for him so soon after what I just went through.

"I'm not going to touch you," he whispers hot into my ear, "Not like they did."

His chest brushes against my back, and my heart surprises me as it sinks. Even after what just happened, what I just experienced, I want him to.

"Even if I need to," he grits out, snaking his strong arms around my frame.

His hard length throbs between us. His fingertips twitch at my sides but keeping to his word, they never do more than graze my skin.

"Wendy," he breathes shakily into the back of my neck. "I want to do things to you that scare me. That should scare you."

My lower stomach clenches. My skin breaks out into goosebumps. I have to force myself to breathe. Sucking in a shaky breath, I slowly turn around and meet his stare. His gaze drops, his eyes touch every inch of my skin in a way his hands never will. Not tonight.

He's admiring, glorifying, openly lusting for what's in front of him.

What he needs.

Who he wants.

Me.

After a moment, Peter looks up and gives me his signature sexy smirk.

Crooking his finger, he gestures for me to follow him. Help-

lessly, I do. Entering another room off the master, I gasp as a waterfall flows down the back wall. He leaves my side briefly as I take in the beautiful sight. Ferns, tropical lilies, hibiscus, and gardenia flowers flow down the rocks setting off one of the most breathtaking waterfalls I've ever seen. All just for Peter. A natural shower full of magic and wonder, like I could never have imagined.

I feel his presence at my back before I hear him. He gently raises my hair off my neck and ties it at the crown of my head.

"Peter," I whine.

"Wendy?" he breathes, prompting me to continue.

"What if I want you to touch me?" I confess. "What if... I need you to touch me, too?"

He groans, low and primal. Coming a step closer, he whispers in my ear, "That's what scares me most. How much we both want that."

"Please," I plead. "Touch me. Touch me like you did at Skull Rock."

His bare chest grazes my back. I suck in a shaky breath. His arm wraps around my center, pulling me close to him, making me realize he's just as bare as I am.

His hard length presses into my ass and I let out a moan. He doesn't say a word, only urges me forward. I take a step, then another until we are under the water. He presses his chest into me, my palms now flat against the stone wall. We stand there, breathing, taking a moment to ourselves as he tenderly kisses the back of my neck. My shoulders. The water is warm, perfect temperature, just like the ocean I hear crashing against the shore outside.

He backs away and my heart aches from the absence of his touch.

"Please," I beg again. I turn to look at him over my shoulder. "You told me once I would never have to ask twice."

"I'll touch you, Wendy," he whispers, his hands now filled with soap. A beautiful mixture of jasmine and magnolia fills my senses as his palms roam the curves of my body. "But not like they wanted to. Not like my body craves. Not tonight."

He reaches the juncture of my thighs, and they part willingly. My center tightens wanting more than he's giving as he tenderly washes my skin. Washes away what just happened. He turns me around, my front to his front now, kneels to the floor, and continues to worship me by tenderly washing my thighs.

His cock pulses and my mouth waters. He looks up, noticing where I am staring and smiles. A mischievous gleam dances in his eyes. Rising, he washes my stomach, my arms, my neck, my breasts. His eyes heating more with every tender touch.

"Promise me," he begs with a shaky breath. "Promise me, no other man will ever touch you like I want to touch you, and I promise you, I'll die before anyone ever puts their hands on you like that ever again."

"I promise," I cry softly.

Right now, I'm willing to promise him the world, even though what I just experienced still has me slightly shaken.

He smiles just before he leans in and places a small kiss against the tip of my nose. When he backs away, I grin and take the soap from his hand, doing the same to his body that he just did to me. First his chest. Then, reaching over his shoulders, I wash his back. I walk around him and drop to my knees. My hands roam his strong muscular thighs. My eyes lift to admire his round ass. He turns and my mouth waters as my eyes land on his impressive length throbbing, pulsing, desperately in need of a release.

It's right in front of me. I can't help myself.

Looking up through hooded lashes, I take his length in my hand and pull slowly from the base to the tip. His head falls back. A deep groan escapes his lips.

"Wendy," he hisses. "Not tonight."

Peter hoists me to my feet and gently pushes us both under the spray of the water. The soap slowly glides down our bodies as he holds me close and looks deep into my soul. So much is said between us without ever having to say a word. Taking a step back, he reluctantly releases me and starts to walk across the room. Suddenly a little nervous, I take a step forward and follow behind him quickly.

"But Peter," I cry as he pulls me from the shower and wraps me in a towel. "You do still want me..." I trail off, "Don't you."

He studies me while he towels himself off. I stand before him vulnerable.

"Want you?" he questions.

I can't find the words to go on.

Want me... Here. In Neverland. In your life In your ... bed.

That's where this is headed, right?

I know I'm meant to sleep there now, but there will be more, if I am not mistaken.

I know I don't know much, and he doesn't know any more than I do. At least, I don't think he does. But instinct tells me I know this. What's expected when you take this next step. My fingertips anxiously twirl around a loose string of the towel as I cast my gaze down to the floor. He takes a step forward. One. Then two more. Until all I am staring at below, are his bare feet.

"Wendy," he whispers, urging me to look up as he places a finger under my chin and I meet his stare.

I know only a little of the birds and the bees from what mother told me back home. If I was honest with Peter, what I'm feeling can only be described as the whole hive, the entire flock, taking flight when I think of what I want from him. What he can give me. Things I never thought I wanted before.

"You make me want what I have been running from my whole life," he confesses, but I am so lost in the clear blues of his eyes it doesn't even register for a few seconds. "No matter how hard I try to fight it, I'm lost to you, Wendy. I always have been. I always will be."

I search his eyes, trying to see if he's lying. I believe he's telling the truth, but my heart is still worried. Still vulnerable. Still so young trying to understand what this all means.

Before I lose my nerve, I say, "Promise me, you'll touch me again." His eyes darken. "The way I want you to touch me." His nostrils flare. "Next time, when I ask you to. Please? And I promise, I will never let anyone else touch me the way I let you for as long as I live."

He wars with himself as he takes a step back. Looking down at the floor, he shakes his head. His eyes close. I swear I hear him talking to himself. Mumbling to himself.

I don't know what's worse, the way my anxiety spikes from the incoherent jumble of words coming out of his mouth, of the fact that I swear he's going to say no.

Side stepping around him, I hurry out of the room and stop only when I hear him call my name. Turning once I've reached the bed, I hold my towel tight against me, a shield of sorts, and search his eyes as he walks into the room.

I find no darkness in his blue eyes. No barriers. Just my Peter.

When he reaches my side, his hand raises, and he cups my

cheek. "Wendy," he breathes, surrendering as his forehead falls against mine. "I promise."

Our eyes lift. Lock onto one another's. My smile matches his and continues to widen as the shadows of night start to fall. But in the far back of his eyes, somewhere that looks like his soul, I see something inside him start to change.

"There is nothing I couldn't or wouldn't promise you," he insists, even though I can tell it pains him to admit it.

As the words leave his lips, as he submits only to me like I do to him, I feel myself falling in love.

I've never been in love. But I swear, without a doubt, this is what it feels like.

"But not tonight," he says, and this time when he denies me, I'm oddly ok with it. "Like I said, let me take care of you." His head nods in the direction of the bed. "Let me hold you," he whispers. "All night, just to know that you're all right."

His eyes flash with the same darkened look I witnessed in them when he entered that room and saw what the lost boys had done to me. It scares me a little, but the tenderness he just showed me is still evident. Still stronger. So, I hold onto that.

"That's all I want."

I nod, knowing that after what I just went through, after what he just walked in on, we both need that more than the kind of touch both our bodies yearn for.

I let my towel drop to the floor and Peter sucks in a shaky breath. He does the same, bearing himself to me. He takes a step closer and wraps me in his arms. His hard length presses deliciously against my lower stomach. His chiseled muscular frame makes my mouth water as it brushes eagerly against mine and I think about all the sinful things I want it to do to me.

"You," he insists, smacking my ass for emphasis, and I giggle. "Under the covers. Now."

I hurry and do as he says. When I'm cocooned in the middle of his bed, even though the sheets are cold, the look he gives me warms me instantly.

He climbs on top of the bed but doesn't get under the covers.

"Won't you catch cold?" I ask worried. He wraps his arm across me and pulls me flush against his chest.

"Wendy, if I get under the covers with you, there is no way I can keep my promise. And I vow to never break my promises, Wendy. Not to you."

I smile and snuggle into him tighter.

"When I finally feel like you're all right, I'll get dressed," he says, "but I'm not releasing you until then."

My smile grows wider, and just before I drift off to sleep, I swear I hear him whisper, "I am not letting you go ever, Darling."

CHAPTER 10
HOOK

"The difference between Peter and the other boys at such a time was that they knew it was make-believe, while to him, make-believe and true were exactly the same thing."
Peter & Wendy
- J. M. Barrie

PRESENT DAY

My blood fucking boils. Her words from before wind their way through my skull, down to my black heart.

"I believed in the wrong boy at the wrong time."

Fucking bullshit!

"And it cost me more than he'll ever know, because he'll never be man enough to understand what he once lost."

Leaning in, my breath releases in harsh waves against her lips. My eyes scan hers. My hands shake.

"Wrong?" My question comes out more like an accusa-

tion as I remember her words from a few moments ago. "*Wrong*, Darling?"

I expect her to back down, much like I did as I studied her from my bedroom window last night. However, I'm quickly learning this *new* Wendy has a fight in her I've underestimated.

For that, I suddenly feel all the more like breaking her.

"You'll never understand what believing in you cost me, Darling."

"Isn't that what we're standing here trying to figure out? Trying to find?" She mocks me.

An evil rage rises from the pit of my gut and spreads across my face into a mischievous, wicked grin. She takes a step forward. Her front now flush with my own. I hear footsteps behind her. Glancing over her shoulder to the crew, I give them a warning with a shake of my head not to come any fucking closer.

"Or," she hisses and my eyes flash back to meet hers. "Is this just another one of your sick games?"

I suck in a deep breath. My eyes widen with madness. A madness she created. One that's only being fueled by her bratty, insubordinate ways.

"Make-believe?" She taunts. "Pretend? Because, I do remember how much you never understood the difference between the two. You say I'm the fool, but you turned your back on..."

"Don't say it!"

"Why? Because it's the truth?"

My hands shake violently. This time for different reasons than rage. For reasons I've always found hard to accept.

I close my eyes, willing the visions of our past away.

She doesn't know I know.

"Always running," she seethes. "Always flying away from what matters most."

"I never ran away from you."

"You never followed, either."

"Didn't I?" I hiss.

She grows silent. Nervous. She can try to deny it all she wants, but deep down I know she knows that's a huge lie. Her eyes drift low between us. My molars grind together viciously the longer I wait her out.

"Seems to me we're both dancing around the same truth," my heated comment condemns us quietly. "Neither of us wants to admit when the truth finally becomes very clear."

Her gaze lifts hesitantly to mine. A scowl darkens her features.

"And how clear is it to you?" she snaps. "Obviously, not very. Not when you have me here, once again making me do your dirty work for you, because you can't seem to grow up enough to do it yourself."

Fisting the ropes around her middle, I pull her backward a few steps until I'm sitting down on a nearby rock. She struggles to break free, digging her feet into the sand, using all her power to stop me. Flinging her across my knee, she lands with a sharp exhale, and shouts my name in an angry warning.

But it's not Hook or Peter that leaves her lips. It's the cold use of my last name that rings through my ears. So impersonal, so distant, when my Wendy has never been so far removed from me.

From us.

My Wendy.

I haven't thought of her like that in years. My thoughts have only been filled with the need for retribution for what she stole from me. For what she pushed away because she didn't wait for me. Because she turned her back on me, a second time, when I couldn't immediately give her what she wanted. What she needed.

My Wendy.

When I look down at her, instantly something inside me softens at the thought of her once being mine. Against my better judgment, I lean forward and whisper into her ear, "Easy, Darling. Or I'll let them watch."

Her eyes lift with and catch the crew staring at us. She goes instantly still. Her breathing stops, and it softens another piece of my cursed heart knowing she'd rather die than relive the past.

"Get out," I yell.

My men look up at me startled.

"But Captain..." Rufio starts.

"Now, or I'll kill every last one of you."

They shuffle out quickly, my focus never wavering off Wendy as she lays still across my knees.

She still hasn't taken a breath. Still needs air. Still needs — me?

Lifting her nightgown, my cock hardens as I take in the curve of her velvet lips. Her bare ass. No panties. No barriers. Groaning, I spank her hard and feel my blackened heart start to beat when she finally sucks in a breath, finally gets the air she needs to keep her here with me, if only just a little bit longer.

"Is this for me?" I growl, as I stroke up the inside of her thighs towards her now dampening core. She tightens them, denying me access to what I've been dreaming about since the last time I had her seventeen years ago.

"No," she hisses back.

Smack!

She sucks in a breath, holds it, and I can't help the chuckle that escapes my lips.

Leaning forward, I whisper in her ear again, "Wrong." She moans as her legs betray her and they slowly start to part. "So fucking wrong, Darling," I growl into her ear. "You'll pay for that."

My hand trails from her ass to the inside of her thigh as her scent rises to greet me. Drugged, drunk on the smell of her desire, I almost lose control. Almost finger her cunt. Almost turn her over and devour her pussy with my tongue before plunging my cock so deep inside her, she'll be screaming for me to stop.

Peter would have no control.

Hook learned over the years that patience, discipline, dominance, it's the difference between a boy and a man.

"Remember, I have ways of making you obedient, Darling."

"Go to hell," she snaps.

A wicked laugh escapes my mouth as my fingertips trail along the outside of her velvet lips, touching only close enough to make her want more, crave more, as her body starts to betray her and she bucks her hips. Swaying them from side to side, Wendy tries to get me to touch her, but again I deny her.

Smack!

"Oh God," she purrs.

"Which one is it, Darling," I smile. "God? Or the devil himself?"

I rub her red cheeks, waiting for a response. Soothing the pain I inflicted when the brat doesn't deserve it. When she still hasn't spoken after a minute, I pull her up and force her to straddle my hips.

"Answer me, Wendy. I don't like to fucking ask twice."

"Funny," she counters, "you used to tell me I'd never have to ask twice. Looks like the tables have finally turned, Pan."

I grab the rope at her back and force it away from her body making her arch her breasts into me. A sharp sound of pain escapes her lips. I wait a moment, some part of me needing to know she's okay. That I haven't hurt her. She looks down at me through hooded lashes, her breaths coming quickly, unevenly. I smile, knowing she wants more, wants only what I can give her, and then lean into her mouth-watering tits. Biting my bottom lip, my cock grows harder at the sight of her hard nipples pressed against the sheer fabric of her nightgown.

"You lied," I hiss. She sucks in a breath and holds it. I blow against her nipples, my dick grows harder as they stiffen until they could cut fucking glass.

She slowly exhales, "Never."

"Hm," I taunt as my mouth hovers over her breasts. Her

hips betray her and she grinds down greedily against my length. "You did, Darling," I grit out, as my hips raise and my cock thrusts up eagerly against the inside of her slick thighs.

"When?" she breathes out desperately.

"When you said this wasn't for me."

She moans out my name as I trail my fingertips across her breasts, slowly circling the tender area around each nipple. "Why are you denying yourself what you want, Wendy?" I murmur against her trembling skin.

Glancing up at her, she sucks in another sharp breath. Her eyes now clear of the lustful spell that she was under a moment before, she whispers, "Why are you?"

Rising up her frame, I pull her back flush against me, cradling her tight in my arms, and insist, "I've never denied anything."

"Wrong," she whispers. "So wrong."

"Looks like we're back to where this all started."

"Aren't we always, Peter?"

That name.

That fucking name.

"It seems like it's the only thing we've ever been good at," her sad voice pulls me under to where my nightmares live. "Me waiting for you to come steal me away so we can start all over again. Only this time, I'm not leaving until we're finally finished."

She attempts to climb off my lap, and I reluctantly let her go. Wendy steps a few feet away and waits for me, glancing at me bitterly over her shoulder when I don't move. Collecting myself, I take a few deep breaths, and when I can finally piece myself back together again, I rise and walk to where she's standing. Grabbing the hook off my belt, I slice through her ties in one clean motion. She gasps as they fall to the floor, then pulls her arms back out in front of her, sighing in relief. Turning, she rotates her palms and tries to bring life back into her aching limbs.

With my finger, I gently raise her chin, and when I have her full attention, I whisper, "This time, Darling, neither am I."

CHAPTER II
PETER

"...And this, as we shall see, led to mischief, because Tinker Bell hated to be under an obligation to Wendy."
Peter & Wendy
- J. M. Barrie

SEVENTEEN YEARS AGO

"*It's beautiful," she whispers in awe.*

But my eyes aren't looking where hers are. My eyes are fixed on her stunning silhouette. Her beautiful profile. The way her hair blows around her shoulders in a spine-tingling way.

There is a dampness on her skin from the mist that excites me in so many ways I never knew it could since I held her last night in the shower. Finally, my eyes land on the breathtaking way the sides of her lips lift into a smile as she gazes out across Cannibal Cove and the Tiki Forest.

"Wendy, nothing compares to you," I suddenly confess. Before

she can turn to look my way, I continue. "You're the most thrilling thing I have ever laid my eyes on. I'm helplessly drawn to you. I have been since before I can even remember. The beginning of everything in my life started the night I first sat at your window. Played music for you while you slept."

She turns, her face is a mixture of shock, infatuation, such intense devotion that I have to advert my gaze.

"Peter," she whispers. "If I had one wish, I'd wish everything in my life could begin and end with you."

PRESENT DAY

I watch her in the shadows as I lean against the trunk of the Kapok tree. Her spine stiffens as she looks out across the forest. It's such a different sight from the last time we both stood here, overlooking what we admired and once beheld as beautiful. Now, our eyes only see destruction, chaos, an impending disaster. Taking a long drag off my smoke, I hold it in until it burns, then exhale as I push my weight off the tree and take a few steps towards her.

"Having second thoughts?" Her eyes flash sharply towards mine, and I can't help but smile. "Last time we stood here, you told me you wished I could be your beginning and your end. Your forever, in a sense."

"You were," she sighs bitterly, as her body turns and meets mine. "I felt alive for the first time when you brought me to Neverland."

My smile widens at her admission.

"But I died when you promised me the world and never came back."

Just when it was starting to beat again, her words reach into my chest and stop my heart.

Leaning in, my eyes search hers and I hiss, "This is *my* world. You're the one that wanted to leave it."

"I left because I had to," she snaps, and I eye her disapprovingly. She rolls her eyes. "You know why. How can you be so heartless?"

"Ah, yes," I shake my head, backing away and walking around her to gaze out across the forest. "How can I forget? Michael. He always was the whiniest one of them all."

"He got hurt," she shouts, but I don't even flinch. How could I show that I care even a bit for a child who took what I needed most in my world away from me? "He wanted his mother. He wanted to go home. He needed a doctor."

Turning quickly, I yell back, "You didn't have to stay, Wendy. Play nurse to a boy who had more than enough attention for just a mere scratch."

"Scratch?" she shouts back. "He received over sixty stitches. One blood transfusion. He was only ten. Not everything in life is a game, Peter. We all don't get to be as lucky as you!"

"What's that supposed to mean?"

"It means not all of us are protected by pixie dust, or whatever the hell you want to call it. It means, we can't all just fly away, dodge danger the way you can."

Her icy stare slices its way through my chest and pierces my soul, making me wish I could tell her everything that I've been afraid to tell her for far too long.

"You were supposed to be watching him that day," she begins to cry. "You were supposed to take care of him."

"The only one I ever made that promise to, was you, Wendy. Not Michael. Not John. Not any of the lost boys."

"If you loved me, you would've protected..."

"Who said anything about love?"

She sucks in a sharp breath and stops talking. I lash back the only way my fucked up heart knows how. With resentment.

Her face flushes a dark shade of red before turning so pale, the longer we stand in silence, the more I worry what I just said might have killed any chance we had at fixing things. Fixing us. No. Not possible. That's some sort of make-believe bullshit that Peter would have thought up. Shaking my head, I take a step forward and go against my better judgment of sticking to the damn plan, because once again, the need to treat her tenderly surfaces, and quickly takes over my brain. My heart.

"Darling..." I begin.

"Wendy," she interrupts me. "Wendy. Not Darling. You lost the right to call me that name a long time ago."

Glaring at her, I take a deep breath and contemplate what to say next.

"Fine," I grit out after a moment. "You may be, right. But if you continue to insist on acting like a little girl, I suppose I should call you by a more fitting name, lass."

Her features harden. She crosses her arms sharply over her chest.

She keeps telling me I'm the boy incapable of growing up, but she's obviously no better herself.

We stand off against each other. Her eyes flare with anger, only fueling my decision to treat her like the brat she's become. Bringing my smoke up to my lips, I take a long inhale. The tip of the cigarette glows red as it sparks and cracks, and my lungs fill with an addiction I've acquired since she's been gone. I study her over the butt end of my smoke, watching her grow more impatient as she waits for me to speak. Her eyes flash from mine to the object held tightly between my fingers as I take my time with my smoke. Eventually, she huffs, stomps her foot, then pushes past me towards the ledge overlooking the forest.

Throwing my cig to the ground, I curse under my breath, turn, and cave. Give into her once again when I've promised myself so many times over that years that I wouldn't.

"Wendy, I..." but before I can finish, the floor falls out from under her feet and she starts to tumble off the cliff.

My eyes widen as she turns back my way and quickly scrambles to keep her footing. The rocks fall with a deafening boom to the ditch hundreds of feet below us.

"Peter!"

"Fuck me, Wendy."

I grab a hold of a swinging vine and shout, "Wendy! Grab this in three. Two. One!"

The vine swings out, but misses, and comes right back to me. She cries out in fear, as the rocks quickly tumble out from underneath her. She claws at what's left of the ground trying to keep from joining them in the abyss below.

"What are you doing?" she demands. "This isn't time for games, Peter. Catch me. Fly out to me!"

A knot works its way up my throat. My mouth goes dry. Looking from side to side, I grip the vine in my hands and swing out to catch her. I'm not sure if it can hold my weight and hers, but damn it, I have to fucking try. Successfully reaching her side, I grip her around her waist tightly. She looks up at me shocked, stunned, not able to piece together what is happening and why, as we swing back towards higher land, I'm not flying like she asked me to.

I barely make it back to the safety of the cliff. As the tips of my toes land, and I come to stand on the very end of the ledge, we stumble at first before I manage to get us balanced.

Taking a deep breath, I look down into her eyes and can tell she's utterly confused. She can't understand why I'm acting this way. Why I won't just fly, use magic like I've always done before to save her. Save us.

If it's even possible to save us now.

Before I can answer the nagging questions left hanging in her eyes, a piercing bright light bursts into a million tiny pieces over her shoulder and starts barreling towards us.

"Shit, duck," I shout.

Hunching down, I shield the back of her head, pulling her face into the safety of my chest. The cluster of light barely misses as it blasts into the vine and severs the connection above our heads. Wendy's yell mixes with my curse as we stumble and start to go down again.

"Fly Peter," she screams.

Instead of wasting time explaining now, my eyes quickly search for a solution. A way we're sure to make it out of this before we tumble to our death. Finding one to my left a couple ledges below, I eagerly strain toward it.

Another flash of light bursts past our heads and slams into the rock ledge just above my right shoulder.

I know that magic. I know the Fae behind it. My jaw

clenches as I turn back to Wendy and grip her tighter against my frame.

"Wendy, do you trust me?"

Her eyes scan mine frantically. Another burst hits the ledge to her right, making her jump closer into the security of my arms. Rocks scatter out from underneath our feet as she grips my frame tighter, holding on for dear life.

"I..." she stutters, looking around us and still trying to understand what is happening and why I'm acting so strange. "I used to."

Bells sound in the distance, quickly coming closer. Glancing over her shoulder, a scattering of bright, golden-yellow light descends towards us at an alarming rate.

"Used to isn't going to work, Darl..."

"Wendy!"

Sternly looking back her way, I savagely pull her closer, her hands hit angrily against my chest. Gathering them in a tight grip with my free hand, I lean in and quickly say, "I once told you I couldn't live with myself if you got hurt. You're still the only life worth saving. So, stop being a fucking brat and let me take care of you, damn it!"

Our fearful gaze lifts as the bells reach a piercing high note. Glancing over her shoulder, our gaze quickly locks back on each others a moment later in terror.

"I trust you," she breathes. "Truth is, I never stopped."

Smiling, I guide her to wrap her arms around my waist.

"Good girl. Now, don't let go."

She laces her hands around my middle, a little tighter than she ever has before, and my heart speeds up. Placing my right hand over hers, I give them a light squeeze and then turn my attention back to our only hope out of this.

Reaching out to my left, I struggle with my balance, from the weight of both of us, as I try to grip a vine that is just out of reach. A few more rocks fall out from under the ledge we're standing on. Her hands begin to shake. Her body trembles as she clings to me.

"Hurry, Peter," her fearful cry spurs my heart back to life as the dreadful mention of my real name falls from her lips.

But this time, it surprisingly doesn't faze me. It fuels me. It makes me want to save her even more. My arm stretches, fingers extending as far as they can. Grunting, I hear the bells pierce my ears as I reach to the left with all my might.

"Peter," Wendy calls out again, this time more alarmed than before. "Please, Peter, hurry!"

She shifts her weight, and we almost tumble off the ledge. With a curse, I pull her tighter against my side, her grip now deathly wrapped around my middle, and try to reach out again. The bells are now screaming in my ears as I take a chance, lean over the ledge with both our weight, and jump, hoping and praying to whoever will listen that I'm lucky enough to make contact with the vine.

Wendy's screams meld with the painful pitch of the bells. Her nails dig into my skin as the vine slips through my fingers and I struggle to grip it. We start to fall, faster, and faster down the mountain. The rope-like vine burns as it slices into my palm the further we tumble.

"Peter," Wendy screams.

Just when I think we've run out of hope, just when I swear we are about to plummet to the bottom of the forest, my hands hit a knot in the vine giving me the extra support I need to grip it just a little bit tighter. I use the weight of us to swing both of our bodies to the left. To safety. To a hidden cave entrance, I used to love to visit when I could still fly.

Releasing the vine as we coast through the entrance, we tumble to the floor, rolling a few feet into darkness. Gravel pierces our skin. Wendy's night dress tears. The leather of my left pant leg hits a snag and rips down my shin. A warm trickle of blood oozes down my leg from the wound. I shield Wendy's head from hitting a boulder as we come to a stop. My body frames her soft delicate figure as I lay on top of her, heaving, breathless, enraged from the thought of what could have happened.

Several rushed breaths leave our lips as they hover mere centimeters from one another. Her heartbeat seems to skip a beat before it starts racing surprisingly faster than my own. Staring into her eyes, I examine her face best I can to see if she's hurt. Turning her face gently in my hands to make sure there isn't even a scratch on the most important thing in my life, a thankful sigh leaves my lips when I find none.

"Peter," she whispers after a moment.

"Wendy?" My questioning eyes search hers in the dim light.

"I can't breathe," she huffs.

"Do you feel faint?" I smile.

She shivers as our memories drift back to a time when the way we felt for one another was not covered up by lies. By secrets. By a truth we've both been running from.

"I'm ok," she finds her breath finally. "I'll be fine."

"You're not."

Her jaw sets with harsh defiance.

"Don't pretend to know what's best for me. Don't make-believe you know how I'm feeling. You don't!"

I open my mouth to speak but the sound of bells in the distance has me quickly shutting it. She glances to her side in horror as I hold her hostage under my large frame.

Fucking Tink.

Ignoring the sounds as they close in, my thumb gently caresses her cheek. Tenderly, I bring her eyes back to meet mine. The innocent, shy girl I fell in love with surfaces, just for a moment.

Her words hurt. I always knew what was best for her. Always knew how she was feeling and how to fix it. How to breathe her back to life.

It kills me to know I can't do that for her now.

"Tell me who did this to you, Darling?"

Her look turns to steel. Her eyes fill with tears as her body trembles beneath me. Pushing against my chest, she forces me off her, and scrambles quickly to her feet.

"You did, Peter." A darkness descends over us. A shadow blocks the entrance to the cave. The sounds of bells stop. "You did."

CHAPTER 12
WENDY

"Fairies have to be one thing or the other. Because being so small, they only have room for one feeling at a time. At present, she was full of jealousy of Wendy... What she said in her lovely tinkle sparkle... I believe some of it was bad words... Tink hated her with the fierce hatred of a very woman."

Peter & Wendy

- J.M. Barrie

SEVENTEEN YEARS AGO

The sounds of parrots and wild birds fill my ears as I follow Peter through Tiki Forrest. Glancing up, a mother monkey glides back and forth through the tall trees, her two infants swing behind her, barely holding on to the vines as they quickly try and catch up.

It all feels like a dream. The larger-than-life trees. The enormous mystical plants. The mist and the thick, cool breeze.

Where sunlight is blessed enough to hit the floor of the forest, flowers smile back up at me.

"Watch out!" Peter shouts suddenly.

Startled, I look his way as his body glides back effortlessly through the air, his arm circles my hip, and he lifts me from the ground just in time to avoid a pit of quicksand.

"Oh my," I gasp. "For a place as beautiful as this, I wouldn't think there would be such danger."

We float down to the ground a few paces in front of the daunting pool of sand. Peter glances down into my eyes, his arm never leaves my side. "There is beauty in danger, Wendy," he grins. "Suspense. Thrill. The rush of the escape."

He's saved me once again from peril. It's exhilarating. Stimulating.

"You like danger," I whisper. "I'm guessing maybe more than you like anything else."

He cocks his face to the side and studies me.

"I'll never deny liking whatever it is that makes me feel alive. Who doesn't love the feeling of letting go until the brink of darkness before being jolted back to life." His thumb runs softly across my bottom lip making me shiver. "Something tells me you desire that too. Light through darkness. Pleasure found with the brush of pain."

I suck in a shaky breath, and he smiles in response.

"Being brought back to life through an approaching self-destruction can be addicting, Wendy." He leans in. "Releasing yourself to the inevitable." His lips hover above mine. "The rush your body gets as your saving grace happens just in time." His breath feathers against my lips, and I close my eyes. "Making you finally take your next breath. Finally feel alive."

His lips crash against mine. Fisting his shirt in my hands, I open my mouth greedily, needing everything he's willing to give me since the last time I tasted his kiss. His tongue brushes against mine and I instantly feel weak. Peter's arms wrap tighter around my waist before he lifts me off the floor of the forest and crushes me against his chest.

His kiss is slow. Tender. Sensual. He takes his time as his mouth brushes lovingly against mine. Savoring. Tasting me in a way that makes me feel cherished, respected, owned.

"Wendy," he sighs as our lips part and we both take a deep breath. "Darling," he kisses me once more, his right hand raising to cradle my face. "Do you mind if I call you Darling?"

"No," I whisper, "in fact," his lips place tender kisses across my face, leaving me breathless. "I like it very much, Peter."

He smiles against my lips before deepening our kiss.

He licks my mouth open. His right hand softly, slowly trails to the back of my neck where he fists my hair in his hand, tenderly pulling my head to the side. I taste carnal need on his lips. A savage demanding power that I can't help but surrender to.

His mouth trails to my cheek. My neck. The dip between my breasts.

"Every night," he murmurs against my skin as he gently sets my feet back on the ground. "I lay beside you, and you never ask me." His left-hand raises, roaming the curve of my breast. He plants a few kisses up my neck to my ear and growls, "Why don't you ever ask me, Darling?"

"Ask... what, Peter?" I reply breathlessly, my mind too clouded by his touch and the way it makes me feel to understand what he's saying.

He groans softly, "To touch you."

His voice hot on my neck, making a shiver rush deliciously down my spine.

"To take you."

My lower stomach quivers.

"I'm trying to be patient, but the things I want. The things I need." He backs away, and his eyes cloud with the darkness I'm growing more accustomed to. More intrigued by. He sucks in a sharp breath before continuing. "I want to be chivalrous and say I'll wait forever. But I won't. I can't."

Nervous, I blurt out the first thing that comes to mind. "We used to enjoy playing games, Peter. Being young. Having fun. Is that all you want from me now? To touch?"

His eyes sparkle with mischief. "I want to play a new kind of game with you, Wendy,"

I swallow hard and try my best to not act childlike. "You do?"

He only nods, his intense stare never wavering off my own.

"What kind of game?" I ask nervously.

His fingertips brush up my arm, leaving a trail of goosebumps in their wake. I tremble slightly, taking in a shaky breath. Worried he won't answer, I open my mouth to speak but he places his finger against my lips telling me to be quiet.

"You like it when I tell you what I want?" he whispers quietly, reading me like an open book, "what I need?"

All I can manage is a simple nod yes.

He smiles as he leans in and whispers against my lips. "I want to taste you, Darling."

My eyes close, imagining him doing so right now. My thighs clench together as a wetness pools there. His mouth moves to my ear.

"I want to memorize every inch of your skin with my tongue. I *want to taste you, touch you places you've never been touched before. I dream of having you spread out for me, only me, to do with as I please."*

I want that, too. But I'm scared to tell him so. His hands roam the curves of my breasts. His mouth grazes the delicate skin on my neck.

"I want to watch you touch yourself."

Dear God. I couldn't. I shouldn't. I desperately want to. Only ever for him, but....

"I want you to show me what you like, and just how you like it. Watch me as I do the same."

My mouth waters at the thought just before his thumb's brushes over my hardened nipple.

"I want to spill myself right here," his fingers lift and trail down the center of my chest and I stop breathing. "Then watch as you run your hands through it, suck it off your fingertips, while you crash over your edge on my tongue. I want to bury my cock inside you. Lose myself to you, Wendy. Only you. "

Opening my eyes, I stare back at him stunned, feeling and needing things I have never dreamt of before. With a wink, he kisses me quickly, releases his grip around my waist, and then urges me to follow after him as we continue to make our way through the forest.

"But..." I stutter at a loss for words. He glances over his shoulder at me, a mischievous smile plays at his lips.

But ... truth is, there is no response to something like that.

So instead I blush, looking down and watching the floor of the forest as we walk further toward wherever it is he's taking me.

We're quiet for a few minutes, and I don't dare tell him what's creeping to the forefront of my mind. The knowing feeling that what he wants to do, the games he wants to play, crosses a definite line. I want everything he wants, too. I'd be a liar if I said otherwise. But I know Peter doesn't want to grow up. Those kinds of games, those kinds of experiences, they'd change everything.

He likes the games he plays in Neverland. Everything he wants, everything he says he needs, it will force us both to lose an innocence we'll never be able to recover. Never get back. It could change him and this place forever.

Reaching a clearing, he brushes a few large palms out of the way before pulling me closer to his side.

"Look." His plea breaks me from my thoughts as I glance out across the horizon. "See that?"

"The ocean?"

"Cannibal Cove," he corrects me. "That's where I'll have my ship one day."

"Ship?"

"Yes, Wendy," he laughs, "all good pirates have to have their ship."

Pirates?

"But Peter, why would you want pirates in Neverland?"

He turns to look at me, confusion etched across his handsome face. "The lost boys and I have played pirates for as long as I can remember," his brow furrows. "For as long as I remember you, Wendy."

"But who are you fighting when you play? Who wins?"

His cocky smile takes my breath away. "I always win. Who else?"

He grips me around the waist and flies me up on a warm breeze to the tree branch above our heads.

My gaze is fixed on him, but he only has eyes for the cove.

"When I am captain of my ship, my crew will call me James..."

"James?" I ask, shocked.

He nods. "Well, Jas for short."

Shaking my head, I glance out across the ocean confused. It is beautiful. The sun is setting on the horizon casting shades of gold, yellow, light and dark blue across the water. The beach is now mostly covered in darkness, but I can see the white tips of the waves crest as they crash against the sandy shore.

"I'll have a first mate named Smee. And if any of the lost boys go against the rules, try to grow up, I'll thin them out."

My body goes rigid. Completely still. He doesn't notice. Only continues to smile at the view. At what I fear is to become of Neverland. As I watch him, my mind can't keep from wondering what he means by thin them out?

Instead of asking him a question I don't think I want the answer to, I foolishly ask instead, "And what about me, Peter? Where do I fit into all of this?"

"Wendy," he laughs. "Silly Darling. You're what we're all fighting over. The treasure that's only ever meant to be mine."

"I don't think I'd like that," I shudder.

Not the treasure part. That has my heart melting. The fighting part. My past at home and what I witnessed in Peter back at Hangman's Tree because of what the lost boys did to me has me very worried.

"It's the only way, Wendy. Not everyone who fights over you wants you for themselves, Darling." I study his face, confused as a tinkling of bells starts in the distance. "Some, only want to take you away, just so you won't be mine."

The bells grow louder, and with them so does the serious expression etched across Peter's face.

"Why would they want to take me away?"

"Don't you know?" he looks at me in disbelief. "Why, to kill you of course."

~

PRESENT DAY

"So, the prima donna graces us with her presence once again," Tinker Bell hisses as she comes to a stop at the entrance of the cave. She puts her hands on her hips, judging me like she always did. Always has.

"I thought you took care of it," A fae I remember by the name of Blaze whispers at her right side.

Another one I don't recognize stands on her left. His bright, crystal green eyes glisten and flicker as they dance across my frame. The look he gives me makes me sick. I take a step back to protect myself, but know they could kill me on the spot if they really wanted to.

"I thought I had," her disapproving stare looks me up and down as she rises to her full height. "Turns out, I was wrong."

Tinker Bell was never the small creature I was told stories about before I first came to Neverland. When she flies, she reduces herself to the size of the sound of her tinkling bells. But when she's standing in front of you, as she is in front of me right now, she has the power to manifest herself into something bigger, something taller than you'd ever imagine so she is able to tower over her competition.

Her slender goddess-like frame seems larger than life as

she gloats silently, still looking flawless after all this time, and still looking down on me like she always has.

"If memory serves right," Pan grits out at my side, "I banished you the last time you came between Wendy and I." He steps between me and the fae. "If you don't remember, Tink, I have no problem reminding you."

Gripping Pan's arm, I stop him from taking another step forward. The sounds of the fairies laughing fills the cave a moment later. Are they laughing because of what he said, or because of me?

"Still so naïve," I hear Tinker Bell chuckle as I turn back to meet her stare. "Still think that you can control him."

"I never wanted to control anyone," I hiss, shaking my head with annoyance.

There once was a time I cowered away from her. I won't let myself do that anymore.

"That's a lie. You wanted control over Neverland. You always wanted control over all of us."

"I wanted Peter," I shout. Pan tenses under my touch. Tink's jaw ticks as she looks back toward him and studies his reaction to the name I just called him. "I would have taken him any way I could have had him."

"Another lie."

"You've always just been jealous," I snap, through with her wrongful assessments.

Her jealous hate still burns bright after all these years. She has always been too filled with envy, jealousy, to see anything but Peter's denial of her when all she ever sought was his approval.

Her eyes widen, obviously shocked that I'm actually

standing up for myself. Before she can respond I go on, "You always wanted Peter for yourself. Always saw me as a threat when you didn't even bother to realize that I wasn't the only danger to your games on the island. Tiger Lily..."

"Was never a threat," she cuts me off laughing. "Still isn't a threat."

She smiles. Something sinister behind her grin makes my attention snap to Pan, but he looks indifferent, unaffected, so I let it slide.

"You're not welcome here," Tinker Bell shouts, making my attention swing back her way. "You never were. You need to leave, before I'm forced to make you, *Darling*."

The name that falls from her lips mocks me in a way that has me taking a step back. Retreating like I always did. It hurts somewhere so deep inside that I back down from her when I promised myself, if I ever returned to Neverland, I never would.

That ends now.

Grabbing the hook at Pan's waist, I slip it from its resting spot before he can stop me and take a step forward. Tinker Bell's eyes flare bright with anger, worry even, for only a small, brief moment before a malicious smile spreads across her lips.

"And what do you plan to do with that?" she snickers.

My hand shakes slightly as I take another timid step in her direction, but it's not because I'm scared. It's because my body is teetering on the edge of control, delighting in the fact that I'm finally doing something I should've done a long time ago. I'm standing up for myself.

"End you," I hiss. "The only way I know how."

She glares down at me as the two fae at her side take an intimidating step forward to protect her. "And how is that?" Tinker Bell taunts.

"Slice off your wings." I make a swooshing gesture, slicing the hook up through the air as I take a step closer.

To my surprise, I'm not intimidated or scared at all when my whole life, I thought I would be shaking in terror if I ever went toe to toe with Tinker Bell like I always dreamed I maybe could one day. Her nostrils flare. Her jaw sets tightly as her eyes never waver from mine.

"I won't stop there, though," I continue, "Without your wings, you won't be able to leave your realm even after Pan banishes you. But your friends, your 'family,' still could. So, I'll end you all, one by one. Until you're at my mercy. The way it should have been all along."

The two fae at her side immediately take a step in front of her to block any advance I might try to make. I grin as I peer over their shoulders at her, loving the slight anxiety I see staring back in my eyes because I put it there. It fuels me. Makes me stand a little taller.

"You don't have that kind of power," she hisses.

"No?" I smile. "But he does."

Gesturing over my shoulder with the hook, Tinker Bell's eyes lift and find Pan's. He's been quiet this whole time. Watching. The two fae at her side start to laugh. The sound of Tinker Bell's annoying giggle fills my ears as I turn back his way and notice he's gone white.

"It would be so easy to correct you, but I'd rather see you die trying to obtain half the power us pixies have over Neverland. A power we've always had. One you'll never take away."

Unable to wrap my brain around what she means as Peter continues to stand next to me silent and pale as a ghost, I slash the hook forward. Pride fills my chest as the three of them stop laughing and jump back in fear.

"Cross me again," I sneer, "and you'll be the one losing all your power."

She studies me for a moment, curiosity, anger rising in her eyes.

"We'll see about that," she hisses. "Boys!"

Her entourage turns and follows her to the cave's entrance.

"Oh, and Wendy?" she gives me an evil smile over her shoulder, "I wasn't lying. If you don't leave, I will make you."

Her evil glare deepens before she takes flight and leaves nothing but a scattering of gold glitter in her wake. It starts to evaporate just as the two men take off after her, leaving Pan and I alone in the cave once again.

"She won't make you," he finally speaks up. "Not as long as I have anything to say about it."

Turning, my body stiffens. "And why should I care?"

His eyes hold a tenderness that I wasn't expecting. Stepping out of the shadows, he says, "I brought you back to..."

"Help you find something," I roll my eyes. "Something you lost. I know."

"Wrong!" he snaps. "Something we both lost. Now, I think there's another reason, another possibility as to why you're here."

"You kidnapped me," I blurt out. "In the middle of the

night. For the second time in my life. Forced me to do things...," he takes a step forward in warning and so I change course, "...and you have the nerve to stand there and act like it was all a predetermined destiny?"

"Wasn't it?"

"Fate wouldn't be so sick."

"Fate has no control," he counters back quickly. "However jaded, or displeased you are with the outcome, Darling."

I glare at him in the shadows, tired of the back and forth. The game.

"Big words, for such a young boy."

Dropping his hook at his feet, I start to walk past him, but he grabs my arm and swings me around to meet his haunted stare.

"The past seventeen years has taught me a lot of things. For one, I'm not against learning," his eyes glance down and slowly, wickedly, trail over my body before rising again to meet mine. "You remember that much, don't you, Wendy?"

"The boy I remember thought he already knew it all."

"The boy you knew no longer exists."

"Prove it."

His jaw ticks. He studies me closely. I hold my breath, a small part of me hoping he actually does prove me wrong this time. When he doesn't respond, my heart sinks.

I'm know I'm foolish to ever entertain the idea of believing in him again. To ever trust him. Still, I can't stop hoping.

Time has shown me a lot, too. The biggest lesson I've learned in our time apart is to not be so naive. To stand up for myself. To believe in myself when everything about my past, about my first time here in Neverland, tried to tear me down and break me to shreds.

I try to shrug out of his embrace, but he takes a step towards me, tightening his grip, and I still.

"Tonight," he insists. "You'll have dinner with me at Hangman's Tree."

"I don't want..."

"This isn't about what you want, Wendy," he snaps. "This is about what we both need."

When I don't respond, he repeats, "Tonight. Maybe then you'll finally see, I already proved to you a long time ago everything you've spent your entire life running from. Everything you've spent the last two decades trying to deny."

CHAPTER 13
PETER

"Wendy, I ran away the day I was born... it was because I heard
father and mother talking about what I was to be when I became a
man. I don't want ever to be a man."

Peter & Wendy

- J. M. Barrie

SEVENTEEN YEARS AGO

"Do you miss home, Peter?"

Her words pierce my heart as I look out across the thick forest on top of Misty Mountain. It's twilight now, and the pixies have come out to play. They dance about with the fireflies, causing a twinkling of magic to be spread out upon the mist. Fog hangs around us as we sit, shielded under the low hanging vines of the weeping willow tree. The thick clouds cling to our clothes. Yet, until now, I hadn't felt cold. I hadn't felt the deathly chill of my haunted past creep across my mind until she asked me that question.

"This is home," I murmur, confusion causing my brows to pinch tight as I watch the darkness begin to swallow up what's left of the sun.

"But..." she begins again. "Don't you miss your family?"

My attention angrily snaps her way. I search her eyes for the hidden meaning behind her words, but can only make out the curves of her face as the darkness around us grows. Her gaze is hidden. I don't know why, but an anxious feeling starts to rise inside me. It spreads quickly across my skin as I struggle to hold onto what I've never questioned before.

Do I miss home?

"No," I snap, shutting the emotion down.

I wish I can take my harsh words back as the moon gently starts to bathe her in its light. Her eyelashes flutter, shame fills her face, and she frowns. It was never my intention to make Wendy sad. That anxious feeling from moments before turns to worry as I scoot a little closer to her, and suddenly feel the need to try and explain.

"Family always wants too much," I start.

Shaking her head, that worry becomes a heavy, uneasy feeling as I reach out and take her hand in mine and she tries to pull away. I drag her closer before she can shut herself off.

Struggling with how to explain, I watch as she stares down at our hands laced together. Something about not having to look her in the eyes to justify my response, gives me the courage to say what I need to.

"They're always trying to tell you what's best for you," I mumble. "How you should behave. How you should respond. What you should like, what you should hate. From the second you're born, they have your life planned for you." She still hasn't looked up, still hasn't cut me off like a part of me worried she would, so I go on. "Maybe that's why I ran away the day I was born. I heard father telling mother he wanted me to be just like him."

"And what was he?" she whispers so quietly I almost don't hear her. "A good man? A bad man? Why didn't you want to be just like him, Peter?"

Something about the way she asks, something about the tone of her voice, gives me an unsettled feeling. Memories resurface. A knowledge that I've tried to suppress for years beckons me closer. There is a sort of hurt to her words. A frightened worry of what I'll say. What we'll uncover. Before I can ask her why, she continues, "If you didn't want to be like him, what would you want to be when you grew up?"

Her eyes finally lift to meet mine. I study her closer than I ever have before as my mind becomes very perplexed.

Doesn't she know? This place, Neverland, it's home because here - I never have to grow up. The lost boys, they don't understand. That's why they're lost. That's why they need me as their leader. Me? I'm not lost. I'm free. In Neverland, there are no rules. Anything can happen.

That's what I love most about this place.

But, for the first time in my life, the look she's giving me makes me question that. It makes me realize there's always been a small hole that needs filling in this make-believe land I can't help but escape to.

"I'm never going to grow up, Wendy." Her eyes grow sad, only this time when I see her expression change it doesn't make me feel anxious. It doesn't make me worry. Suddenly it's clear what's been missing. "And Wendy, as long as you stay here with me, you *never* have to grow up, either."

She smiles for the first time tonight. The unsettling feeling growing between us moments ago lifts as she scoots a little closer.

"I like that," she sighs, leaning into my side as her head drops to my shoulder. "Never having to grow up if I don't want to. After all, so much of growing up is overrated, I think. So much of becoming an adult is corrupt."

I don't dare ask what she means, or how she knows. Instead, I lean my head on hers as our gaze drifts back out across the mountain.

In reality, isn't all I've ever wanted from Wendy nothing but corruption?

I brought her to Neverland with me to show her my world. But I would be lying if I said I didn't bribe her here under false pretenses. I always planned to keep her for myself and never let her go back home. Never let her leave me.

Having her here began with very crooked intentions, and the longer she's stayed, the more I've found the need, the desire, growing inside me to ruin her. Just for me. The way I ruined her that day at Skull Rock.

All those nights I flew to London, laid at the edge of her bed while she slept, played her music, I never felt the kind of power that was between us like that day at Skull Rock. It was a higher kind of magic. An addicting enchantment.

Every touch defiled her. Altered us. Ruined me.

I took a piece of her innocence. Gave her mine in return.

Disgraced us both.

I've never felt more alive, more lured by a power that was beyond my control in my entire life.

Now, every bit of my body, my soul, vibrates with an itch to do it again.

But that doesn't mean we have to grow up. Does it?

It's a thought I've wrestled with for weeks now. It's the reason I stayed away from her after the first time I tasted her lips. It's the explanation for keeping my hands to myself as I lay awake at night, even as her soft, welcoming body wraps around me under my sheets, calling out to every part of my soul to take her. It's the only thought raging through my mind since a week ago, when I took her to Tiki Forest and told her that I'm trying to be patient, but in reality, I only have so much restraint.

"Peter?" she whispers.

I swallow hard, attempting to clear the thoughts clouding my head. Nonchalantly, I glance down at her snuggled closely into my side and press my lips gently against her head. "Yes, Darling?"

"I think one of the things I love most, about being here, about Neverland, about you, is the freeing feeling of never having to grow up. Not if I don't want to."

"And what if one day you change your mind? What if, one day, you decide you want to leave all this behind?"

"I don't know if I ever could."

Her hand tightens in mine, and I instinctively grip hers even tighter.

Bringing our hands up between us and kissing the back of her palm, I whisper, "Good, because I wouldn't let you."

A possessive feeling rushes through my veins as her bewildered stare catches my eye. Selfishly, I lean her back gently against the soft forest floor, covering her body with my own. She's tense underneath me. Her eyes hold a sort of scared curiosity as I grip her waist in one hand and cup my other palm around the back of her neck.

Kissing each side of her mouth, she settles gently in my arms and then sighs. "Liar."

My body throbs. My entire soul fills with the hungry, carnal desire to make good on both threats. To take her innocence and keep her. Make her mine forever. Make sure she never leaves me.

My cock grows, thickens quickly, pulsing between us with impatient need. Kissing across her cheek, I lower my mouth to her neck, and grind up the inside of her thigh. Her body becomes hard. Closed off. Rigid. Her hands that were once running through my hair stop as I take what my body wants. Pressing my hips harder against her center, I hiss when my length forcibly rushes up through the curve between her pussy and thigh.

Whispering in her ear, she lets out a shaky breath as I say, "I'd never lie to you, Wendy. I stole you away with me because it pleased me. Little did I know, I'd never truly be satisfied until I fully claimed you as mine."

She lets out an eager moan and it fuels my appetite. One of her legs rises and she wraps it around my waist tightly. I groan into the curve of her neck.

Maybe that's what I love most about my Wendy. My Darling.

The fact that I know she can't deny me. She's always wanted me to keep her, just as much as I've never intended on letting go.

"Peter," she softly cries, as my lips brush against the curve of her neck. "Maybe we should stop. I'm... I'm worried."

"Why?" I murmur against her soft skin as her back arches into me, begging for more.

She doesn't want to stop, and neither do I. A groan escapes my lips when I feel her soft center grind up against my thickening length. I press down just as she pushes up. A desperate moan falls from our lips.

"I know... you don't want to grow up," she pants. I smile down at her, happy that she finally understands, feeling like a secret I've been holding in far too long is finally out in the open. "But... I want to give myself to you."

My mind struggles to understand what she means as my body only registers what it wants.

Her.

My right-hand falls to her thigh, and I lift it, pulling her nightgown up, and eagerly wrap her other leg around my waist. Pushing up on my hands, I stare down at my cock as it slides across her slick, bare sex.

Wendy never wears panties. Not anymore. She doesn't just to tease me. And fuck, just the knowledge these past few weeks has almost been my undoing.

As my crown hits the spot I haven't been able to stop thinking about since the last time I tasted it between my lips, precum drips against her lower stomach. Her clit throbs. I groan glancing down at the delicious nub I devoured, sucked on, tasted heaven on for the first time in my life when I held it between my lips that night in skull rock before she squirted across my tongue and down the back of my thirsty throat. I repeat the motion, growing even harder when another moan escapes her lips.

"I want to take everything you want to give me, Darling," I slowly thrust my length up her sex and she bites her lip, her breasts bounce with every thrust of my hips, my restraint almost snaps at the breathtaking sight. "Maybe even everything you're not willing to give me, too."

Her eyes widen. "Peter," she pleads. "I'm scared."

"Do I scare you?"

"Sometimes," she admits, and my heart breaks.

"I would never hurt you."

"I know, it's just..."

"What?"

"Oh, Peter," a tear falls from her eye, and I startle. My movements stop as I try to process what she's saying. What she's not saying. "It's not that, it's just ... I don't want to lose you."

Pushing off the floor, kneeling between her legs, my hands fall to the buttons of her nightgown. I start to unfasten the blue fabric confidently.

"Is that all?" I smile, brushing the gown off her shoulders, exposing her breasts to the cool night air, my mouth waters as my eyes take in her creamy, delicate skin. Her nipples are pink and deliciously hard. I brush my fingertips across them gently. A shiver courses through her body as I hungrily stare down at her bare body.

"Stay with me, Wendy," I whisper, gently leaning forward, "and you'll never have to worry about losing me."

Closing my mouth over her nipple, I thrust two fingers inside her. She's mine. Always has been. Tonight, I'm taking what's mine, and nothing she can say, nothing she can do, is going to stop me.

CHAPTER 14
HOOK

"I say, Wendy, always, if you see me forgetting you, just say, 'I'm Wendy,' and then I'll remember."
Peter & Wendy
- J. M. Barrie

PRESENT DAY

T didn't take her that night, nor for many more that followed.

I look at her now, sitting across the large table from me in the dining room of a home we once shared together, and finally understand why.

"Who did this to you, Darling?"

"You did, Peter."

Lies.

The damage was done long before I ever stole Wendy away to Neverland. More men have hurt her over the years

141

than me. It's part of what she was running from that day in the forest, trying to mask her suffering by possibly inflicting a new wound she wasn't ready for. When I realized how fragile she was as she fell apart in my arms, tears falling from her eyes after I forced her to cum again on my tongue, I held her close and whispered promises that could never be broken.

I never ruined her.

I saved her.

What's more, she's mine, and I don't care how many years we've spent apart. Nothing will ever change that.

It wasn't over between us back then, and for as long as I have breath in my lungs, and as much as it pains me to admit it, It still isn't fucking over.

The flames of the candles flicker as they light the room. She brings her glass of wine to her lips, and I do the same. Both of us study each other across the empty space. Both of us wait each other out, wanting to see who will break.

When I brought her here, I wanted to do just that.

Break her.

But Wendy was always broken.

Just like me.

Together, we actually stood a chance.

That's part of the reason why I've always felt called to her. I couldn't see that when she was first here. When I was just a boy, just as lost as she was. But being this close to her again, being forced to remember the night I almost broke her, I see things differently.

"You've changed," Wendy whispers, forcing my thoughts back to the present. Raising her glass, she gestures to me across the table, and I sink back into my seat, retreating into my darkness. The shadows. "Not your manners, or your cockiness," she rolls her eyes, and I grin, "but your appearance."

She studies me closely. I calm my nerves by raising my glass and taking a large sip of wine. Her eyes search mine, trying to make out what her mind is telling her, something I've worked tirelessly to keep hidden. I avert my gaze by setting my glass down, pulling my pack of smokes from my pocket, and then take a generous amount of time lighting up, waiting for her to continue.

"Maybe not," she finally mumbles, and I breathe a little easier.

With a heavy sigh, she sets her wine glass down and pushes away her dinner plate. Leaning back in her chair, she lets her eyes roam around the dining room. I relax slightly, but still keep my guard up.

"Maybe I've had too much wine," she finally confesses.

A light chuckle escapes my lips. Exhaling a cloud of smoke, I gesture towards her with my cig just as she looks back my way.

"Careful," I tease, "the wine in Neverland is not like the crap you must be used to drinking back home."

"What," she huffs, "you going to tell me the fae laced it with magic?" I grin. Nervously, she asks, "You trying to put a spell on me, Pan?"

Avoiding answering her question, I take another long drag of smoke and exhale as I say, "If I was, it would never be as strong as the spell you've always held over me, Wendy."

We grow silent. Nervous. My confession hangs between

us like an ominous fog. After a moment, I push angrily out of my seat, irritated with myself for not being able to stop myself from sharing such a private thought. Glancing back her way, I watch as her gaze lowers to her lap, she fiddles with her napkin before I anxiously start to pace to the far side of the room.

Memories of that night in the forest, the night I almost fucked her against her will, have always hung heavy in my mind. Yes, a part of her was very willing that night. But it never would have felt right. Never would have felt like I had all of her. There was a part of her closed off, and for damn good reason. So, I waited, much like I feel the need to wait now.

There is so much she doesn't know. So many questions I have. Still, what's easy to see, easy to feel, is how much we both still want each other. How much we both still need each other. Denying it is only fueling a fire that's soon to combust if we aren't diligent to talk first. When that match is finally lit, this time, I know it'll be our ruin if I can't make her finally understand the truth.

A truth I am just now realizing myself.

Maybe I'm not as lost as I thought.

Maybe, considering Wendy, I never was.

"I want more," her soft voice finally cries. My back stiffens but I don't allow myself to turn her way. "Of you... I've always wanted more. It's the one thing you've never given me."

Wrong. She's so fucking wrong.

"You've always left me waiting," she whimpers, "Until

one day it was too late." I open my mouth to speak, but she beats me to it. Years of pent-up frustration finally unleashing. "Even then. I waited. I fucking waited."

I hang on her words. Let them strangle me. Ruin me. Her eyes darken, her jaw sets tight. Tears fall down her flushed cheeks.

"Wendy, I ..." she stands abruptly, her chair falls to the floor behind her, and I startle.

"You were all I had, Peter," this time when she says my name, calls me Peter instead of Pan, it does something to my heart that I can't stop. It makes it beat again. Harder, faster, as the pull that was always there between us spins quickly out of control.

Unable to speak at first, I finally manage in a whisper, "You were all I had too, Darling."

"Bullshit!"

"That seems to be your new favorite word," I scowl, my shoulders tensing as she rounds the side of the table and takes a heated step in my direction. "Maybe you want to elaborate?"

"You had Neverland," she takes another hot step closer. "The lost boys." Another step. "The mermaids. Indians. Your beloved Cannibal Cove. Mystic Mountain. Tinker Bell!" On the last one I flinch. "Hell, when it finally all fell apart, you even kept John! You're selfish!" she screams, taking one last step towards me. Pushing against my chest, forcing me a step back, she continues to punch me. I take blow after blow, wishing each hit would once again stop my beating heart. "Nothing but a selfish. Fucking. Boy."

I grab her wrist, use force to restrain her. She pushes against my chest harder, backing me against a wall. Her tear-stained eyes lift, her next words come out on a whisper, "Nothing but a selfish fucking bastard."

Leaning in, my heated breath comes out as a whisper as it feathers against her lips. "Better a selfish bastard than a princess that won't admit when she's fucking wrong."

"I've only ever been wrong about you."

"Really?" I cock my head to the side, still not letting her go. "How so?"

She swallows hard, an anxious blush creeps across her face. "I thought you'd never leave me."

"I didn't."

Her brow furrows. "The fact that I haven't seen you for the past seventeen years would suggest otherwise."

"You can't leave someone that's a part of you, Wendy." It's all I can manage to tell her until she accepts the past for what it truly was. It's a small truth that's bigger than she realizes. "You've always been a part of me, Darling. Even when we both tried to fight it."

Her eyes soften. Her temper deflates as she takes a step back. I keep her wrists held tightly in my grasp.

"When you talk to me like this," she says, closing her eyes, "it reminds me of the way things used to be. It makes me want to believe you."

Her head shakes back and forth, trying to erase the words I've just said. Ones I can't stop myself from finally telling her. After seconds that feel like hours, she opens her eyes and looks at me with a sad smile.

"But time away from you has taught me that's just your

spell, Peter. The enchanting way you've always gotten what you wanted."

"Bullshit." I can't help myself, and bitterly try her word on for size. This time, it's Wendy that cocks her head to the side and studies me. "I've never gotten what I wanted, because all I've ever wanted, Darling, is you."

"You had me," she whispers. "For a long time, you had me, and you gave me up, right after..." her voice breaks. Her eyes harden, never leaving mine.

Pressing her back up against the wall, I lean in and whisper, "Did you really think I would finally have you, give myself to you, and never return to you?"

A shiver runs through her body.

"Oh, Darling, all I've ever craved was you," she sucks in a sharp breath. "I'd never be able to stay away. Fuck, I dreamt of you, touched myself to the thought you until it hurt, desperate to be back inside you, every night we've been apart."

"And Tinker Bell? Tiger Lily?"

I study the hurt in her eyes. My heart breaks, wishing I could change that part of my past. Erase the last seventeen years. Remain abstinent, for Wendy, even if she hadn't done the same in return.

"Never filled the void," I manage. "Nothing can replace the irreplaceable."

She stops breathing and I smile.

"I won't lie and tell you what you want to hear. I'll never lie to you, Wendy. Never hurt you. Not like he did."

She pushes me away so quickly I almost lose my footing.

Grabbing a hold of the table just in time, she storms past me before I can reach out and stop her.

"Fuck you, Peter," she screams. "Not everyone is like you. Lost. You're so damn lost you can't see through the make-believe anymore. Hell, to be honest, you never could."

"I'm not the only one living in a fantasy, Darling," I seethe, following close behind and barely catching the door before she slams it in my face. "Wake up, Wendy!"

She turns, a bitter laugh falls from her lips.

"Right," she mocks me. "Maybe that's it. Maybe I've been dreaming this whole time. This can't be real." Her arms fly out at her sides as she spins in a circle. "Neverland." Her laugh grows louder. "Yeah, fucking right! Only, why would I dream of a place like this when..."

She stops spinning, her heated stare locks with mine as she stands completely still in the middle of the tree fort. A place we used to share with the lost boys before I returned to Neverland without her and took on the role of Hook.

I lean against the wall and give her a cocky grin. She places her hands on her hips. Defiance, annoyance squares off against me as she holds her ground across the room. After a moment, she spins on her heels and stalks off down the hallway.

"Where are you going?" I insist.

"To bed!"

I watch in disbelief as she stalks off in the direction of the master quarters we used to share all those years ago. Slightly embarrassed that she'll realize nothing has changed after all this time, that I left it just as it was, keeping her with me anyway I could, I reluctantly let her go.

"Constantly living in denial," I grunt.

When she still doesn't respond, I yell, "Sweet dreams." Wendy raises her fist, then her middle finger, and flips me off over her shoulder. I turn and storm back into the dining room, mumbling under my breath, "you're going to fucking need them."

CHAPTER 15
PETER

"Of course, Peter should have kept quiet, but of course he did not.
He immediately answered in Hook's voice... 'I am James Hook,
captain of the Jolly Roger.'"
Peter & Wendy
- J.M. Barrie

SEVENTEEN YEARS AGO

I slash my sword forcibly through one of the lost boys and watch him cry out in pain. That'll teach the fucker to go behind my back and tell Tinker Bell where I've been hiding the last few weeks.

Returning home from Kingston Gardens barely a week ago now, all I wanted to do was hole up in Hangman's Tree and be left alone. The lost boys had other plans though, and snitched about where I've been spending my time to the one person I didn't want them telling.

Since Wendy turned her back on me, on all of us, the last thing I needed was to come home to a bitter, angry fae.

The last of the boy's life drains from his face, but it does nothing to ease my pain. He's the third boy I've killed this week, and still it does nothing to ease the ache in my chest. Stashing my sword on my hip, John steps to my side and stiffens. Why he insisted on coming back with me, I'll never know. Especially since he's been gone every night since, disappearing and coming back late after the sun has already started to rise.

"Is there a purpose for all this madness?"

His question pisses me off. Makes me want to tell him to go back home. Return to the Darling household. Stop pretending with all of us here in Neverland.

He was never the one I wanted here, anyway. He only came because it was a package deal. I only ever wanted Wendy. Not her rotten brothers who ended up ruining everything in the end.

But I don't tell him to leave. Truth is, I don't think I ever could. As long as he stays, as long as I give him a reason to never go back home, maybe she'll come back to me.

"Have I ever needed a reason before to do as I please?" I hiss back angrily. Shouldering past him, I start to make my way down to Pegleg Point.

"Ok," he stammers as he scurries to keep up with me. I look over my shoulder and give him a disapproving glare, but don't stop him.

"Logically speaking," he continues, "you don't think it was foolish to kill off one of the last lost boys on the island?"

"I don't need more lost boys, I need...," my voice trails off and I stop walking.

My nightmares resurface. The ones that call to me every time I close my eyes. The visions of Wendy and I at the end. Our end. They keep me awake, tossing and turning, every night since I've been back on the island.

"Never mind," I mutter as I pick up my pace to the lookout point.

"Besides," I call over my shoulder, as we push a few large palms out of our way, coming to the point overlooking the ocean at Cannibal Cove. "You'll be my first mate, John. I won't need anyone else."

"First mate?"

"For my ship."

If I stand a chance of surviving now that Wendy is gone, I can't stay at Hangman's Tree. I have to have a new place, somewhere her memory won't haunt me. I told her once I planned on building a pirate ship out in the cove. Now seems like the perfect time to get started.

"You can't run from your past, Peter," I cringe as he says my name. It makes me think of the way it used to fall from her lips. As if always spoken on a beautiful dream. One that has now become my worst nightmare.

"Watch me," I hiss as I start to scale the point down to the beach below.

"It'll only bring you darkness," John yells above the sound of the crashing waves against the rocks. "Peter, did you hear what I said?"

He's right. But running from my past is all I've ever been good at.

"Peter, I..."

"Hook!" I yell up at John, then watch as his gaze becomes puzzled. "James Hook, Smee. If I ever hear you say that other name again, I'll gut you just like I did your friend."

I nod in the direction of the lost boy whose life I took just a few minutes ago. John glances over his shoulder and takes a step back in fear. I don't give either of them another thought as I continue to climb down the rocks to the beach below.

He's wrong. I turned to the darkness a long time ago in order to escape the hell I knew back home before I ever even came to Neverland. The only difference is now I'm finally finding a reason to embrace it.

～

PETER | THIRTEEN YEARS OLD

"I feel sorry for the boy, honestly," one of the officers says. "His parents were never around. Neighbors say when they were, they were always getting high."

"When were they found? Have the cause of overdose yet?"

I glance over my shoulder, to the three men huddled in a circle in our entryway. I say *our* loosely because there is no *ours* anymore. They give me a sad, pitiful glance, then huddle closer together, whispering amongst themselves so I can't hear them.

Or so they think.

"Most likely, heroine," the taller one says. "If you look at the boy's arms, he might have been high a time or two himself. He's got tracks there to prove it."

I raise my shirt sleeves and shrug. The men behind me are wrong. Not just about my parents, who they are, and how they died. But I've never done drugs.

Never needed to.

I could always escape into my mind, to a world of make-believe that took me away from the hell that tried to suffocate me here in these four walls.

Now, does that mean that my parents didn't hold me down and practice sticking needles into my arms? No, it fucking doesn't. They've been doing that for as far back as I can remember. Always practicing until they got it right. They were sick pieces of shit, that I'm glad not have to walk another day through life with.

Against my wishes, my eyes tear up, my nose starts to run. Sniffling, I raise my arm and wipe my shirt across my nose.

Bitterness fills my mouth and travels south to my stomach. I haven't eaten in days. Almost a week if my math is right. My stomach grumbles loudly in pain.

"It'll be hard to get any orphanage to take him when he looks like that."

Orphanage?

"Agreed, but the kid has no family. No living relatives. If the state won't take him, who will?"

My hands shake as I grip the arms of the chair I'm sitting in, and stare off into the distance. At nothing.

That is exactly what I am now.

Nothing.

I have no one. I will never be anyone. At least, no one that is important. Maybe it would be better if those needles *were* laced with drugs. Maybe it would be better if I got taken away with them.

Or even better, maybe it would be better if I was never born.

I look to my right, and see the door to the backyard swinging softly open and closed on a light breeze.

"Maybe we should take him down to the station," one of the men says.

"Maybe one of the women will know what to do with him."

Women?

My mother was the devil.

My father was worse.

The last thing I want is to be manhandled by grownups, and then put away somewhere where no one wants me. Where no one will ever stay with me. Wait for me. Be there for me, like I want to be there for them.

My feet itch. My legs begin to bounce up and down.

"Let's go talk to him, see if we can get him to come willingly before..."

Fuck that.

I bolt out of my seat so quickly I surprise myself. They yell for me to stop as I run through the room, down the hall, and out the back door. I'm at least twenty feet in front of them when I glance back over my shoulder and breathe easier knowing they don't stand a chance at catching me.

Ducking quickly into Kingston Gardens, I lose them in the dark shadows that are falling at twilight.

My breaths are rushed as I hear them run by in the wrong direction. I quickly dart about, hiding further into the garden. A heavy mist hangs in the air. It twinkles about as the last of the sun's rays shine through. Slowing down, I could swear I hear bells ringing. A sharp light flashes past me and I quickly dart out of the way. When I turn around, a soft voice calls to me from further across the garden and I follow it.

Coming around a corner, I see a young girl, not too much younger than myself, kneeling in a baby blue dress with puff sleeves. A dark blue bow is fastened at the back of her curly auburn hair.

She sings as she spins in circles, something that sounds like a riddle. A game. The urge to play too, to enter her world of make-believe, escape floods me. Her eyes land on mine, and I step out of the shadows, falling head over heels for the magic that I see hanging in her stare. She blushes, realizing I've been watching her, and then quickly takes a bow.

Cocking my head to the side, I follow suit and bow back to her in return.

"Hello," I smile as my eyes lift to meet her stare. "Was that a song you were singing?"

"No," she shrugs as she rises and takes a step closer. "Well, maybe. I don't know." She laughs and I swear the world stops spinning. "I just made it up."

"Do you always make things up?"

"When it pleases me, when I need to escape." She frowns, her eyes grow sad. Something about what she has just said makes me think we might understand each other more than I thought. After a moment, her eyes grow wide with excitement, and she asks, "Do you like to play pretend?"

"Sometimes," I confess.

"What?"

"Oh, I don't know." I shrug. "An island, perhaps, far away from here."

"With mermaids?" she smiles. Her eyes widen playfully.

I nod my head and take a step forward. "And Indians, and pirates."

"And fairies," she sighs, just as a tinkling of bells starts to ring softly through the garden again.

We glance around us curiously as the darkness grows and night sets in.

"Do you have to go home?" I whisper, turning back her way.

"No," she blushes. "I can stay a little longer."

"What's your name?"

"Wendy," she grins. "What's yours?"

"Peter. Peter Pan. It's nice to meet you, Wendy."

I bow to her once again, starting a game I hope never ends.

She giggles, hiding her face in her hands and turning an adorable shade of pink. When she tears her hands from her face and notices I still haven't broken stance, she bows just the same and says, "It's nice to meet you too, Peter Pan. I want to play a new kind of game. Are you in?"

I give her a curious nod, and she takes off through the garden. I chase her quickly, running after a girl I never expected. One, no matter what happens next, I'm sure to never forget.

CHAPTER 16
WENDY

"Mr. Darling used to boast to Wendy that her mother not only loved him but respected him. He was one of those deep ones... in a way that would have made any woman respect him."

Peter & Wendy

- J. M. Barrie

TWENTY-SIX YEARS AGO

"What's it like, Nana?" I sigh dreamily, as I glance out the Victorian window across the room. I smile wistfully as I watch the stars twinkle in the moonlight.

Nana, our nursery maid, has just finished telling me the most thrilling story. My favorite story. One I only got her to tell me because it's my birthday. I turned thirteen today.

Nana, like others in my house, believes it's time I start to grow up. Put away childish ideas and lands full of make-believe.

But something tells me I'll never forget the story Nana's told me over the years. The one about a boy who ruled a world full of magic. A boy I want to know more about. One I hope I never forget, along with his world full of wonder. One filled with secrets, where anything goes, as long as he says so.

The older woman stops rocking in her chair by the window and contemplates my question with a frown.

I heard her talking with mother and father before they left for their party. I know that tonight is supposed to be my last night in the nursery. That I am supposed to forget about these types of things and focus on my studies.

Still, I am hopeful she humors me, if just for tonight.

"What's what like, child?"

"Love," I sigh.

"Your parents wouldn't want me talking to you about such things," she insists angrily.

With a frown, I snuggle deeper into my covers and look out the window behind her head. My gaze immediately falls to the brightest star in the sky, the second one to the right of the moon, and I start to smile.

"I think it's like magic," I whisper.

Nana stops rocking, but doesn't tell me I'm wrong. My gaze stays focused on the bright light as she says, "Some people would call you delusional. They would tell you that love's nothing but a twisted illusion."

I frown again. I've never been in love. I'm still too young, but she has to be wrong.

"That's the best kind of love..." I confess in a small voice. A smile pulls at her lips as she dares to dream along with me and our gazes drift back to the dark night sky. "The kind that can take you

away from reality. Create new worlds to live in. Give you an escape when you desperately need it."

Our gaze falls and meets in the darkness. My eyes water with tears I try daily to never let fall. Especially in front of Nana. Someone who has always been more of a mother to me than the one who gave me life.

When she is around, mother is quick to boast that father is king of all he does. Always gets what he wants. He's someone to be feared. Respected. What exactly he does, I'm not sure. Something with money, stocks and shares he says. But I know he's lying. I know it's a cover up.

Men are always coming and going at odd hours of the night. I hear them as I hide in the shadows, listening to their whispers. His right-hand man, Jake, stays close to his side. Watching everything he does from the shadows. Watching me.

Mother doesn't notice so much. She's always dazed and floating about. Never awake in the morning, always passed out early in the evening. When she's not high as a kite, she tells me that even though my father is harsh, even though he's rough and shows us all tough love, we have to understand we have it better than most.

"We should feel blessed," she says.

Deep down, I know she has to be right because there will come a day when father steps down and Jake will rule. It's something that's been decided for as long as I can remember. Things could be worse. Much, much, worse.

Still, I won't let myself let go of the magic I know exists if I just believe in it hard enough. If I don't let myself succumb to the darkness that seems to be all around me. In my father's eyes. In Jake's eyes.

To survive, I just need to think happy thoughts.

"You're only thirteen, child. What would you need to escape from?" Nana finally asks.

But we both know the truth, and her face falls when I don't answer.

A loud crash on the stairs below has me gripping my blankets in fear. Startled, I sit up in bed just as Nana bolts from her seat and through the jack and jill bathroom to check on John and Michael. Loud footsteps echo up the stairwell and down the hallway a moment later. Sucking in a jagged breath, I retreat into the dark corner of my bed, and press my body up against the cold wall of my room.

The footsteps stop abruptly. An eerie quiet fills the house. My eyes land on the doorknob to my room. A sickness fills my veins a second later when I watch it slowly start to turn.

Nana reappears quickly, her eyes darting frantically to me and then the door. This wouldn't be the first night she stood between me and the evil that lurks behind it. Over the last year, she's refused to leave my side, as if she knows the unsettling feeling we both refuse to acknowledge is right. The difference is, tonight I knew the sinful look in Jake's eyes before he left for the party with mother and father. I felt his lingering touch as he said goodnight to me in the hallway before I retreated for the evening to my room. Nana won't be able to stop him tonight. The thought of her getting hurt makes me suddenly jolt out of bed.

"Nana..."

She holds up her hand, stopping me from coming any closer as the door slams open. My eyes lift and catch the large, towering frame standing in the doorway. I sink back onto my bed with dread. A drunken cloud fills his eyes. Annoyance instantly settles across his features. He stares at Nana in rage. His fists clench tight at his sides as he takes a slow step into my bedroom.

"I thought you were told to be gone by the time we returned," he snarls.

"Didn't feel right, leaving the children all alone in this big house."

Nana stands tall and I shrink back into the darkness, cowering once again into the corner of my bed.

Jake's eyes dart from Nana to me. He licks his lips, and I shudder, gripping the sheets tighter in my fists. Closing my eyes, I pray for a miracle. For the magic. For a chance to escape and never think again about the way he's looking at me tonight. The way he always tries to touch me. The way I know he wants to do things to me that shouldn't be done.

"That's not your concern," I hear him say a moment later. His boots are heavy as he stomps across the floor. I open my eyes wide, worried he's headed in my direction. "You aren't paid for your opinions on what you think is right. You're paid to do as you're told."

His eyes drift to mine and an evil smile pulls at his lips.

"There was an accident tonight." I stop breathing waiting for him to continue. "Mr. Darling won't be returning home." My heart stops. "Ever." I start to shake. "Seeing as I was his right-hand man, I'm now in charge. Wendy is thirteen now. We won't be needing your assistance any longer."

"I take my orders from Mrs. Darling..."

"You'll take your orders from me," Jake booms. Michael starts to cry from the other room. "I'm the master of this house now. This will not be a democracy. It's a dictatorship. In my house, you will respect what I say. I will have as I please."

I lock eyes with Jake and for the first time in my life, wish for the darkness to swallow me whole. Wish for numbness, so I don't have to think. Don't have to feel. Don't have to understand the look in his eyes that terrifies me night after night.

"You'll leave," Jake continues as Michael's cries increase from just beyond the doorway. "Now, Nana. Pack your bags, and never return. Don't worry, Wendy can manage beautifully from here out."

No!

The magic.

Think about the magic.

"No," Nana echoes my thoughts.

Jake's angry stare flashes to our maids. "What was that?"

"No, Sir, I won't be leaving. Not until Mrs. Darling..."

Slap!

I gasp as Jake's fist collides with Nana's face and her head flings back. She loses her footing but grabs ahold of a nearby chair to stop herself from falling to the floor. John has now joined Michael in his crying, and for the first time I feel the harsh reality of how selfish our mother truly is.

She won't come to our rescue. She never comes. It's always been Nana who has stood between us and the monsters that seek to harm us in the night.

Nana grunts as Jake fists her uniform in his hand and starts to pull her towards the door. My maid, my companion through the years, my only friend, digs her feet into the floor and tries to stop him. I hear the faint tinkling of bells in the distance and wonder who could be stopping by at this time of night. Hopeful that it distracts Jake from what he came upstairs for, I sit up in bed and think about joining John and Michael.

Jake wouldn't dare come for me in their room. Would he?

"Don't you fucking move," Jake hisses at me as if he can read my thoughts.

A rattling sounds against the window a moment later, but I'm too caught up in fear, in the terror of what I might lose, that I don't turn to look.

"She's just a child," Nana screams as the rattling grows stronger and the tinkling of bells relentlessly pierces my ears. "I won't let you touch..."

Jake pulls a knife out of his pocket and slash it across Nana's throat. I go to scream, tell myself to move, run, but frozen in horror all I can manage is to tuck myself away further into the corner of my bed.

Jake's eyes find mine as he drops Nana. Stepping over her as if she is nothing, he slowly, maliciously, starts to make his way across the room towards me. Closing my eyes, I focus on the only words that come to mind.

Think happy thoughts.

Think happy thoughts.

"Wendy," Jake whispers low, and dangerously close. "Be a good girl and scoot to the edge of the bed."

I don't hear John and Michael's cries. I don't hear the rattling, the tinkling of bells in the distance. Not like I did before. All I can focus on is the loud beating of my heart as Jake's weight presses down on the bed a moment later.

"If you don't listen to what I tell you," he warns in an intimidating tone, "I will be forced to make you. Like I said, Wendy, I will be respected. This is now my house. And you now belong to me."

Reluctantly, fearing a fate worse than the one I dread is

coming, I feel myself inch towards him.

"That's right," he whispers. I flinch when I feel him touch my thigh. Still not able to open my eyes, his displeasure is evident as he grabs a hold of my wrist tightly, "Respect your new master, Wendy. Do as I say."

When I still don't, he yanks me towards him. I prepare for the blow, the force of my body inevitably slamming into his.

But it never comes.

Weightless, I suddenly feel my body floating through the air a moment later. Slender arms wrap around my waist tightly. The touch is tender. Loving. Magical. The bells sound again in the distance, growing louder as I feel myself gently float back down to the floor far away from where I was just sitting.

I open my eyes wide as Jake lets out a sling of curses. His harsh, strangled voice cuts through the room just before the sound of furniture breaking, shattering around us follows. My stare lands on a shadow, quick, nimble, moving faster than humanly possible as it nips back and forth, attacking Jake, confusing him, and making him stumble about.

John and Michael's cries grow louder again. The boy at my side suddenly speaks.

"Quick, Tink! The other room! Make them see they're not alone. They'll never be lost. They've got you and me now."

I don't look at who's holding me. I don't worry about who stole me away. I can feel the magic. The magic I always dreamed of. With just one touch, I know I'm safe.

My eyes stay locked to the scene unfolding in front of me as the shadow darts back and forth, moving quickly towards us as Jake furiously follows. Before they can reach us, I am lifted again into the air, floating above the madness. Taken away. Escaping, when I desperately need to.

Feeling loved, cherished, when I've never known, never felt the true meaning of the words before.

The shadow tackles Jake, muffling his call for help, and forcing him to the floor. Gently, I feel myself being lowered back to my bed.

"Good work," the boy at my side says next. "Now, make sure he never comes back here again."

The shadow nods, then pulls Jake upright, wrapping his hand over his mouth and tugging him backwards towards the door of my room. The boy by my side releases me. I instantly feel cold without his touch. Stepping forward, all I can see is his back as he gives the shadow more orders.

"I want you standing guard every day, shadow. I'll be here by nightfall. No one comes in, understand?"

He slashes his arm through the air. My eyes grow wide noticing he's gripping a blade.

The shadow nods as he tightens his grip on Jake. The man who was dead set on bringing me harm winces with pain. The shadow pulls him away easily. His head falls back in a quiet laughter a moment later when Jake tries to escape, and then fails miserably. The door to my room closes just as a tinkling of bells reenters the room.

The boy turns to the twinkling light and puts his hands on his hips. "Tink, you stay with the boys. Give Wendy some rest."

He knows my name. But, how?

The bells grow louder, almost angry in tone.

"Tinker Bell," the boy insists in an authoritative tone. "How many times do I have to tell you, you gotta learn to take orders!"

My mouth falls open in awe as the light twinkles its way out of the room, tinkling on and on in an irritated way but, nonetheless, obeying the boy in front of me. When the boy turns, my eyes land on the most charming face I have ever seen.

He bows, and my heart soars. Giggling, I hide my blush as his head lifts, and he gives me a smile. Still bowed over, he gives me a devilish winks, and I bite my bottom lip.

"Hello," he smirks, as if it's all a game. As if we've always known each other.

I'm still too stunned to answer back.

Rising to his full height, he comes a step forward as I push to the edge of my bed.

"You know my name?" I ask, but he only grins in response. His eyes hold a mischievous twinkle as he looks down at me. "How did you know my name?"

"I've always known your name, Wendy."

The way he says my name again makes me forget the way I was feeling moments before. I forget Jake. Nana. John. Michael. Shadows and twinkling lights. I forget everything except for the magic in his beautiful, breathtaking, blue eyes.

"I've come for you every night, since as far back as I can remember."

"Why?" I hear myself question.

"I love to hear Nana's stories," he shrugs with a smile. "And... I always knew one day I'd save you. And in return, one day you'd also save me."

I JOLT awake in a cold sweat.

Pixie Dust.

I knew the wine tasted different. It was laced with Pixie Dust.

When spread across your body, it's the same as having wings. Think happy thoughts, and away you'll go.

Tasting it, drinking it, it acts like a truth serum. You can try to fight it, but it'll always pulls you under. Drags you down. Drugs you to the point of no return. It'll show you things you may never want to see. Show you what you've always been running from.

The darkness in the master quarters is thick, but I manage to make out his shadow across the room. The tip of his cigarette glistens red as he takes an inhale and then snuffs it out quickly on the floor. Stepping forward, a sob falls from my lips as he emerges from the shadows.

"Not such sweet dreams after all, are they, Darling?" he whispers.

"Some parts can be," I sniffle, as he takes another step in my direction.

"The parts about me?"

"Always the parts about you, Peter."

It's a confession I swore to myself I wouldn't make the night he brought me back here against my will, but I can't hide the truth anymore. There was a time when what we had between us was beautiful. I won't deny that any longer.

His jaw ticks at the mention of his first name, but he doesn't correct me.

"I'm not that same boy, Wendy. I don't care so much about games anymore. They irritate me. Annoy me. Cause me to do bad things to good people."

"You'd never hurt me."

His fists clench at his sides. His eyes widen with violence. Not for me, but for some unknown truth he's withholding.

"That's where you're wrong, Darling. I already did."

My mind races to understand, my head still high on the pixie dust, holding me somewhere between now and the past, but all thoughts stop as he takes another step forward until his thighs meet the edge of the bed.

"I hurt you by finally making you see."

Unable to speak, I lay there and take in all he's just said.

Yes, he hurt me. More than he knows. But... I hurt him, too. I know I did. I can accept that now. Problem is, I've been holding on so long to the pain, I don't know how I'll ever let it go.

Leaning in, he brushes a stray strand of hair behind my ear, his thumb gently caressing across the curve of my chin before coming to rest on my bottom lip.

My tongue sweeps across where he just touched. I taste the spell working before I can tell myself to stop. Before I can tell myself that I don't want anymore. But the thing about Pixie Dust is, once you get a taste, once the magic starts to work, a little bit is never enough. You'll always crave more.

He holds out his thumb to me, and like a fiend, I suck it into my mouth greedily. I've gotten a small glimpse of what I've been running from, what I lost, there is no going back now. He groans as my tongue circles his tick digit, lost somewhere between pleasure and pain.

The only way to stop running is to finally turn and face the past.

He pulls his finger from my mouth before sucking his

thumb between his lips, and taking some of the Pixie Dust for himself. A delirious heat settles between my legs. His eyes heat with lust.

"Sleep," he whispers. I lean my body gently back against the pillows.

But I struggle to do as I'm told. Tossing and turning. I'm unable to accept the fact that he expects me to dream about him while he is standing there watching.

My body longs for him. Vibrates with need for him. It's not just the Pixie Dust. It's the truth I'm finally facing. The realization that we've both been so wrong, and I'm not sure I can face the next part without him by my side.

It calls to me, the truth, beckoning me closer. A dream so beautiful it becomes a nightmare in the end.

I groan out in frustration, grabbing the pillow and roughly turning on my side before looking his way and catching a slight smile.

"It was always worth the wait, Darling," he insists, climbing on top of the bed and wrapping me in his arms.

My thighs clench as he pulls me back tighter against his chest. He doesn't push what's building between us any further, just holds me close as if he knows what's coming. As if he knows we need each other to survive it.

Just before I drift off to sleep, I hear him whisper, "You were always worth the wait."

CHAPTER 17
PETER

"The boys on the island vary, of course, in numbers, according as they get killed and so on. And when they seem to be growing up, which is against the rules, Peter thins them out."

Peter & Wendy

- J.M. Barrie

SEVENTEEN YEARS AGO

Fascinated. *That's all I am.*

Wendy is alluring. Tempting. Bewitching.

Besides, I'm always looking for something that entices me. That can keep my attention.

That's all she is.

A beautiful distraction.

I watch as she looks out over Mermaid Lagoon and know I'm wrong.

Breathtaking.

That's what she is.

Too beautiful to ever be tainted by my world.

She laughs as the wind catches her hair and she looks down upon the lagoon. I could search the whole world and never find anyone, ever again, that fascinates me as much as Wendy does.

That means something, doesn't it?

"Back home," John huffs, finishing his climb up to the top of the rock cliff and standing next to my side. "We'd say something like 'take a picture, it'll last longer.'"

A picture?

"What would I do with a picture?" I frown.

John laughs and nudges my side just as the rest of the lost boys reach the top. "Stare at it, you ass. It'll stay just the way you like it, longer than that sister of mine ever will."

My smile grows as Wendy struggles to stand upright. She leans over the edge of the rock cliff, dangerously close to falling over, just to get a closer look at the mermaids below.

I like to watch her dance with danger.

It does something to me.

I like to swoop in and save her, just in time.

Be her hero.

It makes my chest fill with pride.

I also love the look it puts in her eyes.

That startled, loving, excited, flushed expression is what keeps me up at night.

"No," I shrug. "My Wendy will never change. She couldn't. I won't let her."

Just before she falls off the ledge, her shocked gasp reaches out to me. I take flight immediately, swooping in to catch her just as she tumbles over the side of the cliff.

Sometimes, I think she does this on purpose.

I'd be lying if I said I didn't love it.

It gives me an excuse to hold her close.

A reason to feel her skin touching mine.

Fascinating.

My Wendy won't change.

She'll always fascinate me.

"Oh Peter, I was just trying to get a closer look at the mermaids." she stutters as we float to rest on top of a rock closer to the lagoon. "Ever since you brought me to Neverland, I've wanted to get a closer look at them."

"Hasn't the past couple months pleased you, Wendy?" I tease.

I softly release my hold on her, but she grips my arms tight, not wanting me to let go just yet.

Truth be told, I'm not sure how long she's been with me in Neverland. Time tends to stop here. Not like where she comes from. They count the days with a calendar. They even have them named. Seasons when the world turns dark and cold, and later when the sun grows hot, and the days are longer.

We have none of that in Neverland. We lose sight of time as the sun rises. We only slow down when it sets. If I had to think, I'd say Wendy has been here with me now for ages.

I could keep her with me for eternity, though, and it still wouldn't be long enough.

"They've made me so happy, Peter," she says softly. "Happier than I have ever been."

"But..."

"No buts," she insists with a longing in her eye. "Nothing makes me happier than being with you, Peter."

I capture her lips with mine, stealing a moment of time just for the two of us as the lost boys look on. It feels right to kiss her *like this. It feels natural to show her how much she means to me, even as my whole world watches. I've never kissed her like this, out in the open. And so she tenses in my arms as I softly brush my lips against hers one more time.*

"Peter," she breathes, "What about..."

"I don't want us to change, just because someone's watching," she studies my face closely, wondering what I'm getting at. "I like us. Just the way we are. I don't want anything to change that."

She smiles, "Neither do I."

"Peter look!" Michael yells. He points excitedly down to the lagoon. My eyes follow his finger to the water below. I smile seeing Tinker Bell and the other fae down by the water's edge.

I had told them we would be here today; I had hoped they'd come, too. To say things have been decent between Tinker Bell and Wendy since she's arrived would be a lie. Tinker Bell has barely spoken to me since I brought her here. And to be honest, I haven't missed the fae as much as I thought I would. A fact I'm certain she knows since yesterday was the first time I've made an effort since about a week after Wendy's arrival to even go speak with her.

Wendy has yet to meet Tiger Lily, but I've been told by the rest of the tribe she's disliked on that side of the island just the same.

"Is this safe?" Wendy asks scared. "I know how much Tinker..."

"Will do whatever I say," I insist. She blinks a few times and shakes her head in disagreement. Taking her chin in my hand, I force her to look at me. "You and me, Wendy. That's the beginning and the end of everything."

Grabbing her hand, I soar her high before bringing her gently down to the bottom of the lagoon. The lost boys follow quickly behind. Climbing up and over the rocks as fast and best as they can. Looking down at Wendy, I keep her hand held tightly in mine and give her a reassuring smile. She smiles back, but I can tell she's still worried. Still scared.

She doesn't have to feel that way. Not so long as I'm by her side.

"What do we have here?" Chalen, the head of the school asks in a mocking tone.

"Wendy," I assert confidently, never taking my eyes off the beautiful girl at my side. "Wendy Moira Angela Darling."

I hear their whispers, but I only have eyes for my Wendy. That is, until the next one chimes in with a snide remark.

"She's just as pathetic as you mentioned, Tinker Bell. All skin and bone. Nothing like Peter's used to."

My eyes snap toward Penelope's just as I hear the faint tinkling of Tinker Bell's agreement.

What I'm used to?

What on earth can they mean by that?

They go on and Wendy tenses in my arms.

"I wouldn't worry, though," Atlanteia sighs, "it could never last. Look at her. She's nothing but a little girl."

The chorus of women start to laugh. Wendy drops out of my embrace, and I waste no time stepping in front of her, prepared to make the girls in front of me take it back.

"Hey!" Their laughing resolves to a slight giggle as they roll their eyes. "I won't have you talking like that about my Wendy."

"Your Wendy?" Visola echoes. "Oh, please."

Her fin breaks free from the water, causing a wave to course towards where Wendy stands. She props it up on a rock and throws her hands behind her head.

"You tire of things so easily, Peter. It won't be long before

you're back to playing games. Back to joining us in a swim at the grotto."

"Not likely."

Tinker Bell chimes in harshly in her fae voice, masking her words from Wendy and the lost boys.

"Is that what you've been telling everyone?" I ask as the lost boys finally make their way down to the bottom of the lagoon. "That she's nothing but a toy? Something I'll one day grow tired of?"

The women in front of me don't speak. But they don't have to. They stand off against me and the only woman that matters, the only one I'll ever care about. Wendy grows tense behind my back.

"Nothing, and no one will ever captivate me like my Wendy." The words fall from my lips effortlessly. There was a time they might have scared me. But not anymore. "And that's saying something."

I look at the world around me. The magic that once held my attention and realize it's nothing if Wendy is not in it.

"Does that include me?"

My eyes land on Tiger Lily's. Wendy takes a step back, retreating away from the evil that lurks just under her eyes. I reach back and grab her hand, pulling her forward to my side.

"It includes all of you," I hiss, "What she gives me, what I have with Wendy, can't be replaced."

"Hm," Tiger Lily smirks. "Irreplaceable? My dear Peter, nothing is irreplaceable."

Clouds close in. A foreign darkness grows. I look up at the sky just as rain begins to fall.

"Peter," Wendy's voice calls to me. Her startled eyes grow

wide. I glance over my shoulder quickly to see what they are staring at.

Indians. Hundreds of them. Closing in on every side.

"You see, you're not king of Neverland, Peter. You never were," Tiger Lily continues. "There are several here that don't agree with your new way of thinking. The new things you want, instead of the life we were used to living."

Wind kicks up out of the East. I pull Wendy closer. John and Michael protect my right and left. The other lost boys stand close behind.

"You see, we don't like change," the princess snarls.

Tinker Bell and the other fae fly to her side and magnify themselves to their full height. Wendy gasps. Intuitively, I clutch her closer and she burrows into me, allowing me to guard her with my life.

"We don't like to be thought of as... replaceable," Tinker Bell chimes in, glaring at Wendy. "Expendable. Inconsequential."

"Your actions make you insignificant in my world, Tink."

"Oh," she taunts with a mischievous smile. "But it is our world, too. Or have you forgotten?"

The mermaids swim circles below our feet turning the lagoon into a treacherous whirlpool. The darkness surrounding us grows blacker. The wind gusts increase. Rain pelts down harder.

"Peter," Wendy's whispers. "Peter, it's okay if you have to let me go."

Sacrifice.

That's what's needed here.

I can't keep her and them too.

But my life is meaningless without Wendy in it.

"I make this world Tinker Bell," my tone is sharp, dark,

commanding, as I turn back the fae's way. "I allow you all to live in it, and I can take you out of it."

The fairy's eyes glow red with rage. Her sparkle brightens into a piercing light. A ringing starts in the distance and quickly speeds closer. In a blink of an eye, all I can manage is to push Wendy out of the way just as the fae darts for her.

"Now!" Tiger Lily yells.

The Indians close in quickly. Swords drawn, they take out one, then two lost boys with swift fatal blows. The mermaids pull at Wendy's gown as Tinker Bell and two of her men wrestle me to the floor. I yell for John and Michael to help, to rescue their sister, but they're too busy fighting off their attackers to be able to save her.

Tinker Bell releases me and darts for Wendy, pushing her down and making it easier for the school of mermaids to pull her closer towards the rock's edge. I lock eyes with Tinker Bell just as one of her men's wings come in contact with my right hand. With a quick yank, I rip them from his back. My right side is freed immediately as he shrinks back to his normal size.

Tinker Bell's rage is evident as her eyes quickly flash the same shade of crimson as before. My vengeance on her man does the trick I need, and she releases her hold on Wendy and starts to dart back to save the other fae's life. I wrestle him to my side, quickly coming atop him, and pull out my knife. With a flick of my wrist, I slash what's left of his wings from his body. He dies instantly.

Quickly getting to my feet, Tinker Bell's eyes me furiously. "You're going to pay for that," she seethes. "I'll make sure of it."

"Peter!" Wendy calls out from the lagoon just as Tinker Bell darts away, retreating quickly towards Mystic Mountain.

Wendy gestures towards her brothers. John is fighting the chief. Three lost boys now lay dead at his feet.

Wendy screams again, and my eyes flash to Michael. He's wounded. Badly. But still fighting to the death. Wendy kicks at the mermaids trying to make it to her brother's side. John throws her a dagger, she grabs it quickly before it falls off the cliff, slashing it in the mermaid's direction and making them finally bolt back in fear. She jumps to her feet, and I dart forward, knowing that if my Wendy were to be so pure, so heartless, to sacrifice herself for me, she'd do the same for her brother.

"Wendy," I yell, just as she throws herself in front of Michael's attacker's blade. "Wendy, no!"

"Peter," Michael shouts. "Catch her!"

Before the Indian can slash his knife down, Wendy's brother throws her off the cliff. Her screams echo off the rock as her body starts to fall quickly to the whirlpool below. Swiftly, I fly to her rescue, swooping in and catching her just before she can hit the water. Just before the mermaids can get their claws in her.

Floating her to a safe space, out of reach of the madness, she shakes in my arms as I set her down upon a rock. Her face is tucked into my neck. Her breath is warm against my lips as her eyes lift to meet mine.

"Wendy," I whisper. "Darling, remember, I won't be able to live with myself if you get hurt."

Her grip on my biceps tightens.

Sacrifice.

"Remember, you're the only life worth saving, Wendy."

Her body trembles in my arms. I'm completely unaware of my own shaking because of it. Tightening my grip around her, she asks, "More than your own, Peter?"

This time when I answer her, there is no humor in my tone when I repeat the same words I've said to her once before.

179

"Without question, Wendy. I'll always put your life before mine."

"Peter!" John's yell startles us, and we immediately look up. He's standing at the edge of the cliff. All attackers are slain. A knife is clutched tight in his fist. He's staring wise eyed in disbelief as Michael fights the chief and starts to tumble off the ledge a few feet away.

The mermaids have swum off; the water is still. I tell myself to fly. To save him. But before I can, Michael looses his footing and falls. Wendy reaches out to me, and we cling to each other as Michael's body hits the jagged rocks below.

CHAPTER 18
WENDY

"Surely you know what a kiss is," she asked, aghast.
"I shall know when you give it to me," he replied stiffly, and not to
hurt his feelings, she gave him a thimble.
"Now," said he, "Shall I give you a kiss?" And she replied with a
slight premise. "If you please."
She made herself rather cheap by inclining her face towards him,
but he merely dropped an acorn button into her hand.
Peter & Wendy
- J. M. Barrie

SEVENTEEN YEARS AGO

A tapping noise startles me awake. Rolling over, I glance at the window and bolt upright when I see his shadow pressed up against the glass. Throwing the blankets off my body, I wrap my arms around me tightly, bouncing back and forth on each foot trying to keep warm as I make my way towards the window.

After the way we left things, I honestly never thought I'd see him again.

The snow glows around him in the moonlight as it thickly falls to the rooftop at his feet. His eyes hold a desperate sadness as I work quickly with cold hands to unlock the window. Pulling it open, the chilled air blasts into the room, freezing through me, instantly chilling me to the bone.

But Peter never moves, just continues to stare back at me. Broken. Hollow. A shadow of the boy I left a week ago in Neverland.

"Peter," I whisper. He flinches at the mention of his name. "Why are you still standing there? Quick. Come inside."

He doesn't respond. Just looks at me, almost as if he's staring through me. Lost. For the first time since I've known him, he looks so lost.

I try again. "Peter..."

"You left without saying goodbye."

His voice, the way he says the words, it's more chilling than the night air around us. He grips the window tightly in his hands as he leans in towards me. His warm breath hangs heavy on the cold wind as it wraps around the two of us.

"You left, without letting me kiss you goodbye, Wendy."

He moves forward so quickly I barely have time to step out of the way. Jumping down from the windowsill, he turns and closes the window with a loud bang. I glance quickly back over my shoulder, worried that someone might have heard.

"Darling," my name falls from his lips with a hiss. A madness I've never heard before. Looking back his way, an uneasy feeling spreads across my skin, leaving goosebumps as it goes. His eyes

turn dark, unreadable, making me grow nervous as he takes another step forward. "Darling, I hate goodbyes."

"It wasn't..." But I stop speaking as I hear the sounds of the nurse checking on Michael in the other room. My eyes dart to the jack and jill bathroom and I rush to close the door, locking it quietly once it closes on its hinges.

With my back still turned to Peter, I close my eyes and take a deep breath. It wasn't supposed to be goodbye. When I left almost a week ago now, I had every intention of returning. But, with Michael's extensive wounds, how could I ever go back?

I feel his presence at my back and startle. His hand lifts and he brushes my hair off my shoulder. Leaning in, he presses his lips to the side of my neck. I grip the doorknob for balance, my knees grow weak, my body desperate for more of his touch as his soft, warm mouth grazes up to my ear.

"It wasn't what, Darling?" His voice is barely a whisper. His breath hot as it feathers across my skin, making a tingling feeling rush up my spine. "Goodbye?"

The word comes out broken. I open my eyes, stare at the door in front of me as my throat closes tight and tears threaten to fall. I can't lie to him. I can't lie to myself.

"It wasn't supposed to be."

"But now, that's not necessarily true, is it?" he hisses.

His hands grip my hips tight enough to let me know the pain he's feeling, but not harsh enough to bruise me.

"Peter... I...."

"It hurts," he confesses as he sucks in a sharp breath.

I inhale a deep breath of my own, waiting for him to go on, holding it in until it burns. I know all too well the pain he's talking about. His head falls against the back of my own. His hands circle my waist, pulling me tight into his frame.

"I can't breathe without you, Wendy."

He sucks in another sharp breath; his body shakes, as if he's on the verge of tears before a dark laugh escapes his lips. Crushing my body against his, his face falls to the crook of my neck, anger fuels his touch as he grits out, "You've become the air I need to survive, Darling."

Letting go of the breath I was holding, I turn in his arms slowly. My hands tenderly rise to frame his face. His eyes are closed. His brow is furrowed as he lets out a shaky breath. My heart bleeds for him. For us.

He takes a step forward and quickly backs me up against the wall.

"You've always been the air I need, Peter," I confess.

I know I've told him that before, but I feel compelled to remind him now. His eyes open and my heart breaks as I watch them water with unshed tears.

"You've been a part of me so long, I don't know how to live without you," his own confession is like salt on a wound. It's a desperate plea. One I'm not sure I can answer.

"You don't have to," I say, trying to think up any way I can make our world right once again. "You can come back here. Sit on the edge of my bed. Listen to the stories. Play your music for me, and..."

His sad smile causes me to stop talking. Shaking his head, a lone tear falls down his right cheek.

"It would never be enough," he whispers. "Not after I've had a taste of you in my world, Wendy. It could never. Be. Enough."

His head falls against mine and I grab a hold of him tightly, clutching him to me as if my life depends on him. As if our life together depends on us.

"Peter," I whisper. "I told you once I wanted to give myself to you. But the truth is, you've always had me. You'll always have me. Whether it's here, or in Neverland, it's just..."

Footsteps fall down the hall and we both look towards the door to my room. I move to get around him, and he reluctantly lets me go. Tiptoeing towards the door, I rest my ear against the wood and listen. The muffled sounds of men standing guard, changing shifts, echoes back to me through the door.

I don't know when Jake is expected home. I haven't seen him since I came back. My body shivers as I hear the men outside my door talk about when he's supposed to arrive.

Peter's presence suddenly warms my back, calming me as I stand paralyzed by fear of the man he once saved me from. His right-hand raises, turns the lock on the door. He cages me in. His hands press on either side of my frame. He softly rests his lips near my ear.

"I didn't take you that night, Wendy, because I couldn't. I felt the same fear in you that night as I did the night I protected you from him."

I shiver as he backs away and gently pulls me with him. Turning me around to face him, my bottom lip quivers as he lifts my chin.

"I also couldn't take you because something about that night didn't feel right. I wanted to, Darling. God, how I needed to. But I wouldn't do that to you."

My brow furrows as I study him. As if he can see the wheels in my head spinning, he smiles and pulls me closer, guiding me back across the room to my bed.

"I couldn't take you without being able to give you myself in return."

My feet stop in the center of the room. He turns, holds my eye, and keeps walking backward a step or two.

"See, that night," he kneels, and my heart skips a beat. Grabbing a hold of my hips, he licks his lips and focuses on my center. "Fuck, I craved you like I've never desired anything else before."

I have to tell myself to breathe as he looks back up in my eyes and I see so much love, so much desire hanging in them I swear I feel like I am soaring above the world. Flying higher than I ever have before without the help of pixie dust.

"I wasn't ready to give you what you deserve. I wasn't ready to make the kind of sacrifice you need in return."

Reaching into his pocket, he pulls out a shiny object I can barely make out in the shadows. Lifting it up, he urges me to take it, but I stand before him too stunned to even move.

"For you, Darling," he insists. "So you know, you're the only one that I'll ever give myself to." When I still haven't moved, he starts to visibly shake. "Wendy, do you understand what I'm saying?"

"I can't ask you to do that for me Peter..."

"I've never needed anyone before," he cuts me off aggressively. "I've always stood on my own. I've run away, flown away, from anything in my life that had ever mattered before. Not because I wanted to hurt them, but because I didn't want to ever feel hurt in return."

He stands quickly, pulling me against his chest, crushing me to him. It's then that I feel the salt of my tears on my lips. It's then that I feel the desperation, the vulnerability in his touch.

I don't know how I never noticed it before.

186

"Wendy, if you tell me you don't need me, that you don't want me..."

"Oh Peter, I could never know a world where I didn't want you..."

"But you don't need me?"

"I'll always need you," I whisper.

"Then, come back with me."

His hands shake as he pulls my palm up between us and slips the object on my finger.

An acorn button, made out of a metal thimble, sits on top of a shiny ring. But it's not made with the precious metals I'm used to. It's made of iron. Iron to protect me from pixies. Peter brushes his thumb across the top of it as we both stare down at where it rests on my finger.

"To protect you," he whispers. I suck in a shaky breath. "Stay with me, Wendy. Please?"

I glance up at his handsome face and feel my heart break. I can't leave Michael. Not now that Jake is expected home. John left first thing when he heard Jake was coming back. But I can't leave Michael alone to fend for himself. He's too young. I worry about what Jake would do. What he might turn him into. That's if he even stands a chance to recover from his injuries. That's if he isn't permanently scarred.

"Peter, I..."

"I love you, Darling."

I blink quickly, my heart coming to a complete stop. His eyes lift and find mine in the darkness. A sad, vulnerable smile pulls at his beautiful mouth, and I start to cry.

"I'll admit, I've never loved anyone," he confesses. "Not more than I loved myself. At first, I thought it was because you fasci-

nated me so. Then you left, and Neverland hasn't been the same. I can't help but love you, Wendy. I've fought my whole life to not need anyone. To never grow attached. To show the world I am enough on my own."

He laces his hands through my hair, pulling me closer and resting his lips close to mine.

"But I'm nothing if I don't have you." He kisses me softly and I melt into his embrace. Pulling away, he whispers. "My world doesn't exist without you in it. So, please, don't... don't leave me. Not when I need you to keep breathing."

I don't know what to do. My heart is torn. I hold onto him, close my eyes and wish things could be different. I wish for magic to take us away, somewhere Jake doesn't exist, where Michael isn't hurt, and things like mermaids, fairies and Indians can't harm us.

When I finally open my eyes, Peter looks back at me torn. He's on the brink of ruin. It scares me because I finally understand, finally see, I alone hold the power for his destruction.

Before I can stop myself, I whisper, "I'll never leave you, Peter. You'll always be a part of me."

And I mean it. No matter what happens. I'll always carry him with me. Even if we're forced to live our lives apart.

His smile widens. Leaning in, he takes my lips in his and immediately deepens the kiss. Slow. Seductive. His tongue grazes mine in a way it never has before.

He walks me backward until my legs hit the side of my bed. With desperation, he lifts my nightgown quickly over my head.

He was right. It wouldn't have felt right for him to take me before. And as his lips find mine, I wrestle with the thought of if it's right now. If I can live with myself after tonight knowing my heart is his, but my future may never be.

If I only have this night though, if I only know what it's like to be his one time, I want to experience him. Experience us.

I push away all thoughts of reason and give into what was always inevitable.

Grabbing his shirt, he helps me lift it over his head before throwing it to the floor. His belt is next. As I start to undo the clasp quickly, I stop when he stills my hands and forces me to look him in the eye.

"You and me, Wendy. That's the beginning and end of everything."

CHAPTER 19
PETER

"'You just think lovely, wonderful thoughts and they lift you up in the air.'"
Peter & Wendy
- J.M. Barrie

SEVENTEEN YEARS AGO

"Peter," she breathes, "show me how much you love me." Her whisper comes out timid. As if I didn't plan on doing just that. She averts her eyes, starting to work on the buckle of my belt when I stop her again. She doesn't look up at me right away, and her hands tremble as they rest against my skin.

"Wendy," I plead, but she still doesn't look me in the eye. "Darling, look at me."

She shakes her head and bites her bottom lip before starting to undo my belt again. Taking a step forward, I cage her in between *me and the bed, forcing her hands against my stomach to make her stop what she's doing.*

"Look me in the eyes, tell me you don't want this, and we'll stop," I demand. "I said I loved you. I meant it. Loving you is the only thing I've done right so far in my life. I won't fuck that up now."

She raises her face, but her eyes remain closed off. Distant.

"Wendy, I'll take you anyway I can have you. It doesn't have to be like this..."

"Peter," she cries. "I think I could handle you better when you were selfish."

I laugh as my hands come up and cradle her face. A tear falls from her eyes, but she smiles, a sigh falls from her lips as I brush her sadness away.

"I'm still selfish, Wendy, when it comes to you." She lets out a soft sob that scares me. "In my life, I want you, any way I can have you. But if you don't want to do this..."

She sucks in a sharp breath. Her sadness seems to lift. She pulls me closer by my belt loop, and whispers, "Then take me, Peter. Make me yours. Because I'm just as selfishly in love with you, too."

Crushing my mouth against hers, she purrs as my tongue glides eagerly against hers. This time, when I taste her lips on mine it's like coming home. She's my home. My world. My Wendy.

My hands fall to her waist, and I hoist her up in my arms. Her breasts press firmly against my chest, and I groan when her nipples graze across my bare skin.

"Darling," I whisper, as I lay her body back against the cool sheets. "I'm dying to taste you." I run my finger along the thin

fabric of her panties, watching as her wetness presses against the lace. "I'm desperate to feel you wrapped around me."

Glancing up, we lock eyes as I slowly slide the lace down her thighs. I can smell her desire, almost taste it on my tongue, as I look down and see her velvet skin drenched and ready for taking. Licking my lips, I pull back, slowly starting to undo the buckle to the belt she was so eager to free me of just a moment ago.

Our chests rise and fall quickly. The seconds tick by in the most agonizing way as I pull the leather from my pant loops and toss it to the side. The sound of the buckle clattering on the floor somehow increases the tension between us. Slowly, I undo the top button of my jeans as she wets her lips in anticipation, her thighs parting in need.

"I don't think you understand what you do to me, Darling."

I fist my hard cock, grinding into my palm, as her hips slowly rise off the bed. My gaze falls back to her center, and I groan. "Fuck, Wendy. I don't think I can give you nice and slow."

"Peter..." my name comes out as a breathless plea as her hands trail down her stomach, towards her center.

My eyes grow wide as I watch her fingers inch closer to her opening.

"Naughty Wendy," I growl, slipping out of my jeans and kicking them off to join my belt. "Do you touch yourself often, Darling?"

Her fingers stop. Her breaths increase.

"I've never touched myself, Peter."

"Not even when you think of me?"

She bites her lip, and my cock grows thicker. She shakes her head no. Something about the bashful look in her eyes makes me grow impossibly harder, makes me need her more than I ever dreamed possible.

"Touch yourself, Darling," I whisper, fisting my dick and showing her how. "Show me how wet I make that pretty pussy."

She hesitates for only a second before doing as I say. Her fingers slip in between her slick lips with ease. Her head falls back, her eyes close, her middle finger glides into her opening before she works her finger back out, up, rubbing her sensitive nub that I can't wait to suck between my lips as I lick her slowly toward heaven.

"Peter," she purrs, and I can't get my briefs off fast enough.

"Open your eyes," I demand, and she does so instantly.

Her fingers work faster as I grip my cock in my hand, squeeze it, start to work my hand up and down, matching the rhythm of her fingers in her tight cunt. Moisture pools at the crown of my cock. I throw my head back with a deep moan as it thickens. When I look back down, Wendy's eyes are trained on my length. She wets her lips and moves her fingers faster.

Climbing up on the bed, I spread her thighs wider, grip her hip with my free hand and work my other hand slowly up and down my shaft, right above hers. I let her set my pace, keeping my rhythm synced with hers as she plays with that pretty pussy, so wet, so needy, the sight of it coating her fingers makes the blood pump faster through my veins.

"I told you, I want you to teach me what you like."

Our hands start to move faster, chasing a release that's only the beginning of a long night.

"I want to worship you, Darling."

She arches her back. Her wetness slips beautifully through her fingers. Her climax is close.

"*Tell me what you want, Wendy. How you like it,*" I growl.

Leaning forward, I rest my lips above hers, sucking in her air as she in turn takes mine. Our eyes stay locked on each other as we chase our release. She looks down between us, my cock throbs above her hand as she pleasures herself and I work myself hard the same way.

"*You want my cock, Darling?*"

Her eyes flash to mine and her mouth falls open. She nods her head slowly. The same bashful look from earlier stares back at me. My dick throbs in my hand needing to be inside her. Sucking in a sharp breath, I lean closer and whisper, "*Where do you want it?*"

She doesn't say a word, only shows me as she places her hand against her chest.

"*I want...*" *she starts then stops as her eyes close, her thighs spread, and her orgasm threatens.*

"*Fuck,*" *I growl, frantic with the need to feel her, not just watch as she crashes over her edge.* "*Tell me what you want, Darling.*"

"*Cum for me,*" *she purrs.* "*Right here.*"

She trails her finger down the center of her chest and I almost explode with the erotic sight.

"*Christ, you're a naughty girl, aren't you?*"

Reaching down and grabbing her wrist, I stop her pleasure. I'll be damned if I'm not the one that finishes her off tonight. Her orgasm is mine.

She gives me a sad pout, and I smile as I quickly gather her other wrist and hold them above her head. Climbing up her body until my cock slides between her beautiful tits, I reach back and gather some of her wetness. Her back arches off the bed, and she screams out as I stick three fingers inside her.

"Fuck, your cunt is so tight," I hiss, rotating my fingers back and forth.

In and out. Her mouth falls open. Her face looks pained in the most breathtaking way. My hips thrust forward. My cock slides between her breasts and her eyes widen. I finger fuck her pussy harder and stare down into her eyes.

"You want my cock here too, don't you?"

She bites her lip and nods her head. I slip my fingers out of her slick heat and run them up to her clit. She moans my name, and fuck, I almost explode all over her chest.

"Not yet," I pull my fingers back and wrap them tight around my cock. "First, I'm going to cum on your tits," she gasps, her eyes widening in anticipation. "Then, I'm going to watch as you lick it off your fingers while I lick your pretty little pussy."

I fist my cock, jerking off faster and harder than I ever have before. Wendy's hips rise, meeting me thrust for thrust, as if I was already deep inside her.

For the rest of my damned life, I will never forget the way she's looking up at me.

Laid out for me. Willing. Letting me to do with her as I please, because fuck, it pleases her too.

There is nothing more intoxicating in this fucking whole world than the sight of a women desperate to please a man.

Right now, if I asked her to, Wendy would do anything for me, just to see me cum all over her fucking beautiful tits.

"Fuck, Darling, I'm close," I groan.

I grip the hands above her head tighter as my balls draw up, my movements become jerky. Carnal. Hysteric. Her eyes lock with mine and she whispers my name. That's all it takes for my hot seed to spurt out of me, spreading quickly across her porcelain skin.

My head falls back, my eyes close. I crow in pleasure. She screams softly beneath me as I empty myself onto her skin, and my world fades to black. I suck in a sharp breath as the last of my cum empties onto her chest and come back to life. Come back to Wendy.

In a haze, I release her wrists. Greedily, she runs her fingers through my cum and brings it to her lips. I too run my fingers through what's left and raise it to her mouth, watching with sick fucking delight as she wraps her lips around them and sucks them clean.

"Don't worry, Darling," I laugh, "there is a lot more for you to enjoy later."

She looks down at my still hard cock with wonder. The thing is, my dick is always hard for Wendy. One orgasm isn't going to cure me. Not when it comes to her. I could fuck her for hours. All night. And still be rock fucking hard.

"But first," I back away from her body and drop to my knees. Pulling her close to the edge of the bed, I say, "Raise your feet onto the ledge. Spread your thighs, baby. Yes... Just like that. Good girl."

She does as I say perfectly, but I can't help myself and push her thighs wider apart, needing more of her than I've ever been given access to before. Her center grows wetter, my mouth waters in anticipation just as her hips rise with need. Slipping two fingers inside her slick cunt, she cries out from the intrusion. I look up and lock eyes with her.

"Wendy," I sigh, "How will I ever fit inside you?"

Leaning forward, I take her pussy in my mouth, lick up her center, my fingers still deep inside her slick walls. When she cries out, I punish her by sticking a third finger quickly inside her tight cunt. Stretching her to the max. Her breaths come out harshly; her panting increases as I suck her clit in between my lips. Her hands find my hair and she tugs on it, urging me to stop. With my free hand, I slightly rise up on my knees and cover her mouth.

Releasing her clit, I growl, "I'm going to make you cum so hard you scream, Wendy. Now, be a good, naughty girl, whatever the fuck you want. Only cum for me, baby."

She moans into my hand. Slowly, I lower my face back down to her center. Fucking her slowly with my fingers, as soon as my mouth sucks down on her clit she explodes. She bites my hand, screaming just like I said she would as her orgasm courses through her. I force my fingers deeper, curling them, running them through her thick wetness as her center convulses around them. She squirts down my hand, into my mouth with such force I groan out in fucking bliss. Her hips raise off the bed and I release her mouth to force them back down, devouring her cunt until her screaming stops.

She whimpers as I lick up her velvet center more tenderly a moment later. She shakes as I pull my fingers from deep inside her and kiss her slick, sensitive skin.

"What do you want now, Wendy?" I whisper.

Looking up, I watch mesmerized as she pants from her release. Standing, my cock rests at her entrance. I press my hips forward, my cock sliding up, over her wetness, my crown hitting her clit. My dick needs to feel the pleasure that just exploded across my tongue, so I urge her to answer me, "Do you want what I want?"

"Please," she begs, and I'm fucking done for. "Please, Peter, don't make me wait any longer."

Fisting my length, I press slowly into her tight opening for the first time. Her center sucks in my crown easily before we both hiss out when her pussy tightens, unable to take anymore. She cries, her sex unwilling to open further. The pain I feel from needing more, but not wanting to take more if it's going to hurt her, is evident as I lean forward and grit out, "Wendy, Darling, I need you to relax for me."

"I can't," she cries. "It hurts."

I cage her in, my forehead resting against her own. I try my hardest not to press into her any further until she's ready. Against every part of my body that tells me not to say what I am about to say next, I whisper, "We can stop."

She shakes her head. "No, no I don't want to." With tears in her eyes, she finally stares up at me. "I want this, Peter. I need this."

Swallowing hard, I nod. I need this too. We need this. More than we've ever needed anything else before. "I need you to open up for me," I plead, my hips beg for me to thrust them forward, take her when she's not ready, but I force myself to hold back.

"I don't know how," she whispers, her bottom lip beginning to tremble.

"Darling," I smile. "Yes, you do." She looks up at me bewildered. I give her a tender kiss on the lips and whisper, "just think happy thoughts."

She lets out a deep breath and I suck in her air, her legs part and her center grants me further entrance. She closes her eyes and shakes her head. "It burns."

"There is pleasure in pain, Wendy. Remember? I know, because that's how I felt when I finally opened up to you, Darling. To us."

Her eyes open and realization dawns.

"I love you," I whisper. She smiles, her legs part further as I continue to sink slowly into heaven.

"I love you, too, Peter."

"Do you trust me?"

"Always."

"Breathe for me, Darling."

She takes in a deep breath...

"Good girl," I whisper. "Now, let go."

She exhales and with a brutal thrust, I take her quickly, breathing her in as she screams out. She grips my biceps, her nails tearing into my flesh, and I groan. I wait, worried she'll hate me for what I just did. My cock rests deep inside her, and even though my body vibrates with the need to move, to take, I wait, needing to know she's ok before we continue.

When her breathing settles, she leans forward, takes my lips quickly with hers, and whispers, "More."

This time, I let go without no remorse.

I pull out and slam back into her with so much force I nearly break the bed. She screams louder, unworried about who might hear. She holds on to me tightly, whispering softly for me to keep going as I give into the most carnal need I've ever known.

Blinded by the way she makes me feel, I selfishly mark her. Claim her. Fuck her so hard and raw that I worry it might scare her until I look down in her eyes and see the same need, the same desire to be taken hard and fast staring back up at me.

"You like when I fuck you hard, isn't that right, Darling?"

"I love everything about you, Peter," she pants as I thrust inside her. Her body softening. Opening up to me. "Ever since the first day I saw you," she breathes as her body thrashes up and down on the bed, my hips moving faster as our climax builds. "But

this," she gently stops me, placing a hand to my chest and I still. "This, Peter, is my favorite part."

She smiles up at me, her words reminding me of the night I stole her away with me to Neverland and my heart explodes.

I link my fingers through hers and smile. "The beginning of forever." Her hand starts to shake, so I kiss her and slowly start to move again, in and out of her delicate center. "Stay with me Wendy. Stay with me, forever."

She doesn't say another word, just stares up at me longingly. A sort of sadness hangs in her eyes that I don't understand. Maybe because what we're doing changes everything? Maybe because after tonight she won't love me anymore because of it?

Lifting her up, I sit on the edge of the bed and force her to ride me. I match her thrusts with harsh ones of my own. Our bodies are slick and warm, a heavy contrast to the cold night air around us.

When we crash over the edge, she grips my shoulders as her head falls back with a scream. I pull her closer and spill myself so deep inside her, I know she'll forever be marked by me. So deep, I know she'll have no choice but to stay with me. And I with her. Forever.

CHAPTER 20
WENDY

"The reason was so simple, 'I'm fond of her, too. We can't both have her.'"
Peter & Wendy
- J.M. Barrie

SEVENTEEN YEARS AGO

TWO WEEKS LATER

"Say it," he smirks. I giggle as he holds me down against the bed. His rock-hard length slides up my swollen sex causing a moan to escape my lips. "Say it, Wendy, or I'll take you again."

His lips fall to my neck, and he kisses me tenderly, his weight pressing deliciously into me as his erection grows. My legs part willingly, although I don't know if I can take him again tonight.

After the first night we spent together, Peter never went back to Neverland. He stayed in Kingston Gardens across from our house. Every night he's met me at my window, and we've laid awake until morning exploring each other in ways we never thought possible.

After the first time tonight, I was surprised when the second quickly followed. When I tried to catch my breath, he kissed a path down my body and feasted on me until I screamed into the pillow. With my lungs still burning, aching, matching the throbbing between my legs, he thrust inside me a third time. How he's ready to go again now, I'll never know.

"I love... um, sunsets," I tease.

"Wendy," he groans, his face falling into the crook of my neck in frustration.

"I love... watching the sunrise."

"Darling," he pulls back, a mischievous gleam in his eye. "You've been warned. I won't tell you twice."

Smiling, I reach up, touch his face, and concede.

"I love a boy named, Peter." My heart beats faster as his smile grows. "Because he taught me the best things begin and end with him. With us."

"Always."

He rolls us over so that I'm sitting on top of him, his impressive length sliding up between my folds. I bite my lip. I'm so beautifully sore, I'm not sure how I'll get out of bed tomorrow. But if staying in bed lets me keep Peter, I see no issue with my predicament.

"I can get used to this view," he smirks, his large hands raising to mold my breasts. His thumb grazes across my nipple and I stifle a moan. Peter's nostrils flare as his eyes grow wide with need. Rising up off the bed, he takes my nipple in his mouth and sucks down gently, rolling the other between his fingertips.

"I can get used to the way you, what did you say?" I gasp as he sucks down harder, "Worship my body?"

"If only you knew how long I've been waiting to idolize you this way." He rolls us back over so that he's in control once again. Grabbing my wrists, he pins them above my head and leans in close with a grin. "The things I think about when it comes to you are downright sinful, Darling."

"Hm," I tempt him, raising my hips and acting like I can take more than I'm willing. "I've been waiting for you to take me this way even longer than you think." He cocks his head to the side and smirks. "I think I can take all the sinful things you're thinking of and more. Because, Peter," I whisper, leaning forward and nipping his bottom lip between my teeth, "I guarantee I've thought of them, too."

In one swift move, he flips me onto my belly and grips my hair, pulling my head back gently.

Leaning forward, he growls in my ear, "There isn't a place on this body that I don't plan to memorize." His finger traces down my spine. Wetness grows between my legs as he reaches my backside and I suck in a sharp breath when he trails his finger down further to my opening. "There isn't a place on this beautiful body I don't want to put my cock."

"Peter, I..."

"Will you let me, Darling?"

His voice is soft, gentle, just like his fingers as he spreads my cheeks and dips his finger down further into my center, running the moisture back up across my ass.

"I want to fuck this tight ass," he enters a finger inside me, and I start to scream so he lowers my face to the mattress, covering my mouth and making me yell into the pillow.

"Do you want me to stop?" He asks through rushed, heated breaths. I think about it for a moment but don't answer. "Just tell me, Wendy, and I'll stop. If you really wanted me to."

To my surprise, I shake my head no. He groans as he pushes his finger in further. I moan, the sound muffled by the pillow, and then stop breathing. His body leaves mine, but he keeps his finger in place. I'm about to move when I feel him spread my thighs, then lift me up gently to my knees. His mouth finds my center a second later, and he licks upwards, pulling out his finger as his tongue runs along my ass. I suck in a shocked gasp.

He groans, sticking a finger in my center, he curls it, twisting as he runs it in and out of my sensitive flesh. "God, I can't stay out of your pussy. It's my new favorite addiction."

He adds another finger, and my fists clench the sheets tightly.

"God, Darling. I know you can't take anymore, but please," he begs. "Will you make this tight, pretty pussy cum for me?"

My legs part on instinct, unable to deny him. I didn't think I could take anymore, but if sex is what he wants...

He leans down and whispers into my ear, "No, Wendy, I'm not going to fuck you."

A part of me is happy, because honestly I don't know how I could take it, but another part of me feels a void I never thought I would.

"I just want to make you cum." I feel my walls tighten at his words. He feels it too, and sucks in a shaky breath. "Naughty Wendy, you like it when I make you cum, isn't that right, Darling?"

I grip the sheets tighter, his fingers fuck me harder, my hips rock instinctively back and forth against his palm, meeting his punishing thrusts and I scream again into the pillow.

"Fuck, Wendy, you're so wet it's dripping down my hand, sweetheart." He groans in frustration. In satisfaction. "You're so wet I can hear how much you need me inside you." The slick sounds of his fingers thrusting in and out of my center, coated with my desire fill the room. "How will I ever get enough?" he groans. "Fuck, I want your pussy for breakfast," he backs away, replacing his fingers with his tongue. I cry into the sheets as his fingers circle my clit, faster and faster, his mouth devouring me like a fiend. "Lunch," he groans, as I hear him reluctantly take a breath. "Spread your legs wider for me, Darling," I do as he says, and feel the void of him for only a moment before he slides under my legs. "And dinner." Sticking his fingers back inside me, he pulls me towards him and whispers, "Now ride my face, Darling, and give me a meal I'll never stop fucking craving."

It only takes a moment, just a mere second before I'm crashing over the edge, yelling into the mattress. He forces my hips down against his mouth, groaning, and drinking up every last crop. Peter moves my hips forward and back when I can't find the strength to move them myself. After a moment in the most beautiful heaven, my body starts to slowly come down, and it's then that I feel his hand at my ass. He spreads my cheeks, gathers my wetness from my cunt, and forces his finger inside my tight virgin hole. Another orgasm rips through me stronger than the first as he sucks my clit back between his lips. I try to pull away, try to escape. But he holds me against him with so much strength, so much force, I give in and swear I'm about to pass out for a moment before I start to feel myself come back down from the high.

"Fuck," he grits out underneath me. He pulls my body down flush with his own. "If I was a dying man, granted the wish of one last meal. Your pussy would be the only thing I'd crave, Darling."

Still panting from my orgasm, he grins, "You riding my face, Wendy, is my new favorite thing."

I let out a light laugh, breathless and still dazed from my orgasm. He kisses me. I taste myself on his lips and it causes a new kind of buzz to travel through my body. His lips are soaked with my flavor, and it makes my center throb. It lies to me, telling me I can handle more, that I want more, but I know there is no way I can. At least without a small break first.

Suddenly, there is a loud pounding on the stairs. Boots climb toward us quickly. I look up to the far side of the room just as Peter glances over his shoulder. We scramble to our feet. Hurry to get dressed. Peter pulls on his jeans. I'm just about to slip my nightgown over my head when the door to my bedroom is kicked open.

"Well, well," Jake sways in the doorway. "What do we have here?"

I was told he wouldn't be back until next week. I was still hoping for some more time with Peter before he returned. Before he ruined everything.

Peter helps me pull the nightgown over my head and then quickly grabs my hand, pulling me to his side. Jake glares at him and takes a step forward.

"I heard you were back, Wendy," he says with a tisk, taking another slow, calculated step into the room. "Thought we could pick up where we left off. See someone beat me to it."

Peter instantly steps in front of me and stops Jake from coming any closer. "Men like you don't deserve to live," he seethes.

"And boys like you should have been killed in the womb, and

not have been allowed to be born to become someone else's problem."

A cry falls from my lips as I grip the back of Peter's arm.

"Boys like me?" he questions with hatred.

Jake pulls a flask from his hip and takes a drink. Replacing the cap, the liquor gives him the courage to take another step forward. Peter tenses, and I freeze.

"Our parents didn't love you," Jake's revelation makes Peter's hand in mine begin to shake. They're brothers? I tremble at his side as Peter's stance hardens, "No orphanage would take you," Jake takes another step and Peter takes one forward in challenge. I grab out to him, trying to stop him, but it's pointless. "No one could ever want you."

"Wendy wants me."

Jake's laugh is pure evil as he stumbles to the side and barely catches his footing. When he does, he takes another drink off of his flask, studying us closely over the top in the darkness.

"Funny thing," he slurs, gesturing towards the two of us. "Your shadow seemed to be under the same impression. That is, until I convinced him otherwise." My eyes widen as I look up at Peter, but he doesn't give any inclination that he's phased.

"Amusing really," Jake continues. "Watching a shadow slowly die. Bringing it fully into the light until there is nothing left. Nothing but the truth."

Something in the room changes. A darkness begs to be let in. And it isn't from the man across the room. A man that has threatened to take what I don't want him to since we first met.

It's from the boy that stole my heart. The one that showed me unconditional love, maybe for the first time in my life. The boy that helped me believe in magic when I desperately needed it to save me. When I needed him to save me.

"Wendy would never leave me," Peter insists, and my heart aches. "She's going back with me. To Neverland. We'll be happy there, and..."

"Right," Jake laughs and my stomach grows sick knowing the truth that Peter doesn't. But he feels it, the change, the inevitable reality that I have been trying to hide these past few weeks we've spent together.

I can't go back. Michael needs me. Peter does too, and Lord knows how much I need him. But Michael may need a kidney transplant. His wounds are getting worse, not better. Maybe, one day, I could return, but not right now. Not when I'm needed more here. By my brother's side.

Peter turns to look at me, as if questioning what I never thought he would. What I hoped he wouldn't, at least until we had a little more time together.

"Well? Tell him the truth, Wendy," Jake slurs, coming a step closer. "Tell him, he's wrong. You won't return to Neverland. There is no such thing as fucking magic."

I flinch. Peter's eyes search mine frantically. There is a darkness in them that I've never truly recognized before. One I've only seen in his shadows. Now, it's all consuming, but I hold onto the little piece of light I can see in the back of his soul to find the courage I didn't know I had in order to do what I have to. In order to break his heart.

Because, right now, it looks like the only way.

"I can't leave with you Peter," I suddenly blurt out before I can stop myself. He studies me, hurt, confusion, darkness creeping closer.

"Why?"

It's such an innocent question with a gut-wrenching answer. One I'm not sure I can ever give him, because I know it will ruin him. Destroy us. I glance to my side and see triumph in Jake's eyes and my back instantly stiffens. A hardness grows in my heart as I reluctantly look back Peter's way and tell him the only thing I can manage to say. The harshest truth I've ever had to swallow, the one I know will force him back to Neverland.

"I lied to you," his brow furrows as the darkness comes closer. *"I don't believe in happy thoughts anymore, Peter. I don't believe in magic."*

How could I when everything we had changed in an instant? When I came home to a nightmare that won't let me wake up? When the magic, the world that I always dreamed about, ended up stealing from me any chance I'd ever have of believing again, the outcome made it impossible to stay with him.

"That's a lie," Peter demands, and my hands begin to shake. *"I don't believe you, Wendy. I know you're lying."*

"Believe what you want," Jake insists, Peter and I instantly glance his way as he once again starts to come closer. *"But Wendy is staying here, with me, for reasons you can't understand. Reasons,* a boy, *will never understand."*

Peter pulls me behind him and squares off against Jake. An enemy we've just learned is his own flesh and blood. His older brother. "You'll never touch her. I won't let you."

"We played that game once before," Jake laughs. *"Didn't work out for you then. I can guarantee it'll be the same this time."*

"You touch her, and I won't hesitate to kill you. I've killed for a lot less."

209

"You'd have to be a man to kill, Peter," Jake hisses. "It goes against all of your principals."

Jake begins to circle us like we're his prey. All the while, Peter keeps me shielded, turning us to keep me away from the man that's threatened me since the first day we met.

"Never growing up," Jake's eyes widen with a sort of hysteria. "Maintaining innocence." He stops circling and looks us up and down. "I'd say that's all good and done away with, now. Don't you think? Or are you still keen on pretending?" Leaning in, he adds, "You can't shove your cock inside a virgin cunt and still think you can run off to Neverland like nothing's changed."

Peter steps forward in challenge, his hand quickly goes to his hip where he keeps his dagger. But Jake stops him as he steps forward and immediately continues.

"Maybe you were always more of a man than you thought, Peter. Thinning out lost boys when they didn't do as you say. Taking young girls, turning them into women, when it pleases you. Discarding them when you're done. We may have more in common than you think. So, fly back to Neverland, trust me when I say Wendy will be in good fucking hands."

Jake's eyes find mine and he rubs his palms together, licking his lips for emphasis. A menacing smile spreads across his face as he tries to come closer. A threatening look gleams brighter in his eyes. He's determined. This time, nothing's going to stop him.

In an instant, everything in the room changes. It all happens so fast I don't have time to react. Peter lunges forward, tackling Jake to the ground. Jake pulls a knife and I scream. He rolls Peter on to his back, the alcohol giving him an advantage as adrenaline fuels his rage. He pins Peter to the floor so he can't get to his weapon and my heart beats out of control.

I fling myself on Jake's back. Grabbing around his throat, I attempt to choke him. My feet kick at his sides as strongly as they can.

"Wendy, no!" Peter's voice is all I hear as I wrap my arms around Jake's neck tighter and squeeze, but it still isn't hard enough. Jake backs away from Peter and tosses me easily to the floor. My head hits the side of a table in the process, causing me to black out momentarily. When I come to, I see that my distraction worked perfectly as Peter brings his knees up and kicks Jake to his back across the room.

He rushes to my side and holds me against him, searching my eyes. "Darling, are you ok?"

I nod quickly, my hand rubbing the spot that hit the sharp wood. I feel a warm wetness and pull my hand away, noticing blood staining my fingers. Peter glances down just as I see Jake begin to move across the room. Looking back, Peter's eyes find mine and the small piece of light that I held onto a moment ago completely goes black in them. His jaw ticks as he pulls his dagger from his hip. With a loud crow like I've never heard from him before, he turns quickly and charges Jake.

They both fall backward; this time Peter pins our attacker in place. He holds his weapon up to his throat as Jake tries to force his grip back with all his might, but it pierces his skin and I instantly hear Jake scream out in pain.

I look up just as the nurse rushes into the room. She takes one look at the madness that's unfolding, her eyes widening in fear, and then dashes off down the hallway, screaming for the guards.

"No!" I yell after her, rushing to the door and feeling my foot trip over something in the process.

Jake!

He manages to grab hold of my ankle and pull me backwards. I hit the ground with a loud thud, my head smashes into the floorboards before I immediately tell myself to turn over and kick at his grip. Peter looks up, worried for my safety, he loses control of Jake for a moment as our attacker reaches up with both hands and tries to pull me closer, keeping me from stopping his rescue.

I glance up at Peter. My eyes holding his as panic, madness, starts to set in. I scream as Jake's strong arms succeed in clawing me towards him. I kick back, grab out to anything to keep myself out of his clutches. Peter looks on stunned, as if out of his body, out of his mind. He takes one final look at me, glances down at his brother Jake, and then takes his dagger and harshly runs it through his side.

The sound that pierces my ears is nothing I will ever forget. Peter crows violently, as he pulls his dagger free. Jake's screams thunder through the room. He lets go of my ankle, his hands quickly fall to his wound. But before they make it there, Peter takes his sword, grabs Jake's hand out to the side and runs it through the center of one of his palms. Jake's yell roars through my ears and matches the one that falls from my lips as I scurry to back away from the scene in fear.

Peter glances up my way, his jaw clenched tight. His eyes hooded, dark, vicious, as he grabs Jake's other wrist and pulls it up above his head. Without hesitation, he pulls a knife from his ankle and stabs it through his other palm just as I hear boots coming up the stairwell.

"No one touches what's mine and lives," Peter hisses, leaning in towards Jake and making his brother look him in the eye. He twists the blade in his palm and Jake screams out in agony.

The sounds of the guards coming closer grow louder. I look over my shoulder and hear the nurse talking frantically, telling them what she saw. Instantly, I find my feet and rush to Peter's side, pulling him from Jake's body as he writhes in pain on the floor. His side wound is losing blood quickly. His hands are pinned in crucifixion for his sins. With trembling hands of my own, I pull Peter to the window and open it quickly.

"You have to go," I insist, and he stiffens. I look at him with pleading eyes, but he doesn't back down. "Now, Peter. Before they catch you"

"Wendy, you've seen what I'm capable of. Believe me, I can take them. Besides, I'm not leaving you. Ever. You can't make me."

I knew as much. I prepared for as much. But that doesn't make this any easier.

"Playtime is over," I hiss out angrily as the sounds from outside the room continue to come closer. I look towards the door. My anxiety growing with each second that passes. "I'm never going back to Neverland. I am needed here. They need you..."

"I need you."

My heart stops beating. Hanging my head and turning back his way, I force the tears back as I glance up into his eyes.

"I don't need you, Peter. Not anymore."

He takes a step back as if my words cut him.

"I need to grow up," I whisper.

His brow furrows.

"I want to grow up. I don't want to live in a world of make-believe anymore. Of magic."

His face hardens and instinctively I reach out to him. My heart bleeds for hurting him. I wish I could take back everything I'm saying. But it's the only way to get him to leave. To save him. Because I would never be able to go on living if anything happened to him. If I knew he was no longer breathing in my life. He was right. Everything begins and ends with us. I can't let this be our end. Not yet. As much as I am not ready to say goodbye, I'll never be ready to watch him die. He flinches away and it only causes me more pain.

"But, what about the beginning and the end, Wendy..."

"We've run our course, Peter. This is our end. Neverland, it's not enough. It'll never be enough..."

"I'm not enough?"

The look in his eyes kills me as I turn and see two guards enter my room. Three more are hot on their heels. They kneel by Jake and then look up at us. They start to charge, and I immediately push Peter towards the open window.

"Please!"

"No!"

"Peter, you have to go."

"I told you, I'm not leaving you. I love you, Wendy."

"Oh, Peter," I cry, swallowing down the tears and trying my best to sound convincing. "I could never love a boy that refuses to be a man."

The guards reach our side and try to grab him, but he flies up in the air quickly. One pulls me back, another reaches for him a second time, but he floats just out of reach and out into the night.

"You lie," he screams. "I know it! You can't fool me, Wendy. I see it now. Not everything is make-believe. Even if you don't believe me, I can tell what's real!"

Quickly pulling his ring from my finger, I throw it with all my might and watch with my heart in my throat as it flings out the open window and falls to the ground in the night.

"Grow up, Peter," I manage, tears flood my eyes, my heart

strangles me, killing me slowly for having to do this to him. "It was all make-believe. This whole time. Nothing but an illusion. Deception. A sick spell."

As hard as I try, I can't stop my tears from falling. They rush out of my eyes angrily as I stare back at him. I fight to break free from the guards, but they hold me back harshly. They yell at him to come down or they'll draw their weapons.

As much as it kills me to say what I'm saying and push Peter away, deceive him when I never thought I could, it would surely end me if he ever got hurt, if I ever had to live in a world where I knew he didn't exist.

"Go back to Neverland, Peter. And take your silly magic with you."

I can't stand to see him fly away. Turning my back on him, I rush to Jake's side, hopeful it delivers the final blow. On my knees, I fall apart, breaking for the boy behind me that I always feared one day I'd loose. I close my eyes and cry out, devastated that in the end, it was impossible to keep him.

I hear gunshots and start to shake. Crying harder, I hear Peter yell for me. Begging me to turn. To listen to him. But I can't.

As they pick up Jake's lifeless body and start to walk out of the room I follow. I walk away from the boy that I couldn't stand to watch become a man. He wanted to sacrifice himself for me, but I couldn't let him. I leave my room, abandon the nursery, and surrender my heart to a fate that was always supposed to be our end.

I can't take you with me, Peter.

I have to push him away to protect him. To keep him just the way he is. Maybe that's part of the magic of love. The illusions at

215

the beginning, they keep us breathlessly delusional until the very end.

Maybe Nana was right.

I know I'll always love Peter. But I can't take him with me. And where he's going, I no longer have the strength to follow.

CHAPTER 21
HꝎK

"That was the last time the girl Wendy ever saw him. For a little longer, she tried for his sake not to have growing pains, and when they met again, Wendy was a married woman...
Wendy was grown up."
Peter & Wendy
- J.M. Barrie

PRESENT DAY

Wendy cries in her sleep as I gently brush my fingers up and down her bare arm. She whispers my name. The pixie dust is beginning to wear off and a shiver courses through her body. My high depleted a long time ago and for endless hours I've been laying here watching her.

"Peter," she cries, and it pulls at my heart, but her next words break it fucking wide open. "I'm so sorry."

Clutching her to my chest tightly, I whisper in her ear. "Wendy," she doesn't wake up, just continues to sob softly, I say, "Darling, come back to me."

She turns over, clutching herself tightly to me like a monkey. Her arms pull me closer. Her right leg quickly drapes over my side. I smile into the crown of her head and drown in her. In this moment. A moment I thought I'd never get back that night seventeen years ago when everything between us was destroyed.

"Peter," she cries harder. "I'm so scared," my brow furrows as I feel her grip tighten. If she's still sleeping, I'll never know. "I can't lose you twice," she sobs.

"You never lost me, Darling," I confess, a reality that breaks my heart as I admit it. "You never could."

She shakes her head and pulls me closer, giving me the hint that she's lucid now. She doesn't speak for a moment, and in the past that might have made me nervous. But not now. Not after we've already lost everything yet, somehow, made it right back here. Home. To each other.

"I pushed you away..."

"We pushed each other away," I correct. "That ends now."

Picking up her hand, I raise it to my lips and kiss the ring that still sits on her finger. "I thought you got rid of this."

"I couldn't, not after I had to let you go," she starts to cry. "I searched endlessly for it in the garden below my window until I found it."

"You don't know how happy it makes me to see it sitting again on your finger." I brush my thumb back and forth across the metal like I did the first day I put it on her hand. Her palm shakes in mine. Her body trembles.

"You don't know everything..."

"I know enough." She shakes her head again; a sob escapes her lips as she burrows her face further into my shoulder.

She's right. I don't know anything. I don't know much past waiting day and night, in Kingston Gardens. Going to her house when I thought it was clear only to be turned away, time and time again, by her mother or the nurse. I don't know more than the rage that filled my veins the day I saw her finally emerge with *him*. The man I thought I killed only to be forced to watch *him* touch, once again, what was mine.

My own brother.

The thing is, I don't need to know more. What I've finally realized about Wendy being my beginning and my end is, there is no need to worry about the middle. My life began with her, and it will end with her. All the rest can go ahead and fuck right off. She's everything to me. Nothing she has to say can change that.

"I need to tell you..."

"You need to tell me nothing," I insist as I pull her closer.

"But, Peter, I..." she pulls back and looks me in the eyes, but the look I give her stops whatever confession was lingering on her lips.

My resolve crumbles more and more every time she calls me by my name. Every time the word leaves her mouth, more and more of the darkness fades. Jas Hook will always be a part of me. But Wendy will always bring out my best side. It's a truth I can no longer run from. One I don't *want* to fly away from. Not anymore.

"Do you want me to tell you everything about the past seventeen years you weren't here with me in Neverland?" She startles, the fog starts to lift a little bit more out of her beautiful eyes. "About Tinker Bell. Tiger Lily. A promise I broke. A darkness that I couldn't help but succumb to."

"But I forced you to it..."

"Just like, I'm sure, I did the same to you."

She cocks her head to the side with tears still in her breathtaking eyes. I can tell she doesn't believe me. She thinks in some way it could have all been prevented. Maybe it could have. But our course was predestined by things outside of our control. The only thing we can both do now is hold on tighter than we ever have before, and this time, never let anything tear us apart.

"Love doesn't mean you won't sometimes break the one who stole your heart, Darling. But true love means you'll stick around to pick up the pieces. You'll apologize when you've hurt the one you love and be grown up enough to admit when you've wronged them."

She goes to speak but I silence her by placing my finger to her lips.

"I broke the day you pushed me away, but I should have seen the way you were breaking in return. I wasn't old enough then to understand, but I am now."

Her eyes grow curious.

"I waited in Kingston Gardens, for days, months, years, Wendy. I only let Tinker Bell warm my bed in order to steal the Pixie dust I needed to get back to you. Every time I'd make the trip, I'd save a little, just in case I needed to return to Neverland."

Her grip on my arms tightens as more tears fall from her eyes.

"I told you I'd never leave you. And for a long time, I didn't. I couldn't."

My voice breaks on my last words and I cast my gaze downward while I attempt to gather my emotions.

"How long," she whispers, and I look up. "How long, Peter?"

I could never lie to her and won't start now.

Swallowing my pride, I confess, "Eight, maybe ten years." Her gasp grabs ahold of my heart and strangles it. "Long enough to watch two little girls grow up before my eyes. Long enough to know, there are some secrets even a mother cannot hide."

She cries harder and I let her break. Her chest rises and falls quickly. Her sobs steal her breath away. She tries to cover her face, but I force her to look at me. To look at a man who had to realize the truth from afar, who watched his children being raised without him.

"I wouldn't let myself take you back with me for the sake of our daughter's," I continue, my voice thick and shaking with emotion. "After what happened to Michael, after the way I continued to watch John turn more towards an impending darkness, I wouldn't do that to them. Bring them here. They were safer with you, Darling."

She sucks in a deep breath and accepts the truth she thought I didn't know. The one that fueled the darkness inside me even more over all these years.

"He never touched me," she finally sobs. "Jake. He never touched me, I swear it. I wouldn't let him. By the time his wounds were healed I was four months pregnant. He came for me, and I pulled a gun on him."

Her eyes grow furious as memories flood back to the present and I have to tell myself to remain calm.

"I was prepared that time," she continues. "He took one look at my stomach and told me he'd gut me."

My hands grip her harder and I see her flinch in pain. But she doesn't tell me to stop, doesn't flinch away. With all the hatred I feel inside, I couldn't loosen my grip even if I tried.

"He told me he'd rip your child from me with his bare hands, then force me to watch as he stole its life away, too. Then, he'd take mine slowly, making sure to make me suffer. I dared him to try. He fought me. Forced my hands down low, trying to get me to drop the gun. It went off, shooting him in the leg, right near his crotch."

I smile with vengeance for a penance well served, at the hands of *my* Wendy.

"It bought me more time, but not enough," she shakes her head and sighs. "The twins were born at seven months. I told him if he came for them, if he came for me, this time I wouldn't miss. I'd shoot him through his heart, then finish him off with a bullet through his head."

"Why didn't you send for me? Why didn't you try..."

"You always came for me Peter, I didn't know how."

For the millionth time in my life, I kick myself for not attempting to go to her after that day I saw her walk from her house with her mother. With Jake. With two small newborns I eventually realized were *my* daughters. It's a thought that has mangled my black heart and tempted Hook to grow more throughout the years.

"He eventually made me a promise." She takes a deep breath and levels me with a serious stare. "He'd leave us alone, wouldn't lay a finger on me or my girls, *our girls*, if I never returned to Neverland."

My hand raises and caresses the side of her cheek. I smile when I notice her shiver. "You protected what mattered most. A job that should've been mine, Darling."

"He told me he'd kill you."

My smile widens. "Death comes to all of us." Our eyes search each other, exposing something so beautiful, so pure, so raw, it hurts. "But Darling, not all of us *truly* get the chance to live."

On instinct, we pull each other closer. My lips rest above hers as she breathes me in, taking my life with hers, both of us finally exhaling all doubt, inhaling all hope for our future and holding it inside until it burns itself back to life.

"You can't have life without air, Wendy," I whisper. She attempts to pull me closer, our lips grazing each others softly as I roll on top of her. Framing her face with my hands, she wraps her thighs around me, and I groan. "Let me be your air, Darling. Let me show you love like I didn't get the chance to before."

"My life doesn't matter if you're not in it, Peter," she cries as my lips fall to her cheek and I kiss a trail downward to her neck. "I tried living, tried merely existing, if only for our daughters." My movements still when she mentions the girls I've never known. Not the way a father should. "But it was hopeless. Torment. A nightmare, living every day without you in my life. Without you by our side."

My face lifts and catches her teary eyes. "You and me. The beginning and the end, remember?"

"And what if this is our end?" She stammers nervously. "Even though we were apart, I knew that the magic could still exist. If only in my mind, we were somewhere beautiful, still together. I don't want it to end. Oh God, what if this is our end, Peter?"

With a sad smile, my lips lower to hers and I whisper, "Then we'll meet it together, Darling."

CHAPTER 22
WENDY

"'Certainly not. I have got you home again, and I mean to keep you.'"
Peter & Wendy
- J.M. Barrie

I haven't tasted his kiss in seventeen years. In fact, I haven't tasted any man's lips but Peter's. I still remember the way they felt against mine. Over our years apart, I stayed up nights replaying all the times we spent together in my mind. I tortured myself with the memory of his lips, his kiss, the urgent and demanding way he stole my breath away all those years ago, night after night.

This time, when he gives me air, breathes me back to life, he does so with the diligence, the mastery, the unrushed and breathtaking attentiveness of a man. Not a boy.

I feel it from my head to the tips of my toes as his mouth slowly presses against mine and I open up to him. His tongue caresses mine in a way that makes me intoxicated, higher than I've ever felt before. His mouth deliberately memorizes every curve of my own, every taste of my lips, in an agonizingly beautiful way he never has before.

It's not the rushed touch of a boy who is eager to try new things. His touch isn't laced with excitement, wanting to go where no one has gone before. It's slow. Gentle. Rough, only when he wants it to be.

Every touch of his hands, his mouth, his body pressed up against mine is calculated, purposeful, hypnotic. I curl into him and feel, for the first time in seventeen years, like I'm finally *really* breathing. Like I'm finally alive.

When he was a boy, Peter was cocky, witty, innocently charming and undoubtably caring. When he took my innocence, he was darker, daring, unhinged and hungry to push limits.

So was I.

The mystery of the man who now diligently holds me in his arms, the one who is exploring my body in ways he never took the time to before, is one that will never be solved.

As a man, he's darker than he was as a boy. Daring, unhinged in the way he handles the lost boys and his crew. Always restless and pushing limits.

But his caring touch, as his hands gently roam lower down my curves, is what will always leave me enchanted. The quiet and intense way he takes his time, knows just where to touch, taste, doesn't rush, will always leave me hypnotized.

"Wendy," he breathes, as his face falls to my neck. I arch up into him and feel him simultaneously thrust up my center. My hands claw at his back, wanting more of him than he's giving, but also wanting to take it just as agonizingly slow as he's allowing.

For the first time, we're not rushing. Not running. Not flying away from a past or present we can't change. We're only embracing each other.

Darkness and all.

"Darling, you were breathtaking before," his lips kiss a trail down my neck, his hips slowly thrust up my center causing a moan to escape my lips as I arch up, meeting his hips eagerly with my own.

"Now," he releases a growl, his hands roughly grip my waist, and he pulls himself slowly away, looking down into my eyes. "Let me show you, tell you, all the ways you've changed, and everything about you that takes my breath away."

He looks down and starts to undo the buttons on my night gown just like he did all those years ago, and I can't help but smile.

The beginning and the end.

His eyes lift, caching my grin, and a mischievous one spreads across his face as well.

"I'm not used to this side of you," I whisper as he unclasps the last button. His rough hands fall to my waist before gently pulling my nightgown up my sides and over my head. He tosses it to the floor at the side of the bed. When he looks back down into my eyes, his stare holds mine for a breathtaking moment before lazily, slowly, grazing down across my face, my neck, to my breasts and he licks his lips.

"Your body deserves slow and gentle, making up for all

the years I couldn't touch you," he whispers as his finger slowly trails down the center of my chest, stopping at my right breast. He circles my nipple. Tugging it gently between his fingers. His eyes lift, "Before I fuck you hard, ruthless, punishing us both for the time we've spent apart."

My thighs clench. My center dampens. I bite my lip in need and his smile grows.

"These tits," he growls, as he palms my breast in his hand and my eyes roll back with pleasure. He molds them firmly, every caress thrilling me as I suck in a breath and stare back up into his eyes. He squeezes harder as his face falls forward, and I feel his breath feather across each breast as he whispers, "Fuck me, they're perfect. Full. Soft. Perky," he licks my right nipple and I let our a sharp hiss.

Molding both breasts up into his palms, he diligently sucks one then the other into his mouth. His hot tongue swirls around each sensitive nub, making my head fall back against the sheets as my eyes close and a moan falls from my lips.

"Mmm," he groans, licking his lips and I let out the breath I didn't know I was holding. "But these hips," his hands fall, and he grips just below my waist. "Full. Thick. Fuck me, they make my mouth water like you'd never believe." He kisses my left hip as his fingers trail down and dip into the sides of my panties. "I love your stomach," he whispers, leaving gentle kisses as his lips graze across to my other hip, and he slowly starts to pull my panties down my legs. I whisper his name as his face falls lower and he discards my underwear next to my nightgown on the floor. "Your thick thighs, fuck, they make my cock so fucking hard,

Darling," he spreads my legs gently, slowly, and places a tender kiss inside each of my thighs. A shiver rushes up my spine as he starts to kiss his way towards my center.

"Tell me, Wendy," his breath feathers across my clit. "Do you still taste as good as you used to?"

"I...," I start to pant, before he slowly pulls his finger through my slit, making me lose all train of thought. "Oh," I gasp, as he slowly circles my clit before tracing back down and pressing one finger tenderly inside me. "Oh, Peter..."

"Fuck, you're tighter than I remember," he presses another digit inside my slick center, and I stifle a scream. "God, your pussy was always the death of me," he releases a low growl, as he steadies himself on the bed and rhythmically pulls his fingers in and out of my sex.

My hips rock into his palm, wanting more, needing him to put his mouth on me. His thumb rubs my swollen nub and I feel my climax building quickly. All too soon, he pulls his fingers from inside me. I look down. A wicked smile tugs at his mouth as he reaches up and swipes his fingers across my lips.

"Answer me, Wendy," he insists as I open my mouth and suck myself off his hand eagerly. "How does that pussy taste, Darling?"

I let out a moan and his eyes widen.

"That good, huh? Fuck, let me try."

Leaning forward, he sucks his fingers from my mouth to his, his free hand presses against my sex. A groan escapes his lips as he sucks my tongue into his mouth, tasting me there. His fingers press back inside me, one, two, three, and I let out a scream down the back of his throat. He smiles against my lips before backing away, leaving me panting, truly breathless, and then slowly descends back down my body.

"Fuck," he hisses, his fingers pressed deep inside me, barely fitting as he curls them deeper, and finger fucks my center. "Everything about you is better than before. But this pussy," he sucks in a sharp breath as I prop myself up, watching him, admiring his fingers as they pull out and then press deeper inside me.

"This tight, soaking wet cunt." He looks up and smiles, "It's my favorite fucking part."

His fingers pull me closer to orgasm. My center tightens.

"Now, be a good girl and cum when I say so."

I barely have time to blink before his mouth is on me, sucking me quickly towards heaven. He pulls his fingers from inside me and hoists my legs over his shoulders, devouring me completely as he licks up my slit, fucks my center with his fingers, and sucks my clit into his mouth like he'd die if he was denied it.

When I'm close, barely a second away from crashing over the edge, he stops abruptly. Pulling away, he smiles up at me, his face wet from my pleasure and only slowly presses one finger back inside me when I'm no longer dangerously close to crashing over the edge.

"I've done nothing but dream about this pussy for seventeen years, so you'll do as I say and let me enjoy you." He licks up my center and I hiss, so ready to fall over the edge it's killing me, "You'll let me take back what's mine."

He places a soft kiss to my clit, another one lower against my velvet lips, before his tongue enters my center and he fucks me with it while staring deep into my eyes.

I feel my center clinch down. I tell myself to do as he says. I want to enjoy this, too. But it's been too long, I'm too close, there is no way I can hold out much longer while watching him pleasure me. He licks up my slit again and I try to drop my legs to the bed, but his strong hands grab my thighs, keeping them flung over his shoulders. He shakes his head as he licks up my center and once again sucks my clit in his mouth.

"Peter," I plead, "Peter, please," my head falls back, and I close my eyes, not able to watch any longer. "I'm so close, I can't…"

In an instant, my legs are dropped to the mattress. Before I can open my eyes, he has me turned on my stomach.

"Hands on the headboard," his tone is harsh, fierce, and I follow his demands instantly. "Spread your legs. Wider, Wendy."

Smack! I gasp out as his hand roughly spanks my ass.

"I want to see that pretty pussy, Darling. I said wider, damn it!"

I spread my legs as wide as I can and lean forward, gripping the headboard for leverage.

"Good girl, just like that."

Silence stretches in the darkness. My heart beats wildly. A low growl escapes his lips. "Fuck, you have no idea what the sight of you like this does to me."

I feel his weight leave the bed, but I do as he says and stay in place. My center throbs with the need for release as I hear his zipper slowly lower. I hear the rustling of clothes hitting the floor, boots being discarded, before his weight settles behind me again.

His cock is larger than I remember, he runs it slowly through my wetness, making my clit throb with the need for release. He slowly presses his crown into my opening, and I moan. A chuckle falls from his lips as he pulls out, then repeats the process, only giving me a slow tease and making my pussy crave the feeling of being full.

"I remember the first time I tasted your pussy, Wendy," he presses in a little further and I bite my lip. "The first time you sucked my cock."

"Peter," I beg, as I thrust my hips back, pleading for him to fill me, but again he denies me.

"I remember the urgency, the desire, the need to take you, explore you, even though we weren't ready. Even though we were so young."

His cock leaves my entrance, and he runs it back across my ass. I suck in a breath and press back into him, making a groan escape his lips. He hisses, his hands grip my hips as he breaches my tight hole and I silently let out a small scream.

"I remember how bad you wanted me to touch you, taste you, just as much as I wanted you, too."

He leans forward and places a small kiss to my lower back. He guides his cock lower, his crown sucking inside my velvet lips again. I grip the headboard harder, my center threatening to explode without help if he holds out on me much longer.

"But now," he leans forward, his lips resting against my ear, "I take what I need, when I want. And as much as I love the taste of your pussy, it's been too long since I've been inside your hot little cunt," he presses in a little further, and we both release a deep moan as pleasure builds, ecstasy threatens to explode. He takes a deep breath and then whispers, "Get ready, Darling. This time, there is no holding back," he presses inside me further and I suck in a sharp breath. "This time, I'm not fucking stopping."

He thrusts all the way inside me so quickly, so harshly, I scream just before my head drops to the headboard. He's quick to anticipate though, and my forehead bounces off his hand instead of wood as he protects the impact.

"Fuck," he grits out, finally fully seated inside me, our breaths start to even out as we both get used to the feeling.

"Was it always like this?" he breathes against my neck a moment later.

"Like what?" I manage, my hips pressing back against his, letting him know I'm ready, wanting, needing him to move.

"Heaven, Darling. Fucking paradise."

He pulls slowly out of me before tenderly, gently, pressing back in, making every nerve inside my soul tingle with need.

"Immoral," he breathes, his movements picking up pace. "Carnal."

He thrusts harder, faster. My arms straighten. I use all my strength and brace for each blow.

"Fucking magic, Wendy."

He wraps his arms around my middle and pulls my body from the headboard. Keeping himself fitted snugly inside me, he sits back on the bed. His hands roam up my hips, my waist, to my breasts as he kisses my neck and I ride his length lazily, with such diligent purpose I hear him suck in a sharp breath. He groans, moans, *growls* into my skin. His hands roughly mark me as he grips my breasts, pinches my nipples, and I feel him slip perfectly in and out of my wetness.

"Darling," he grips my waist tight, making me come to a stop. "Fuck, you ride my cock so good, I won't be able to last. I already want to spill myself inside you."

I thrust back down on his hard length, and he releases a sharp groan. "Good," I moan, as his hips rise, urging me to keep going.

"You want me to cum for you, Wendy?"

He grips my hair in his hands tightly, forcing my head to the side. Taking my lips with his, his hands lower to my clit and he starts to rub me up and down, back and forth, in diligent circles, making me purr with ecstasy.

"You first, Darling."

He lifts me off his lap suddenly, turning me to face him. Fisting his cock, he guides me back down over his length and we both lightly cry out from the feeling. His eyes hold mine as we get lost in each other's souls becoming one. He gently brushes my hair out of my eyes, framing my face tenderly with his hands.

"Wendy, I've finally realized, I was never *lost*," my brow furrows as I study him, and he smiles. "Everything I've ever known began with you. As long as I have you, I'll never be lost," he smiles and leans in closer. "I found what I was looking for. You. It's always been you. Because loving you? It's like coming home."

Tears fall from my eyes as he renders me completely speechless. His thumb brushes them away before gently running across my bottom lip. I suck in a breath, and he smiles.

His gaze fixated on my mouth, he asks. "Do you feel faint, Wendy?"

With a laugh, I say, "I've accepted the fact that I'll never be able to breathe properly again when I'm around you. I'll always feel like I'm about to faint, Peter."

His grin deepens, his eyes hold a light I haven't seen in them since I've been back in Neverland.

"Remember, if you needed air, Darling," his lips lower to mine. "All you had to do was ask."

This time, when his lips meet mine, the same sense of urgency we felt all those years ago rushes back. Eager to follow because we know where it's taking us, we quickly start chasing a connection that we've been craving and denying ourselves for far too long.

He lays me back against the sheets and my legs widen. I take him in, urging him to move faster as his thrusts pick up speed, deepening to a painful depth inside me. My hands clutch him closer. We don't say a word because there is no need. Everything we can ever say is expressed between us without words as we stare into each other's eyes and he claims me. Takes me.

Maybe for the first *real* time in our lives.

Our souls exposed. Hearts united. There are no lies between us. No secrets. Not anymore. I start to cry from the beauty of everything that I'm feeling, that we're finally experiencing. A magic most of the world will never know.

His jaw ticks. His brow is slick with sweat as it furrows, as he holds me closer and never looks away. Everything we could ever say, ever apologize for, is exposed, is felt as he loves me in a way I've never known before, and I desperately, wholeheartedly, love him back.

My screams fill the room. He crows louder than ever before.

We hold onto each other tightly and let go of the past, finally coming back to where we belong. Finally coming back to us. And finally, after all this time, feeling like we're coming home.

CHAPTER 23
WENDY

"'The last thing he ever said to me was, 'just always be waiting for me, and one night, you'll hear me crowing.'"
Peter & Wendy
- J.M. Barrie

H is heartbeat stirs me awake. The rhythmic feeling of his fingers tracing gently up and down my bare arm makes me smile. With my head rested on his chest, my mind replays everything that's happened since I've been back in Neverland. Everything that I thought I knew, now seems so different. The pixie dust has worn off completely and with it, a new day dawns. What it holds for us, I don't exactly know yet. Even though that thought makes me nervous, I try to push it aside, focus on just the two of us. Here. Together. After all this time.

It's nothing short of a miracle.

Nothing short of pure magic.

His hand stills. His movements come to a complete stop. I suck in a breath wondering what he's thinking, but before I can ask, his hand starts moving again. I try to tell myself to not read too much into everything. In reality, I have to face the fact that, whatever happened between us last night, as perfect as it was, is not guaranteed to last.

Not if he doesn't give up Neverland.

Because I can't stay here. And something tells me he won't follow. And if he does, he won't stay. Not forever.

Still, in the after glow of our love making, I can't help but hope that somehow we will be able to write a different ending to our story this time.

"Even when I close my eyes, you're still with me," I hear him whisper, his voice heavy with sleep. Sexy. Raspy in a way that dances deliciously across my skin. "I've had the same dream for years. Only it doesn't really feel like a dream now."

Again, his fingertips start to run up and down my arm and goosebumps break out across my skin. They're a premonition of sorts. As if I know what he's going to say before he has a chance to say it.

He whispers, "There was a little girl, and we were running through Kingston Gardens. I was chasing her because she stole my heart the moment, I saw her."

Visions flash before my eyes. It's almost as if I can see what he's talking about. Almost as if I was there, too. Almost as if he's right, it's not a dream, but something bigger, greater, that we're both finally realizing.

"It was you, Wendy," he confesses so quietly I almost don't think I hear him right. "It's always been you, Wendy."

My mind is neither here, nor there, as I struggle with

what he's just said. But if that were true, we didn't meet all those years ago when he appeared one night at my window and lulled me to sleep with music as he sat on the edge of my bed. If that's true, we've been tricked. Manipulated. Deceived.

All this time.

But by who?

Only one thought comes to mind, and my breathing stops as I ponder what it all means, why we haven't seen the truth before now.

We've never taken pixie dust as a drug before. Only ever to fly when needed. It's a truth serum, alright. Because right now, a whole lot more than I ever imagined is starting to make sense.

Staying in Neverland isn't safe. But going home means losing Neverland, saying goodbye to Peter for good.

Or does it?

"Penny for your thoughts?" he whispers, his hand lazily dipping lower under the covers. He cups my ass and pulls me closer to him. I smile, telling myself to let go of everything my heart won't stop worrying about. "If you don't hurry up and tell me," he says after too much time has passed, "I'll have no other option but to force it out of you."

He teases me by pinching my ass and I blush.

"Really?" I giggle into his side. "And how would you do that?"

"Hmm," his voice is filled with mischief, as he takes my hand in his and lowers it to his crotch. A low growl escapes his lips as he starts to work my hand up and down his thickening shaft. "I told you once, I have ways of making you comply, Darling. I can think of at least three right now that make me want to teach you a lesson, all of which involve different tempting holes on your body, just so you know to always answer me when I ask you a question."

I don't know where my confidence comes from, but before I can think better of it, I hear myself whisper, "Maybe I *want* you to teach me."

I grip his dick harder through the sheets and he lets out a hiss.

"Watch it," he warns, spinning quickly to cage me underneath him and pinning my hands on either side of my face. He presses me firmly into the mattress and my whole body vibrates with need.

"I'll tell you this," he teases with a smile in his eyes. "They all start with your mouth on my cock."

He leans forward and kisses the side of my lips. My body arches into him, wanting more, but he denies me.

"And how do they end?" I breathe out desperately when his lips lower and I feel him kiss a trail down my neck.

"I think I'd rather show you," he whispers. His hot mouth covers my nipple as he sucks down slowly, lazily, and I let out a whimper. My center tightens, my wetness grows, and I push my hips up into him. He lets out a light laugh as his mouth crosses over to my other breast and he repeats the same torture.

"Something tells me you'd like that, too," his hips thrust into me, and I close my eyes, letting out a deep groan when I feel how hard he is against my thigh. "Best thing is, we have the rest of our lives for this kind of show and tell, Darling."

My body stills, but if he notices, he doesn't let on.

The worry I was trying so hard to deny a few moments ago is now back, full force, and I can't ignore it this time. He lets go of one of my wrists and trails his hand down between us, gently pressing his fingers against my clit and rolling them in circles. When I don't respond to his touch, his head lifts. I feel his stare on me, but I can't force myself to open my eyes and look back.

"Wendy, look at me."

I bite my bottom lip and try to tell myself to do as he says. I try to convince myself that I'm worked up over nothing. But when that nothing is the one thing that you've been running from for so long, you can't help but be consumed with fear. He releases my other wrist and both his hands come up to frame my face gently.

"Wendy," he tries again, but for the life of me, I can't tell myself to do as he says.

I can't look him in the eye and deny what my heart desperately wants any longer.

Him.

It's always him.

Because deep down, I've always been afraid that it's always been too much to ask.

"Wendy," he says sternly this time, his hands gripping the sides of my face tighter. "For fuck sakes, talk to me."

"It's always been pointless, hasn't it?" My eyes finally open, brimming with tears.

He stares back at me confused, studying me closely. His eyes search and try to understand the painful truth we've always been too scared to look at.

"What has been pointless?"

"Us," he pulls back slightly, as if I've hurt him, but he doesn't remove his hands from my face. "There's always been something working against us. Something keeping us apart." He considers what I've said but doesn't speak. "*Someone* keeping us apart. From the start, it was pointless. Coming here. Following our hearts. Falling in love. I can't keep you because you won't come with me and..."

"Wendy..."

"... and I can't stay here," I blurt out before I lose the courage. "I can't abandon Jane and Margaret," my voice breaks as my hands raise and grip his.

His eyes implore mine. Hurt. Confusion. Destruction. It all stares back at me as he weaves his fingers through my own, our hands interlaced just like our hearts, and he holds me still underneath him.

"Jane and Margaret are all grown up," his words tumble out, as he tries quickly to grasp hold of reason for the both of us. "Your mother has long ago passed. Michael is crippled, but he could run the family business. There is no need to..."

"I grew up too," I lash out. "Without you. We all grew up, Peter. Not just our bodies, but our minds, our hearts. I can't stay here and pretend. I won't live in Neverland with you and forget about the other half of us that's missing this time."

It's a reality he hadn't yet considered, and I see recognition as it finally registers in his mind. There is more than just the two of us. He wasn't there to raise our daughters. Odds are, he won't be there to walk with them the rest of the way through life either. But I will be. I won't leave them behind. Not like he's always left me behind.

"What are you saying?"

His eyes darken as he stares down at me. My anxiety thickens and my breaths come faster as I try to tell myself, if only for once in our life together, I need to tell him what I want. I need to tell him what I need. Because what happened before was also partly my fault. I never asked. I never told him. For fear that he'd give himself up for a life I was so sure he never wanted.

"I need you in my life like the air I breathe, Peter," tears fall from my eyes, and I watch as his stare traces where they fall. "But I can't stay with you in Neverland."

"Can't or won't?" he lashes out with a sad, hurtful tone and my pulse quickens.

After a moment of staring into his eyes with him waiting for me to respond, with a shaky voice I whisper, "Won't."

He releases a heavy sigh and closes his eyes. After taking a few deep breaths, he nods his head, agreeing with something still left unsaid.

His eyes open, tenderly lowering to mine, just as his thumb brushes gently against my cheek. He shocks me when I see a smile slowly pull across his handsome face. A smile I totally wasn't excepting. "Love is a two-way street, Wendy. I won't have you give up anymore of yourself for me."

Swallowing hard, I blink a few times in shock and ask, "What are you saying?"

Spreading my legs apart with his knee, he rises up and guides himself towards my opening.

"Give," he whispers, as he thrusts forward, "and take, Darling," I cry out as he fills me completely, beautifully stretching me to a painful high.

His hips start to move harshly, and I grab onto his arms,

bracing myself, and preparing to take each passionate thrust.

Before I lose my courage, I stare deep into his eyes and whisper, "Come home with me."

He gathers me into his arms, lifting me gently and giving himself the leverage he needs to go deeper. My head falls back, and a small scream escapes my lips.

When my eyes once again meet his, he groans, "Stay in Neverland with me."

His lips trail down my chest, his teeth mark me, claim me, as his length pulses and throbs while he forces it slowly in and out of my sex.

We stare in each other's eyes and before too long he starts to smile. Gone is the man, before me sits the boy with fear in his eyes. He pleads, "Stay with me Wendy, and I promise to go wherever you go."

"I could never leave you, Peter. Even when we were apart, you always had my heart."

He smiles. "Summers in Kingston Gardens?"

"Winters in Neverland?"

A future suddenly unfolds before us that neither of us expected.

"I'm going to spend the rest of my life making you happy, Wendy." He lays me back against the sheets and slowly starts to make love to me. "And when this life is over. I'll find you and love you even more in the next."

He doesn't say another word, only does exactly that. Loves me wholeheartedly, just like he said he would. No barriers. No secrets. Nothing holding us back. When we crash over the edge this time, it's into a new beginning that promises to somehow be brighter and better than our first.

CHAPTER 24
TINKER BELL

"I don't know whether the idea came suddenly to Tink, or rather she had planned it on the way, but she... began to lure Wendy to her destruction. Tink was not all bad: or, rather, she was all bad just now."

Peter & Wendy

- J.M. Barrie

"And do you think they suspect anything?" My eyes bore into his, a dark glow strengthens between us as I implore his mind to tell me what he's thinking.

To tell me if he's lying.

"No," he mumbles, shaking his head and taking a step forward out of the shadows. "They're too obsessed with each other," my hands shake in rage, "too captivated, infatuated, to ever see straight. To ever see past what they have between them."

"Just like they were before," Tiger Lily sighs in displeasure next to me.

I turn her way, my patience wearing thin as my hands grip the arms of the chair I'm sitting in. My knuckles turn white as my heart beats out of my chest. Envy rushes through my veins, fueled by a hatred that's only strengthened since Wendy's been back in Neverland.

"Just like they've always been," Tiger Lily continues. My teeth clench and I hiss out a heavy sigh. "Just like they always will be. As long as she's still breathing."

"So, we stop her breathing," I hiss out with no regard for the person in front of me.

The one who has been playing sides since the very beginning. One that came to me with a thirst only I could quench all those years ago and paid for it willingly. He sold his soul in order to get what he wanted most.

Me.

The chance to rule Neverland as King.

My soldiers step out of the shadows, hands on their weapons, ready for me to say the word. They've been waiting eagerly, just as long as I have, to take back the island. Only problem is, I believed it could be done without killing the little tramp that took what I've always wanted.

Who I've always wanted.

"Any objections?" I scowl as I look around the room.

The person in front of me shuffles his feet. Looking to the floor, he bites his bottom lip.

"I told you, no one harms Wendy," he grits out.

I glance towards Tiger Lily, who is studying him closely. Slowly turning back his way, I try and read his mind as best I can, to see why he's so keen on standing in our way. But the bastard has a block, a wall up. There's something I can't see past for the first time since I've known him, and it infuriates me to no end.

Wendy has been a problem since before she first came to the island. Since she first cast a spell on Peter that's been impossible to break.

I took him from his family all those years ago when I fell in love with the boy who used to play every morning and long into twilight in Kingston Gardens. The boy who believed in a world no one else knew existed. A land no one else would ever trust in. Except him.

He stayed with me, loved only what I could give him. Neverland. A place where all his dreams could come true. That is, until the day he felt the pull back to his homeland. It was the day the pixie dust I cast on him wore off and something stronger grabbed ahold of him tighter than I ever could and promised to never let go. I feared then what I now realize was always inevitable.

It would never let go. *She* would never let go.

Wendy. Fucking. Darling.

They played together once as kids. Wendy was maybe ten, eleven. Peter thirteen.

They discovered each other just as I discovered Peter.

I knew what I had to do the moment I saw the way he looked at her. The second I realized she'd always win.

Casting a spell on both of them, I thought I erased their memory and stole Peter away with me to Neverland for good. To keep him for myself. To keep him away from anything that could ever come between us.

It wasn't long after Peter came to live here that he started flying back to her. He'd sit on her bed at night and tell her stories of their time apart, thinking he was telling her stories of a life he's always lived, always been a part of. One I gave him, and one I hated to admit he only wanted to share with her.

I loved him first. I saw him first. There was magic in his eyes unlike any other's I had looked in before, and there was no way I was going to let a spoiled little brat by the name of Wendy Moira Angela Darling come between us.

That bitch grew up privileged. Her family was well-known about town. Her father was king of the underground. Peter's was as well. They were business associates. Colleagues of sorts. They called on the fae more times than they should have been allowed.

Jake was always a pawn. He was a boy who loved the life of the fae enough to risk his own life in order to sit beside me in Neverland one day. He played his part nicely until Peter stole Wendy away to Neverland, fell in love with her, lost his innocence and started to fall into darkness.

I knew he'd never touch Wendy. Jake's only ever wanted to be exposed, explored, desired by the hands and hearts of the fae. A fact I've dangled in front of him for years to get what I want.

Just like I've done with the fool staring anxiously back in my eyes now.

Jake was supposed to keep Wendy as far away from Neverland and Peter as he possibly could. A job he failed at, when Peter stole pixie dust and left to go back to her.

Everything was right in Neverland until *she* came along.

248

Until she bewitched the only boy I'd ever loved with her *Darling* charm and then stole the only thing I've truly ever wanted.

The boy with enchantment in his eyes. A boy who believed in make-believe so much he couldn't tell truth from reality. One who would always believe in magic.

But my spell was never as strong as the magic between them because I never planned on Wendy being the only truth he'd ever need and the air he needed to survive.

"I never wanted anyone to get hurt," the person before me finally stutters. "It was never my intention to…"

"You knew what you were doing when you started playing sides," I sigh in annoyance. "You knew it would eventually come to this."

He looks up at me, a hesitance still hanging in his eyes.

Leaning forward, I rest my arms on my knees and level him with an intense stare. "We made a deal. What I want, for something you want. You've been diligent to bring us information. For that I thank you. But if you turn your back on us now, if you try and take back a promise you made…"

"Fools make promises in the heat of passion."

"Lucky for me, it was never about passion between us. Only sex. Sex you've paid for, like a good servant. Up until now. So, cut the bullshit because I'm tired of the damn back and forth. You're either with us, or against us. I'm taking back this island. Even if I have to kill Peter in the process."

Leaning back in my seat, I watch as his eyes fill with hatred. His jaw clenches in rage. "He's the only friend I've ever known. I've changed my mind, I don't want…"

"Do you always stab your friends in the back?" I hiss. "If

that's the case, seems to me I've been smart to watch mine since the first night you came to me, begging, offering anything in exchange for a night in my bed. For a chance to rule Neverland instead of him."

"I was young..."

"So was Peter. So was Wendy. Now look at the mess they've made of things. No fucking excuses."

"I don't want Wendy to die."

A wicked smile pulls across my lips. "Who said anything about death? I'm only talking about taking away both their reasons for breathing."

"I don't want to be the reason Peter suffers."

"Why?" I snap. "They've made the rest of us suffer. They've danced around in their own little world, playing make-believe while they interrupt the rest of our lives. They're so consumed. So smitten. They're so fucking intoxicated with each other it makes me sick. I warned her once. She mocks me by staying. I ruled this island before her, before him. It's time I take it back."

"You'd kill the one you say you love," he steps forward, courage and loyalty painting his features as he begins to yell in madness, "all because he couldn't help but fall in love with a girl who gives him something you can't?"

"Something I can't!" I boom.

Standing abruptly from my seat, I flash across the room and I'm at his side in an instant. He backs away in fear and I follow, forcing him into the darkness. Forcing him back into the shadows. Forcing him to understand. Forcing him to give me what I want and stop with the fucking trouble his disobedience is sure to cause.

"I gave Peter a whole new world, one he saw and believed in before anyone else did," I seethe. "One filled with a boy's wildest dreams. No girl was ever meant to follow. I gave him everything and he'd rather have her! What can she give him that I can't?"

"She makes him feel alive," he whispers, his stare imploring mine and my eyes widen as his words hit me harder than expected. I flinch back in shock. "She's his reason for living, Tink. Can't you see that. His reason for breathing."

"And Neverland isn't?"

"Some kinds of magic won't captivate you with your eyes. The strongest kind of magic is one you feel. It's the way he feels for Wendy that he doesn't feel for you, doesn't feel for Neverland, that will always win. Always take him away. Always call him home. No spell you cast will be strong enough to stop that."

"Time has passed for spells, John. I think you finally realize that."

Wendy's brother looks at me defeated and lowers his head. He knows the promise he made. If he won't keep up with his end of the bargain, there is only one thing left to do. And that is to collect what he owes me the only way I know how.

"Now, tell me what you know."

He takes a deep breath, and I can feel the block that was there moments before finally start to lower. He complies beautifully. But I'm too heated to not inflict pain. To not make him suffer for trying to stand in my way. My brain searches John's quickly as he starts to crumble to the floor at my feet.

"She's my sister," he cries. "I can't do what you're asking."

"You sacrificed your brother to us before." I smile and he cries harder, clutching his head as I extract what I need.

His back arches and he screams out, fisting his hair in agony as he starts to writhe in misery at my feet.

"Your shame made it impossible to stay home with him when he got hurt. Returning to Neverland, you knew what was required of you."

"I honestly thought he'd forget about her," he screams, visions of Wendy and Peter together flashing from his mind to mine, showing me their night together, their plans for escape.

But there will be no escape for any of them. John included.

"Your job was to keep him from her. Build the darkness. Turn him into Hook. Not someone who is weak, who would go running back to that whore Wendy Darling the first chance he got."

"I didn't think..."

"You never think!" I shout. John screams out as I tower over him, my mind racing through his at a lightening rate.

"I'll help you kill, Peter," he pleads. "It never sat right with me the way he left Wendy all alone. Just, please, please, listen to me. I'm sorry, I..."

"Apologies are too late," I suck in the last bit of information I need just as John's eyes roll back in his head, and his body falls to the floor. His breathing stops. I cock my head to the side, study his seemingly lifeless form, and then shake my head in disgust.

Pitiful. His last words were as weak as Peter has become. They were a confession. A plea. An attempt to make amends for something he never had control over in the first place.

"Is he dead?" Tiger Lily asks as my men come, collect his body, and haul him away.

"If not, he'll wish he was if he ever wakes up."

Turning, I make my way back towards Tiger Lily. She studies me. Arms crossed over her chest. A look of annoyance etched across her face. "Are you done playing games?" She sighs. "Because I'm growing tired of waiting."

"Don't worry," I smile. "We haven't been waiting in vain, Princess. I've seen all that I need to see. This time, no one will stop me from taking back what I want. The end is near, and I'm going to enjoy watching every second of Peter and Wendy's magic finally burning out."

CHAPTER 25
HOOK

"'I want Peter Pan, who first gave the brute a taste for me.'
'Some day,' said Smee, 'the clock will run down and then he'll get
you.'"
Peter & Wendy
- J.M. Barrie

The smell of smoke and ash wake me from a deep sleep. Wendy lays next to me, her body intertwined with my own as I sit up suddenly disturbed. I look to the door of the bedroom and my eyes widen. Smoke billows underneath the sill and I startle. Shaking the woman at my side, I gently say her name as anxiety begins to take over and worry quickly turns my insides sour.

"Wendy," I urge, but she doesn't stir. "Darling, wake up."

She rolls to her side. I pull from underneath her, swinging my legs over the side of the bed and grabbing my pants from the floor.

"Peter," she whispers in the dark, "what is it?"

"Quick, get dressed," I pull on my pants and button them quickly.

Grabbing her nightgown from the floor, I urgently place it over her head as she shuffles to the side of the bed. She pulls it down as the smoke increases and starts to fill the room faster than before. The sound of wood cracking and popping can be heard coming from the other side of the door.

"What's happening?" she asks.

I urge her from the bed and grab her hand, pulling her behind me as I quickly make my way to the door. She starts to cough, the smoke thickening around us as I place my hand on the knob and curse, pulling back quickly as it singes my skin.

Turning and glancing over Wendy's shoulder, I nod towards the bathroom, and she gets the hint. Taking off quickly, she bolts from the room and I run after her. Entering what I once thought of as my own private oasis, I've suddenly never felt more trapped in my entire life as she spins around and looks back at me with fear in her eyes.

"What do we do now?" she screams in terror.

My eyes lift and catch the waterfall. The only way out is up. Swiftly, I pick her up in my arms and carry her to the shower. She grips me tightly as I come to a stop at the base of it and take a deep breath.

"You can't carry me up the rock wall," she laughs. "Just fly. What are you waiting for?"

"I can't," I confess finally, watching as her face drains of color. "I haven't been able to in years."

She urges me to put her down and I reluctantly let her fall out of my arms but keep her close.

"What? But how? Why?"

"I don't know," I shrug as the crash of wood crumbling to the floor echoes from the other room. "After the first time we were together intimately, I started to feel the magic leave me. It didn't all happen at once. Just, slowly faded over time."

"How did you get back and forth from Kingston Gardens to Neverland?"

"I stole pixie dust, from Tink, when she'd come and stay the night."

I swallow hard not wanting to confess any more than I have to. From the look in Wendy's eyes, I would say she gets the hint.

Suddenly, I feel the heat from the other room and turn just in time to see flames engulf the door to the bathroom. Wendy looks over her shoulder and notices the same. She takes a step closer and anxiously grabs my hand.

"I'd say you didn't so much as steal it, more like she let you take it in exchange for something I don't want to know the details about."

I look back her way and frown. "I don't like the way that sounds."

"I don't like the fact that she knows what it feels like to have what's mine."

I smirk and pull her closer. "I'll never live that down, will I?"

She glances back over her shoulder at the fire that's roaring to life at a rapid pace. "If we make it out of this," she anxiously stammers, "I promise to never bring it up again."

"If we make it out of this," I chuckle nervously, "I promise to never stop making it up to you for as long as we live."

She looks back in my eyes and smiles. "Deal."

Kissing her lips softly, I urge her to my back and guide her hands over my shoulders. "Hold on tight, Darling. I may not be able to fly, but I swear I'd lay down my life before ever letting you slip through my fingers again."

She does what I say just in time as the bathroom succumbs to the fire. Quickly, I start to scale the wall, pulling us stealthy through the water as flames threaten to ignite at our feet. She screams as one singes the hem of her night-gown but is quickly quenched by the waterfall.

I struggle at first with her holding on to me. A few rocks crash to the ground breaking into pieces below, but I'll be damned if I'll ever give up before at least making sure she reaches the top unharmed. Pushing through the heavy downpour from above, I pull us higher, higher, until I can almost see the stars in the night sky.

My arms shake. Wendy trembles. My name leaves her lips in a desperate plea. I glance back into her eyes and see she's just as worried as I am that we won't reach the top alive. My foot slips, and I lose my grip on the rock to my right. The bolder falls out from under my feet and explodes with a deafening boom once it reaches the bottom. Wendy screams as I tighten my grip, balancing us both on a small ledge.

"Darling," I hiss out through clenched teeth, hoisting her up, "grab a hold of the top, quickly."

She looks up stunned and sees the ledge. With all the strength I can manage, I heave her up in my arms and give her a boost. She grabs ahold of the soft earth and claws her way to freedom just as my left-hand slips and I start to fall.

"Peter!"

I claw at the cliff, my hands unable to grasp hold of the one thing I need to stay with her, the ledge, and then tumble a few inches down the side of the wall. But before I go down completely, my foot hits a rock and gives me the sudden stop I desperately need. Looking up, I see her clutching her chest in fear. With shaky hands, I start to climb my way back to her. Back to where I always belonged. By her side.

It takes me longer than it did the first time. My arms threaten to give out as I grunt out through the pain. The water, which was once refreshing compared to the hot flames of the fire below, is now nothing but an obstacle I can't wait to be rid of. Wendy urges me to keep going. To come back to her. Finally, my hands touch the grass at her feet, and I pull myself up quickly. She kneels, helping me up by my arms and dragging me away from the cliff.

When I can catch my breath, I steal a kiss and pull her to her feet. Glancing behind me, I watch as Hangman's Tree burns quickly to the ground and smoke surges up the waterfall, floating around our feet. A tinkling of bells can be heard in the distance and my vision goes black with rage.

"Tinker Bell," I hiss.

"She won't let you go without a fight." Wendy shakes at my side. "Tiger Lily. The mermaids. They've all always wanted you for their own, Peter."

"The only one who has ever *truly* had me is you, Wendy. Nothing they try to do can change that."

"It's not safe here," she whispers, looking over her

shoulder and taking a step closer. I wrap her in my arms and glance around us just the same.

"You're right, but I can't fly us back to Kingston Gardens. Not until I get my hands on more pixie dust. I used the last of what I had to bring you back to Neverland."

The sound of bells grows louder, and I grab her hand, taking off quickly towards the mountains.

"Where are we going?" she yells behind me as my feet rapidly pick up their pace.

"Somewhere we can escape if we need to," I yell over my shoulder. "Somewhere Tinker Bell can't hide."

We hurry through Never Wood, bypassing Mystic Mountain and coming to the thick, tropical forest before Cannibal Cove. Monkey's scream and chatter above us as they swing through the thick trees. Large animals scuttle through the thick brush at our sides. Bats click as they swoop through the night near our heads. Wendy shrieks in fright. Looking up, I notice the moon is full, high, and bright in the sky, as we make our way towards the one place Tinker Bell doesn't have memorized like the rest of the island. Wendy's hand tightens in mine as we come to a stop overlooking the cove.

It doesn't seem like so long ago that we stood here, gazing out across the same shore and I told her of my plans to one day have a ship and be feared by a crew of men. The ship was my only solace the years we spent apart. The only place Tinker Bell never visited.

Tiger Lily was allowed on deck from time to time. But she was escorted to and from my quarters, and never left unattended. Now, it looks like the Jolly Roger is our only chance at survival. I clutch Wendy's hand in mine and turn to look sternly in her eye.

She doesn't say a word. Only nods her head, as if she knows it's our only option. With a smile, I pull her swiftly behind me and start to make my way down the hill towards the seashore.

"I told you, Wendy, all good pirates have to have a ship," I joke, as our feet hit the sand. Dropping her hand, we both take off running towards the water.

"You also told me that I'm what everyone is fighting over." She glances over her shoulder just as a faint tinkling of bells can be heard once again in the distance. "You weren't wrong about that, either."

Our toes hit the water and we start to wade through it quickly, pushing through the tide desperately with the need to make it to the Jolly Roger as fast as we can.

"Only this time, Darling," I shout, as I jump into the waves, Wendy follows suit as we start to swim to the ship. "I'm not letting them take what's mine. You're a treasure I've waited for my whole life, and the only way I'm giving you up this time, is over my dead body."

CHAPTER 26
HOOK

"A strange smile was playing about his face, and Wendy saw it and shuddered. While that smile was on his face, no one dared address him; all they could do was to stand ready to obey."
Peter & Wendy
- J.M. Barrie

The best way to catch a fae is to tempt them. Dangle the treat they want most in front of their face. Put it on display, out in the open, in the middle of nowhere, where you can slam the lid closed on their magic, finally containing their mischief, and stopping them once and for all.

Wendy is what they want most.

A special treat that's guaranteed to stop all their magic forever if I execute my plan correctly.

Standing back in the shadows, I watch her body tremble with slight fear. It does something to me. Seeing her on edge like this. Waiting for the inevitable. Waiting for me to save her. Just like all those times before. The delight I always felt back then when I would rush in and rescue her just in time once again breathes life back into my veins.

Tick Tock.

Tick Tock.

For the first time in seventeen years, I don't fear the time that passes. I know I can save us. Take back our beginning. Make a new ending. That's all that matters.

I knew she needed saving the first time I looked into her eyes. A part of her soul called to me. Always brought me back to her. But the truth is, she saved me, too. Long before she ever came back to Neverland and fell into my arms by some magic neither of us will ever understand. She saved me from a fate I'd rather die before I ever meet at the hands of Tinker Bell and her army. Or, at the mad clutches of Tiger Lily and the Indian chief. The mermaids and their tainted lagoon. The whole island can go to hell for all I care. Because all I've ever truly cared about, and ever will, is *my* Wendy.

She saved me from myself, from falling so in love with this place that I couldn't see anything else. It took me seventeen years to realize *she's* where I belong. No matter if that's here, or back where we both come from.

All that matters is that after all this time we've spent apart, we'll finally be together. Someplace different. Someplace new. Without the foolishness of this place.

Losing Neverland isn't the end. It's only the beginning.

As I hear the loud tinkle of bells closing in, I clutch the hook at my side and watch Wendy's back stiffen with pride. With determination. With challenge. We both know there is no way out of here without putting up one hell of a fight. If our time apart has shown me anything, it's that Wendy's a fighter, just like I am.

And together, we're invincible.

"Loyal to a fault," I hear Tinker Bell say as she lands on the deck of my ship. My eye catches movement in the shadows on the far side. Tiger Lily emerges, some of her men follow close behind.

Tinker Bell is soon flanked by several other fae that fly to her aide, The mermaids scream in the distance. They circle the ship, making it impossible for us to swim to shore if we need to in order to make it to safety. Rain begins to fall as the sky grows darker overhead. The mermaids wake starts to create large waves, the ship begins to sway roughly back and forth, as we all wait for Wendy to speak.

"My allegiance has always been to Peter," she says, her spine stiffening when Tinker Bell takes a step forward in challenge. "Pity, I can't say the same about the way he's treated you."

The fae laughs and shakes her golden locks, her eyes blaring bright red when she looks back Wendy's way. "Peter was no good as a boy, and even more pathetic as a man. Hook I could deal with, when he was warming my bed."

Wendy takes a step back as if what Tinker Bell just said struck her across her face. Figuratively, I guess it did. The sting of it can be felt from where I stand nearby in the shadows, waiting impatiently for what's coming next.

"He showed promise," the fae sighs with annoyance. "For a while. Until I noticed pixie dust missing and assumed the worst." She cocks her head to the side and smiles wickedly at Wendy. "Or should I say best? After all, he brought you back with him this time. And *this time*, I'm prepared to end what's been standing in my way for the last seventeen years. This time, Darling, you won't be escaping Neverland alive."

"Peter will..."

"Hook!" She snaps, correcting Wendy as more fae hit the deck. Tiger Lily reaches her side and grins, challenging Wendy with an intimidating stance. "Hook, Darling. Peter was weak. A pathetic soul who only believed in what we told him. Make-believe, Wendy. We could shift his mind to whatever we wanted. Make him think about only things only we told him."

"Even make him think about me?"

Tinker Bell's eyes widen. Her face fills with rage. It's a question she obviously wasn't expecting. One she doesn't want to answer. But one I suddenly need to hear the truth about.

"No, Darling. Not you. You were the one thing we didn't account for. The one thing that always kept complete control of his mind."

The group starts to step towards her. I give my second in command across the way a firm nod. He lifts his chin and turns, making his way down below to the gallows to get the other men. I looked for John when we first came aboard the ship and couldn't find him. My eyes scan the ship deck, searching him out again, but he's nowhere to be found.

"I never controlled him, not like you're thinking," Wendy insists, and the group stops walking.

After a moment, Tinker Bell says, "You did, more than you think."

"It was never my intention..."

"Oh, we know that," Tinker Bell snaps. Grabbing out in a flash, she angrily pulls Wendy to her side. I tell myself not to react, but when I see Wendy start to struggle in her grasp, I anxiously take a step into the moonlight and slowly start to make my way across deck.

Tinker Bell looks up. Tiger Lily does as well and catches my eye. Both women smile triumphantly, as each of my calculated steps take me closer to an impending fate I was too blinded to see because of my love for Wendy. One that could do more harm than good before I somehow think of a plan to get us away from here to safety.

"It was never his intention either," Tinker Bell hisses out.

"What wasn't?" Wendy struggles against the fae's tight grasp but Tink never lets go. She holds my stare as my feet quicken their pace. I know that look in her eye. In fact, I know Tinker Bell better than anyone else. Even herself.

"To lose what matters most," the fae grins. I break out into a run as Tinker Bell's eyes fall back to Wendy. "What he treasures most in both your world and ours."

"You mean me?"

I push my feet further. Faster. My heart pounding as my eyes widen with fear.

"Of course, Darling. Who else?"

A wicked smile plays across the fae's lips as she leans in closer. I see the glimmer of the dagger as she raises it. It glimmers in the glow of moonlight as my body propels itself in front of the blade. A crow rips from the depths of my toes, up through my lungs, and barrels out as I throw myself in front of Wendy.

The blade slashes through my skin, digging deep,

twisting in even further as I turn to face Wendy and push her out of the way. Wendy's eyes widen as she takes in what's just happened. I grab on to her, the weight of my frame forces us both to the floor. The dagger sticks out of my side, and she screams when she sees it. She yells for help as my men's feet finally hit the deck and start making their way towards us.

Tinker Bell releases a heavy sigh. "Looks like there *is* some of the boy still lurking inside the man after all." I grunt in pain, rolling off Wendy and staring up into the wicked fae's eyes. Wendy cries, clutching me close, but careful not to push the blade deeper into my side. "Or is it the other way around?" Tinker Bell seethes as the rain pelts down harder, and the wind picks up. "The man lurking inside the boy? Maybe you've had us all fooled this entire time. That's part of your charm, isn't that right, Peter? The magic of Neverland, Hook?"

My chest rises and falls quickly as the pain intensifies. Pulling the dagger slowly from my side, I wince in pain. Glancing dow, I see blood start to stain Wendy's nightgown. Her hands drip red as she gently examines my wound. Tears stream down her face, her hands shake. Taking her hand in mine, I brush my thumb across the ring sitting on her finger. She smiles down at me sadly, and my heart fucking constricts in my chest. Strangles me. Pulls me closer towards my impending death.

Pulling her hand slowly down my side, diligent to never take my eyes off Tinker Bell the entire time, I guide her palm to our only hope. Tink glances over her shoulder at Tiger Lily, a look of triumph is exchanged between them. Wendy's tearful eyes raise instantly and catch mine as recognition hits when her hand reaches its mark. She sucks in a deep breath just as my men reach our side. Looking back up, she glares up at Tinker Bell in challenge.

Wendy slowly rises to her feet. Her nightgown is soaked, hanging onto her like a second skin. She squares off bitterly against Tink. Her hair is drenched from the unrelenting rain, stray strands fly about in the wind. I swear she's never been more breathtaking than she is now, standing up for herself. Standing up for us. Struggling to stand, I start to force myself to my feet, but fail. Cursing, I try again. I need to be by her side for what's coming next. I need to be the man she's needed all this time.

"Fascinating, really," Tinker Bell goes on. "The one who has had us fooled this entire time, is the fool himself."

"The only fool here, Tinker Bell, is you," Wendy shouts as I quietly pull a knife from my boot once I can make it to my knees. "You've been trying to control a boy, a man, who doesn't want you. Will never want you."

I hear the chatter of the other fae and attempt once again to rise to my feet. But the pain in my side paralyzes me, and I stop abruptly, hissing out from the strain. My feet give out slightly. I start to tumble. Wendy notices and instantly leans down to help me.

"Peter saw nothing else but me until you came along," Tinker Bell screams. "I put *magic* at his fingertips, and he *still* chose you!" Wendy urges me to put my weight on her, in order to help me stand. My eyes catch Tinker Bell's. I watch as they grow sad as Wendy and I lean on each other, but I have nothing left in my heart that could ever care for her again. Not after the way she's always stood between me and Wendy. "I even had Hook for a while..."

"You never had me..."

"Until I let him get word that you were alone. I knew he couldn't resist you. He'd bring you back to us. Where I could finally finish the fight we started. Kill you. Control him. Once and for all."

A flash of lightening lights up the night sky. A crash of thunder rumbles endlessly in the distance.

"A person is not something you can control," Wendy insists. "It's not like..."

"Magic?" Tinker Bell snaps. Wendy flinches from the use of the word. "Magic is something I can control. And with you out of the way, Neverland will finally be the way I always wanted. We'll have Peter. He'll rule by my side as Hook. And you'll be nothing but a dream he only vaguely remembers, but can finally no longer make his way back to."

CHAPTER 27

WENDY

"It was the terrible tick tick of the crocodile, and immediately every head was blown in one direction: not to the water whence the sound proceeded, but toward Hook."

Peter & Wendy

- J.M. Barrie

Tinker Bell pulls a second blade from her side and thrusts it in my direction. I jump back just as Peter steps between us. It slashes his left arm, and he crows out loudly. His signature sound thunders through all of Neverland making the entire island grow eerily silent. Even the storm stops for a moment. Rearing back, he stabs forward with a blade of his own, but misses. Tinker Bell reacts quickly, bringing her sword up once again and striking down with a fatal blow.

He falls to the floor, and I scream. Without thinking, I pull the hook I took off his waist from behind me and strike when the fae isn't looking. When her head is downcast and she's staring at Peter's dead body.

Dead.

My Peter.

Dead.

Vengeance is all I know, all I feel, as I swipe the hook up and clip the fae's wings. She screams out in shock, and something takes over me. Something breaks inside me. Darkness consumes me. My heart stops beating as I think of Peter and all we shared laying on the floor at my feet.

Taking her wings is not enough. Will never be enough.

Brutally, I dig the hook into Tinker Bell's side, twisting and forcing it deeper and watching as her light starts to fade. The tinkling of her bells can be heard roaring through Neverland as I plunge the hook deeper. Her life starts to slip through my fingers and I find the blood in my veins surges with delight as she falls to the floor. Her army, the other fae, they start to scream. Their bells pierce the night sky, echoing into an angry chorus all around us.

But the crew of the Jolly Roger hold them off. Ripping their wings from their bodies, they force them into submission as they start to descend on Peter and me. Tiger Lily's Indian cry thunders through the night as she charges forward with her men, and they close in on Hook's crew. Their screams meld with the yells of the crew, with the tinkling of the bells, as I fall to the floor and roll Peter onto his back.

Blood flows out of his side from the cut of Tinker Bell's sword. Instantly, I begin to cry as I look up towards the night sky. I send up frantic prayers for a miracle. For a second chance. Hell, a third even. I plead with God for some kind of magic to bring him back.

A hand lightly grips my fingers and I jolt. Looking down, Peter's eyes flutter open before quickly closing again. My eyes widen in shock as I try to pull him into my lap, but he's dead weight, and I'm not strong enough.

"Peter," I scream. "Peter, come back to me."

"Darling..." My name is faint on his lips as I try and pull him to sitting.

"Peter, please, stay with me."

"Always," he coughs out with a harsh laugh. Blood coats his lips.

I smile through my tears, before looking up frantically and noticing Tiger Lily's army growing stronger.

"We have to go," I panic. "Can you stand?"

He opens his eyes and tries, but fails. I prop him up on my shoulder, and somehow manage to hold his weight, as he attempts to stand one more time and begins to walk towards safety. My eyes find Tiger Lily's and her face hardens. My hands are stained with Peter's blood. Tinker Bell's blood. If I need to shed hers too in order to leave this island, so be it.

"They won't be able to hold them off," Peter says. I trace his line of sight to see him looking at his men. "With Smee here, maybe. But without him, they don't stand a chance."

Tiger Lily starts to make her way towards us, and I flinch. "What should we do?" I stammer, quickly looking around us for an escape.

My eyes land on our only option just as Peter's does as well.

The plank.

"But the mermaids?" I ask.

"They won't bother us now that Tinker Bell is gone."

I listen for them in the distance, but don't hear them as loud as before. Maybe he's right. Peter starts to walk towards the plank and I follow, helping him the best I can as we struggle across the short distance of the deck. The mermaid's screams have quieted, but the water below still rages with the storm. I shake my head with worry. "I don't think we could make it."

Tiger Lily screams Peter's name. We turn just as she starts to charge toward us. Peter grips my arms sternly and forces me to face him.

"Wendy," he pleads, "Darling, do you trust me?"

There was a time I thought I didn't. But truth be told, there is no one and nothing I could believe in more than Peter Pan. More than Hook. More than Neverland.

Even as I stand in the middle of this make-believe world, and it all comes crashing down around us, there is no way I could ever deny it's magic. His charm. The undeniable pull all of it will always have on me.

"The beginning and the end," I smile. "That's why I never stopped waiting, Peter. Why I never stopped believing. I've always trusted you."

He smiles and gently steals a kiss. But there is no time to savor it, and we quickly pull apart, glancing up just in time to see Tiger Lily taking her last couple steps towards us. Frantically, I look back Peter's way and see his eyes have never wavered from me.

"If this is our end," he says with a sad smile, "then we'll meet it together, Darling."

Suddenly, he forces us over the edge of the boat, off the plank and into the crashing waves. The water is a light crystal blue. Sparkling in a way I have never witnessed before. I hold on to him tightly. The current is desperate to break us apart, determined to tear us away from one another.

His lips find mine under water. I breathe into him. He exhales into me. Both of us give each other the air we need to survive as we're sucked under by a rip tide and forced out to sea.

My fingers start to slip, the tide pulls me away stronger than before. Peter's wounds force him to flinch back as he struggles to hold on to me while the waves crash and tear into us relentlessly. He tries to keep me by his side. Struggles with all his strength. I watch his eyes as he labors constantly, attempting the best he can to keep a tight grip on me.

All too soon, I feel him slipping away. He's ripped from me for what I fear is good and there is nothing I can do to stop it.

Desperately, I try to cling to him as he's pulled from my grasp. Our fingers claw out to one another in one last attempt to hold on. To come back for each other. To stay together like we had finally promised.

My lungs burn without him. Without the air I need to survive. The ocean pulls me under, succeeds in severing all spells as it wrenches us apart and takes him away from me forever. I suck in water as I try to push my way to the top. My lungs feel heavy. A fire slowly starts to suffocate me as my body grows dangerously weak. My mind screams it can't go on. But I try one last time to fight my way back to the top. Back to life. Back to Peter. Back to the air I need to survive.

A dizzy feeling takes over.

A dense fog settles, creeping quickly through my brain.

I stop fighting.

I close my eyes.

I think happy thoughts.

And one more time.

I believe in the magic I once saw in the lost boy's eyes.

I feel my body become weightless. My chest start to burn from the inside out and the darkness finally wins.

My last thought is my favorite happy thought.

Of the boy with magic in his eyes and danger in his soul.

Peter Pan.

CHAPTER 28
WENDY

"You know that part between sleep and awake? That place where you still remember dreaming? That's where I'll always love you. That's where I'll be waiting."

Hook

- James V. Hart

A soothing, rhythmic, humming noise nudges me from my dreams. I smile knowing, feeling, understanding the shift in the room before I even open my eyes. The music is gentle, low enough for only me to hear and not wake anyone else in the house.

I sit for a moment, a blush creeping across my cheeks, my body awakening in a different kind of way for the boy who I sense sitting on the edge of my bed.

When I still don't move, his foot gently rubs against mine and my smile grows. The bed shifts with his weight as he sits down on the comforter. My head lulls from side to side with the rhythm of the music he plays. But it only lasts a few more moments before he stops.

"Keep playing, Peter," I whisper before I can stop myself.

My mind urges me to listen. To understand things my heart's denying coming to terms with.

I've been here before. Said this before.

More than once, I'm guessing.

"You're almost at my favorite part," I breathe out wishfully as my eyes open.

"What part is that, Wendy?" The lost boy stares back at me with a mischievous smile. Before I can answer he says, "Want to know my favorite part, Wendy Moira Angela Darling?"

Breathless, I stare at his mouth and whisper, "Part of what, Peter?"

"Of you," he smiles, inching closer and brushing my hair out of my eyes. "Everything," he whispers, and I sigh. "Everything about you is my favorite part. Part of living for, part of breathing for, part of dying for."

A frown pulls at my lips, my mind races, my heart tells me not to listen. I know what he's saying. I can feel what we both don't want to understand. It's covered up by an enchantment. A beautiful allure that keeps pulling us back before we ever get to the truth.

"There is beauty in danger," he smiles. "Suspense. Thrill. The rush of the escape."

My mind still struggles, but I feel myself start to smile, start to understand, as I stare back lovingly into his eyes.

"I want to play a new kind of game with you, Wendy," he grins, a mischievous smile pulls across his handsome face.

"Will you show me your world, Peter?" I ask without thinking, blushing as I wait for him to respond. His smile grows as he scoots a little closer on the bed.

"Will you stay with me?" he asks nervously. "Wait for me."

"I've been waiting my whole life," I confess. "I'll always be waiting for you, Peter." When he only looks at me adoringly, and doesn't say a word, I ask timidly, "Will you always stay with me? Wait for me?"

"Always," he answers instantly, and my heart soars.

The boy's eyes fall to my mouth. He slowly brushes his thumb across my bottom lip and my body tingles. A jolt courses through me, awakening parts of me I don't yet understand.

"The magic was never really gone," he whispers. "The magic was always just you and I."

"Do you think we can capture it?" I whisper back. "The best parts? The worst parts?"

I swallow hard, my hand clutching his tightly, needing to know the truth, needing to know if we have a chance to live again. Breathe again. Be together again.

"Can we rewrite our story?"

"Of course," he smiles as his lips fall to mine and I breathe him in.

They stay there, suspended above my own, as we take a moment to just breathe each other in.

Soon, he smiles, and his eyes light up with the magic that never fails to take my breath away. Never fails to make me believe. To make me think happy thoughts.

With his lips hovering above mine, he slowly sucks all

the air from my lungs before exhaling and breathing us both back to life when he says, "My favorite part, Darling, is the best part. The part that begins and ends with us."

The End

Keep reading for an extended epilogue and a sneak peek at Book 2, Saving Tink, Jake & Tinker Bell's story.

Preorder
Tinker Bell & Jake's story,
Saving Tink, releasing October 15, here!

An extended version of
Losing Neverland is available!
Titled Lost Boy, the added chapters are easy to find and marked with an asterisk*
To read the extended version visit here!

Losing Neverland is coming to audio **fall 2024!**

EPILOGUE

TINKER BELL

I watch him through the portal in anger.

My breathing is labored. My body aches from fighting for my life.

I loved Peter.

I loved Hook more.

We were supposed to rule together. Neverland was always meant to be ours, no one else's.

"What about the magic?" Blaze says, "What if Peter finds his powers again, and..."

"There is no such thing as magic," I scowl. "Not anymore."

That's not entirely true. But there isn't enough magic in all of the world, not just Neverland, that can save Peter and his precious Wendy from the hell I intend to unleash on them next.

"There's no telling how long it will take before they reach each other," he insists.

"Then we'll wait," I hiss back. "Days, months, years if we need to. Nothing can save them now. Not their pathetic happy thoughts. Not pixie dust."

"Maybe we should find a way to take them now when they're vulnerable?"

Shaking my head, a wicked smile tugs at my lips.

"Too easy," I hiss. "When I take them down, I want it to be a fair fight."

"All is fair in love and war, Tinker Bell."

But he's wrong.

They tried to kill me. They honestly thought they won.

But despite popular opinion, cutting off a fairy's wings doesn't always necessarily result in death.

It looks like I was one of the lucky ones.

Holding onto my side, I let out a groan as I stand. I ache from where Wendy pierced me with Peter's hook. A wound she inflicted hoping it would be the end of me. It might have been, if Tiger Lily hadn't gotten me to the healer back at her camp so quickly.

"We'll need a bigger army," Blaze says as I take a few steps closer to the portal.

"Maybe I can be of some help."

Blaze and I spin around quickly. He pulls a dagger from his side and steps in front of me. Rising on my toes, I glance over his shoulder, and my eyes widen.

"After all, this is my fight, too."

I reach in front of Blaze, place my hand on his wrist, and guide him to lower his dagger. He shoots me a questioning glance over his shoulder, but does as I instruct. How this mortal found the portal to our lands, I don't know. But I have my suspicions.

"You were no help to us before," I sigh with a roll of my eyes. "Odds are our chances won't be any better if we join sides."

"So much confidence for someone who just lost a battle they've been waiting seventeen years to win."

My head cocks to the side. I study him with a scowl.

"You lost the battle for us long before I ever had to step in and try to make something of the broken pieces," I hiss. "Why would I trust this time would be any different?"

"You wouldn't," he smiles smugly. "But," he gestures towards the portal. "Better to take your chances than to face off against something that almost killed you the first time, am I right?"

Turning back his way, I bite back. "Why would I leave something this important up to chance?"

"Exactly," he snaps. His brows raise. A smirk pulls across his handsome face. But indecision gets the better of me, and I let the silence stretch between us.

"You don't want me," he shrugs, "Then I'll go..."

"Jake, wait," I blurt out quickly before I can stop myself.

He turns, and I regret the decision I'm silently making before the words are even out of my mouth.

"If you promise..."

"Promises have never been my problem before," he smirks, stepping further into the room. "Breaking them has always been your specialty, Tink."

"You know what, forget it."

I spin on my heels and release a heavy sigh. Focusing back on the portal, I decide it's better not to take his help than to be held prisoner and indebted to Jake, Peter's ruthless older brother.

Blaze leans into my shoulder and says, "he's not the first choice, by any means, but..." he nods in the direction of the portal, of the scene unraveling before me, "We might need him," Blaze reluctantly whispers.

Slowly turning back around, my anger grows as I see Jake standing still in the middle of the room. He didn't leave like I hoped he would. No. Instead, he stayed, knowing that I might cave. It makes accepting his help that much harder to swallow.

He fiddles with the tip of a dagger in his hands, rotating it around on his palm like it couldn't slice him open with one wrong slip of his wrist. That's something the Pan boys always had in common. Danger. Escape. They've always been addicted to it. He waits for me to speak, and I hate him even more for it.

"Jake," I finally sigh. His eyes lift, and he grins. "You loved Wendy once. How can I be sure you won't change sides?"

Something dark flashes across his features. It startles me. It makes me take a step back. His gaze slowly rises up and down my frame. His jaw sets firm as his eyes land back on mine. Something has changed since the last time we met. Something's different. But being so frail from the fight and losing my wings, my powers are still regenerating, and I can't search his mind to find out what it is.

"You can't," he seethes. "But it looks like I'm your best bet. Only choice. Maybe even, your last hope."

I cross my arms over my chest and roll my eyes.

"What's it going to be, Tink," he teases. "Are you going to deny yourself what you need most? Or do you have the courage to roll the dice?"

"This isn't some kind of game," I spit back.

"Never stopped you before."

I glare at him, and to my surprise, he has the audacity to take a few steps forward until we're toe-to-toe. Leaning in, he places his lips next to my ear and whispers, "What are you waiting for? We're wasting time, Gidg..."

"Don't call me..."

"Gidget."

His nickname for me has always grated on my last nerve. A reference to being a girl, and when I shrink down to my smaller size. *A Gidget.* I roll my eyes as he pulls back and gives me a wink that makes me want to haul off and slap him across his ruggedly irresistible face.

"Alright," I whisper, trembling slightly when I notice his mouth hovering dangerously too close to mine.

Sucking in a shaky breath, I try to disguise the effect he has on me. But Jake's smile grows knowingly, and I hate him even more for it.

"I'll take that bet," I hiss. "This time, don't make me regret it."

**Preorder
Tinker Bell & Jake's story,
Saving Tink, releasing October 15, here!**

An extended version of

Losing Neverland is available!
Titled Lost Boy, the added chapters are easy to find and
marked with an asterisk*
To read the extended version visit here!

Losing Neverland is coming to audio fall 2024!

SNEAK PEEK AT SAVING TINK

JAKE

T don't need a clock to tick off the tense seconds as I stare into the Gidget's eyes. No, the beating of my nervous heart will do just fine.

Standing across from Tinker Bell, after years of bent up frustration, years of not being deemed worthy enough to stand in her presence, I unbutton my suit jacket and cross my arms over my chest.

Trying my best to put on an air of indifference between us, my plan is to wait for her to speak first. It's about power, after all. And as long as she shows her cards before mine, I stand a chance at keeping the control.

My breaths become shaky.

My legs slightly wobble.

Cool it, Jake.

It's been a long time since I've come face-to-face with Tinker Bell.

A lot has changed. Things she'd never imagine. Not even in her wildest dreams.

By the look in her challenging gaze though, a lot has also stayed the same.

Since the night Peter stabbed me in the gut, crucified me against Wendy's bedroom floor with his daggers, I haven't laid eyes on the pixie. Before, it was always about her part of our bargain. Keeping Wendy away from Peter, that is.

Now, I grin remembering a promise she made me nearly two decades ago.

"Regretting things already," I tease, trying to cut the tension building between us.

Although, if I'm being honest, the tension is what keeps me coming back. Keeps me thinking of her, longer than I've ever thought about any woman.

Centered in the middle of the Misty Mountains, Tinker Bell looks down disapprovingly on me as she sits outdoors on a gold throne with plush pink pillows. Located in the center of a clearing, thick woods encircle us as I stand at the bottom of her dais. Moss covered steps lead up to the throne. Lush green vines grow wildly, entangling themselves throughout the shiny metal. Roses adorn the greenery as it spreads out to the sides, then reach high above her head offering an overhang of sorts, and giving her an air or royalty, regalness that I'll never be deemed worthy to touch.

Not by her at least.

Not even after I expose a truth, a curve ball, I'm sure she's not expecting.

My eyes drink in her long, thick thighs as they cross over one another, and the cut in her dress reveals more than I've ever seen of the pixie. My mouth waters. My throat tightens as my gaze rises and I study the curve of her hip. I memorize the way the fabric of her sparkling gold dress dips into the v between her legs, tucking it away for secret pleasures I'm sure to indulge in later tonight. Her small palm comes up to clutch her side a moment later, and she lets out a tiny wince of pain. It's the only thing that succeeds in bringing me out of my greedy trance as my eyes shoot up to meet hers.

For a brief moment, I silently chastise myself for thinking of her so indecently at a time when she's hurting.

If only she'd let me close, I'd be able to take all her pain away.

When the discomfort in her side seems to have subsided, she releases a soft sigh and studies me closely. With an irritated roll of her eyes, she finally huffs, "you're not worthy of being something I'd ever regret, Jake."

Her words burn harsher than I imagined, and if I'm being brutally honest, I've imagined more of her than I ever should have since the last time we met. Things she'd say, things we'd do, if I was ever so lucky.

"In the interest of saving time," she sighs, exasperated, "tell me how you can rectify your past wrongs, and actually prove helpful this time against Peter and Wendy?"

Being cast aside and regarded as unworthy again gets to me.

Storm clouds quickly close in. The sky grows dark as midnight. Rain pelts down harshly. The rose vines, enhanced by magic, close their petals and retreat into the gold. Tinker Bell takes one look at the sky, crosses her arms over her chest, and frowns.

A smile pulls at my lips as I stand before her getting more drenched with each passing second. But for the satisfaction of winning whatever war this is building between us this time, it's worth it.

"Seems the Gods decided to grace us with a little rain," I smirk, having the upper hand.

"If you think me getting wet is going to make me surrender," a new mission gets mentally added to my "things to do with Gidget" list, she says, "you lack what little brain cells I thought you had, Griffin."

"Griffin?" I cock a curious brow her way as the rain continues to unleash. Griffins are magnificent creatures. Half lion. Half Eagle. "Why Gidg, to think all this time you thought of me as having the power, the wisdom..."

"More like the greed, the hoarding..."

"Only when it comes to you, Gidget," I wink.

A lightning bolt illuminates the dark sky. If I'm not mistaken, I see the little pixie jolt in her seat. She covers up her slip by rising the next second and slowly descending the throne.

The rain soaks her gown straight through to her skin. I keep my eyes trained on hers, not trusting myself to let them roam the curves of her body the storms has so graciously uncovered for me. It takes all the control I have not to sneak a peek. But, if I were to ever see her bared to me that way, it would only be by her choosing. Not due to foolish games.

Despite the rumors, I am a gentleman after all, and even the most courteous and honorable ones only have so much restraint. Especially when it comes to a woman they've dreamed of touching for decades. Swallowing hard, hanging onto my last thread of self-discipline as she takes her final step toward me, I let myself sneak a brief peek at peeks of her breasts before sucking in a sharp breath.

It's then that she recognizes the small scar on my right temple just above my brow. The one bestowed on me by a higher power when my life suddenly changed all those years ago. To be honest, since arriving in Neverland last night, I'm surprised it's taken her this long to see it.

Shocked, she takes a rushed step back, but then curiously leans forward, cocking her head to the side to try and get a better look. Against my better judgement, I reach for her hand. To my surprise, she doesn't steal it back away. I don't want to scare her off when I've finally got her this close, but standing next to her after all this time, it's making it hard to think clearly.

Looking down, I study her small palm in mine. As my fingertips entangle with hers, the rain stops immediately. The warmth, the fire that I felt between us all those years ago simmers and grows. The clouds part. The sun comes out. A warm breeze tangos seductively across our skin, drying us instantly. High up in the nearby trees, birds begin chirping.

"Jake, I..." she stammers.

"What," my nervous gaze lifts to her shocked one, "you've never seen a demigod in the flesh before?"

She retracts her hand immediately. Confusion. Anger. Resentment fill her features. "How..."

"Simple really," I grin, side stepping around her, I climb the steps to the dais. "Let's just say Peter's inflicted wounds the night he crucified me for all to see were more a Gods send than injury."

Sitting down on her throne, I cross my right leg over my

left knee and lean back in her seat. She whirls around and furiously puts her hands on her luscious hips. My mouth waters with the greedy need to touch her there. Taste her there.

"Demigod?" she demands. I can sense her inner wheels working. The bitter bite that's sure to be thrown my way next. "Please," she rolls her eyes, "what moron decided to make you a God?"

God?

"I do love the way that word falls from your lips," I taunt, making her cheeks flush, and her eyes fill with an adorable embarrassment. She crosses her arms over her full chest, her mouth opens to bite back, but I cut her off. "Peter wasn't the only infidelity our father had. Seems our mother, or rather the woman we were raised to believe was our mother, was neither to both of us." I pause, letting those facts sink in. When she still stands there with indifference in her eyes, I go on. "My father had an affair with a fate," I explain. She blinks, as if the word is not registering. "You know, Clotho, Lachesis, and Atropos?"

"It's been a while since I've been acquainted with the Greeks, but yes, Griffin, I know who the fates are."

I hold my hand against my heart, pretending to be wounded by her once again calling me a Griffin. Sure, Griffins are greedy and known for hoarding, as she so harshly pointed out. I'm well aware because of our past Tinker Bell would be inclined to view me none other than *that* way. But Griffins are also know for their loyalty. Their protectiveness. Their power and wisdom, especially in times of war.

Maybe, subconsciously, she's testing me. Seeing if I'll

stand up to the name when she needs me to most. Before I can ponder the thought further though, she snaps, "get out of my seat."

When I don't budge, she stalks angrily up the steps towards me. The fire in her eyes burns a yearning to life in my soul as her breathtaking stare holds mine. Reluctant to let her get the better of the situation, I hold up my hands in surrender, and rise just before she reaches me. I barely get out of the way before she sits down.

Not that Tinker Bell sitting on my lap would be a bad thing, but...

"The fates preside over human life," she breathes out annoyed as I step to the side and shake the vision of her straddling me from my mind. I look down and notice a thought she intends to keep secret settle into hers. Her frustration evaporates, for the moment, that is, and she says, "If what you say is true, it's no wonder Peter's mother, Morgan Le Fay, sought your father out to have an affair with him. Perhaps she was hoping he'd share whatever he took from them," she eyes me curiously. "Or did he save that to spare you?"

A low chuckle escapes my lips. "The fates do personify the birth, life, and death of humankind, but no, my father was able to persuade another to help in my time of need."

She leans back in her seat. Eyes me curiously, mockingly even Through fluttering lashes she asks, "Pray tell, God Jake, who is it that changed you, then?"

Leaning toward her, I brace a hand on each side of her throne and breathe her in. She smells like a sweet summer breeze on a lonely night. Comforting. All consuming. She holds her shoulders back, becomes a pillar of strength. But even the highest pedestal cracks and breaks with time. After a moment, as my needy gaze roams the curve of her face in silence, she starts to worry her bottom lip between her teeth. My eyes fall and take in the lush lips that have haunted my dreams for close to twenty years, and whisper, "God Jake, huh?" her face blushes the most captivating shade of pink. "Next time those words fall from your lips, Gidget, they'll be said with pleasure, not feigned interest."

She opens her mouth to bite back, but I move away quickly and continue, "when I was injured, my father thought surely my wounds would heal quickly because of who my mother was. That's when he divulged his secret, and told me the truth about where I came from. To be honest, I don't think he would have ever told me otherwise. We both know Peter was his favorite, since as I grew it seemed I didn't inherit any Godly traits like other demi children should."

I shrug and give her a weary smile. She offers me one in return. The fact that we've both never felt good enough when it comes to who we care about most is the common thread between our – arrangement. Or so it seems.

"But as days turned to weeks, weeks to months, and I was only getting worse, my father made a deal with Hermes, the son of Zeus. Being a cunning trickster, it worked for a while, but it didn't heal me completely. Hermes in turn went to Hera, Zeus's sister and wife, the Goddess of women, marriage, and childbirth. She agreed to heal me, with the aid of Chronos and Karios, the Gods of time, and Ambrosia, that is. The only thing, commonly made into food or drink, and given by the Gods that will ensure immortality. Of course, there was an exchange made. Something my father wanted for something the Gods wanted as well. A small price to pay, my father would say, for saving the life of who he believed was his only son since Peter left us all for Neverland ."

Tinker Bell's eyes lift. Understanding, awe, disbelief even stare back at me.

"What was the exchange?" she asks.

I swallow hard, not wanting to think about it. "It's nothing for you to concern yourself about," I smile sadly. When she eyes me with concern, I add, "trust me."

Rolling her eyes, she releases a heavy sigh and says, "well, all that's fine. I'm glad your father got what he wanted after all this time. A powerful son to take over the family name. But I'm sure your cover is blown after entering into marriage with Wendy. She must have uncovered it over the years you two *shared* together. So, I'm not sure how you'll be of help to us. If you were a hidden weapon, perhaps, but..."

"Wendy never discovered it," I insist sternly.

Her eyes flutter to mine. "You were married to her for seventeen years. Surly she wondered why you never aged?"

I shrug. "She never got that close to me." My jaw ticks as I hold her stare. "I never wanted her that close to me, Gidget."

She studies me. Attempts to read my mind like she was able to all those years ago. But if there is one thing I mastered immediately upon becoming immortal, it was the ability to put a shield up to keep prying minds like hers out.

"I'm guessing you're the one we had to thank for that shower earlier," she glares at me, and I can't help but grin. Of course I was. "What other powers do you have up your sleeve, Griffin?"

"Enough," I taunt. When she doesn't respond, only sits there and continues to stare at me with cool disdain, I say, "enough to make you the greedy one, Gidget. When it comes to me, that is."

Her lips quirk into a mischievous grin. "Perhaps. But until then," she rises, and boldly brushes past me, "You report to Blaze. If he gives me even one reason why I shouldn't trust you, I'll make sure you'll never get the chance to stand in my throne room again."

She makes it down the steps and starts to stalk off across the clearing.

"You're forgetting something, Gidg."

She stops. But she doesn't turn. After a moment, when I'm sure I have her undivided attention, I calmly say, "A promise is a promise after all."

This time, she makes no effort to disguise the shiver that I see deliciously run down her spine.

"Whatever I want, I get it," I grin, though she doesn't turn around to see the mischievous gleam in my eyes. "Wasn't that the arrangement?"

I descend the steps in front of me with practiced patience. After all, I've waited for this moment for close to twenty years, and turning immortal has taught me a thing or two since our first meeting. Patience is definitely a virtue. The only sound between us is my heavy steps and the birds chirping overhead as I make my way towards her. In fact, I think the pixie is so stunned, she not only forgot that tiny fact, but also forgot how to breathe. Coming up behind her, I lean down and place my lips next to her ear and whisper,

"And I was once reassured how seriously your kind takes promises, remember?"

She twirls around quickly. Placing her hand on my chest to put some space between us. The connection of her skin on mine heats quickly and she jolts back as if burned. Jaw set tight. Eyes troubled, angered, disturbed, she sneers, "I need an ally, Jake. Not a lover..."

"Still hung up on Peter, huh?"

Her eyes widen. I try to read her, but she gives me a look that would baffle Zeus himself.

"I need to know what you can do for me on the battle-field, not the bedroom, Griffin," she sighs.

"Try me," I sneer.

She only smiles, "that I will."

Without another word, she turns and struts off in the direction of her hidden cottage on the highest Misty Mountain peak. I watch, entirely not done yet with this conversation, but wise enough to know I need to let her go. Patience. Virtue. This isn't over. What's been building between me and Tinker Bell all these years will never be over. After a moment, I hear footsteps behind me, and sense Blaze, one of Tinker Bell's henchmen.

"I'm rooting for you, Sir," he surprises me by saying. "I never liked Peter much. Not even when we were forced to."

With a heavy sigh, I turn and start to make my way towards him to take my place in Tinker Bells army as just another one of her pawns.

For now, that is.

"Careful," I warn, "He's still my brother, after all."

A brother I've been at war with since the day we were born.

Preorder
Tinker Bell & Jake's story,
Saving Tink, releasing October 15, here!

An extended version of
Losing Neverland is available!
Titled Lost Boy, the added chapters are easy to find and marked with an asterisk*
To read the extended version visit here!

Losing Neverland is coming to audio **fall 2024!**

ALSO BY...

DESTINED HEARTS SERIES

Catch
College/ Sports/ Virgin
A Modern Day Cinderella Story
Read Now

Indecision
Small Town/ Opposites Attract
Read Now

Devotion
Small Town/ Opposites Attract
Read Now

Reckless
Enemies to Lovers/ Second Chance/ Angst
Read Now

Deliverance
Military/ Romantic Suspense/ Second Chance
Read Now

Rebellion
Dark/ Romantic Suspense/ FBI
Read Now

THE DOMINANT LOVE DUET:
Dark/ Mafia

Amico
The De Luca Family's Secret Heir
Book 1
Read Now

Amante
The Moretti Family's Ruthless Empire
Book 2
Read Now

STAND-ALONE NOVELS:

Resurrection
Psychological Romantic Thriller
Justin & Rose

Read Now

Peaches
Rom Com | Chick-Lit
Billionaire| Fake Engagement| Enemies to Lovers
Office Romance
Read Now

~

NOVELLAS:

Lifeline
Vampire/Slayer
Read Now

Flirty Sexy Love
3 erotic short stories in 1 novella
Read Now

FOLLOW ME ON SOCIAL...

TikTok
Instagram
Facebook
FB Group
Twitter
Website
Mailing List